RUTHLESS

STEEL DEMONS MC BOOK EIGHT

CRYSTAL ASH

SDMC series playlist

All American Nightmare - Hinder
Notorious - Adelitas Way
Hail to the King - Avenged Sevenfold
O Death - Ashley H
Joan of Arc - In This Moment
Radioactive - Imagine Dragons
Bad Company - Five Finger Death Punch
Love Me to Death - No Resolve
(Don't Fear) The Reaper - HIM
David - Noah Gunderson
Apocalyptic - Halestorm
Blue on Black - Five Finger Death Punch
Machine Gun Blues - Social Distortion
Wanted Dead or Alive - Chris Daughtry
I Get Off - Halestorm
You Shook Me All Night Long - AC/DC
Nobody Praying for Me - Seether
Loyal to No One - Dropkick Murpheys
Crazy in Love - Daniel De Bourg
Be Free - King Dude & Chelsea Wolfe
Raise Hell - Dorothy
Coming Home - Skylar Grey

Listen on Spotify at:
crystalashbooks.com/sdmc-playlist

Prologue

JANDRO

FIVE YEARS EARLIER

"Where are you going?" I stood in the doorway, watching my sister Angelica throw clothes into a suitcase on her bed. She ignored me and grabbed a small wooden box next, one that I knew was stuffed with letters. "Angie, come on, answer me."

"Oregon." She flashed me a glare but otherwise remained steadfast in her packing, tucking clothes around her letter box as if it were a precious relic. "Not that it matters to you."

"Why wouldn't it matter?" I crossed my arms, watching her from the door.

"Because it's clear you're happy here." Angie jerked her chin at me. "In this wasteland with that vest, those patches, all your guns. Not all of us can play gangster, Jandro, so I'm out. Alma and Josie decided to come with me too."

I leaned my head back until it thunked on the doorframe, closing my eyes with a resigned sigh. I'd seen this coming for months, but still wasn't prepared for it to be real. All the women in my family were scared, frustrated at being cooped up in the house, and always needing a man to look out for them. Me and my club brothers stepped up to protect them without complaint, though we still hated that it was needed at all.

Years had passed, a decade almost, since it was considered safe and normal for a woman to go somewhere alone. The Collapse had only made it worse.

"You'll be safer if you stay," I argued. "The club will protect you. We've already secured this whole block so everyone who lives here can come and go without issue."

"Yeah? And what happens if someone bigger than you rolls up, huh?" My sister paused in her packing to stand squarely in front of me, hands on her hips. "What if the fucking Steel Demons finally meet their match one day?"

"It won't happen," I insisted. "It's been almost a year since anyone's tried to fuck with us, and we're just getting stronger. Our protection is secure."

"Right," Angie scoffed, turning back to the suitcase on the bed. "Denial won't get you anywhere these days."

"If a militia threatens this area, we'll get you all out," I said. "You can stay with us, where you'll be safest. Look at Reaper's sister, Noelle. She's adjusted fine to MC life."

"I don't *want* to adjust to MC life, otherwise known as squatting in hotels when you're not riding around on your loud-ass motorcycles!" Angie's fists balled up at her sides. "You think our fifty-year-old aunt and uncle would be up for that too? Praying with their rosaries in a filthy room while you bang your whores next door?"

"It's not like that," I protested. "Well, not *all* the time," I amended. "One of the guys is married with a kid and has another on the way. It's pretty family friendly actually." I decided against telling her about Big G's wandering eye but the point was, his kids *were* safe and taken care of.

Angie unclenched her hands and took a deep breath, her voice softening. "I just want to live a normal life, and not worry about getting kidnapped or raped every time I walk outside."

"You think there's none of that up in Oregon, sis?" I gave her a hard look. "You think it's some kind of utopia up there? *Nowhere* is safe anymore. The safest place you'll be is with us. We're armed to the teeth and we'll protect our own. That's the whole reason Reaper started up the club in the first place."

"Oregon was establishing independence before the Collapse ever happened," Angie shot back. "They saw this coming and they prepared. And even if it sucks," she shrugged, "oh well. It's close enough to Canada."

"How are you gonna get there?" I demanded. "'Cause I ain't giving you a ride through Nevada. You think here's bad? *That* desert is a fucking wasteland."

Angie wrung her hands in front of her, looking nervous for the first time. "Drew's picking us up. Tonight."

My jaw fell open at the same time my hands fell limply to my sides. "So *that's* what this is about."

"Don't, Jandro." Angie's jaw clenched with the warning.

"You give me this whole spiel about safety when you're about to run off with some guy you've never met? Taking our sisters with you? Unbelievable, Ang." I rubbed my forehead with a groan.

"He's not some stranger, Jandro. He's my boyfriend. You've talked to him!"

"On the phone," I reminded her. "He could be anybody! Most likely, he's a trafficker getting a three-for-one deal."

"I said, *don't!*" Angie moved with lightning speed to square up in front of me, dark eyes murderous and jaw set tight. She only came up to my chin, but was older than me by two years and wouldn't hesitate to pop me if she got pissed enough. When we roughhoused as kids, she was always the scrappiest fighter.

"Damn it, sis." I shook my head at the expression on her face. "You're really gonna do this, huh?"

She and this kid Drew started talking on the phone last year when he accidentally dialed a wrong number. When all the phone companies went bankrupt and the cell towers stopped working, they kept in touch by writing letters. I should have known he put this in her head the moment she stashed that box in her suitcase.

Angie's face softened just a fraction but she didn't back up. "I know you're worried, but you're suspicious of the wrong person." She stepped away, returning to her suitcase. "You should worry about those bikers you're rolling with now."

"Don't try to deflect, Ang," I warned, my temper

flaring. "I've known most of the guys for years. Plus, Reaper's a hardass about club law. We do what we have to, and that does *not* include luring women to the so-called safety wonderland called Oregon."

"He is *not* luring me, it was my idea!" Angie slammed the suitcase closed and whirled around, dark curls whipping her shoulders. "Anyway, what are you gonna do? Keep me prisoner here?"

"No." I slumped against the door, defeated. "If you're gonna go, I won't stop you."

"Then why are you being so up my ass?"

"Because if you go," I let all the sadness bleed out into my voice. "I know I'm never gonna see you again."

There was a long pause as my sister and I just stared at each other. "Jandro," she finally said, as if chastising me. "I'll write to you."

"Not if you're dead," I answered curtly. "Not if you're chained up in some sicko's basement, or drugged up constantly 'til you're a zombie."

She sighed, the sound heavy and tired. "Is there anything I can do to make you feel okay with this?"

"Stay," I pleaded one final time. "Just…don't run off with him. Hell, he can even stay here for a few days so I can meet him properly before you go."

Angie shook her head and my heart sunk. "I can't stay here another fucking day, Jandro. I'm so, so sick of it here."

"I'm sorry, sis. That's just how the world is now," I told her sadly. "You've heard the radio reports. The whole country's fucked."

She shook her head adamantly. "I don't believe that.

There has to be a better place, Jandro. And for me," she pulled in a shaky breath, "that's in Oregon, with the man I love."

I'd never felt anything like that moment before—that awful paradoxical feeling of knowing my sister was already gone, despite standing right in front of me. Nothing I said would make her budge. Trying to talk her out of it would only drive her further away.

So I did the only thing I could do at that moment— pulled Angie into a hug for the last time.

"God, please, *please* be careful," I begged her. "You get even one weird feeling, you hit the dirt and run back here, okay?"

To my relief she hugged me back, the anger melting out of her as she patted my back. "I've thought about this for months. Trust that I know what I'm doing."

I bit down hard on the inside of my cheek, not wanting my last moment with her to be an argument. After one more tight squeeze and a kiss on her forehead, I released her.

"Write me as soon as you can," I said on my way out of the room. I didn't bother with goodbye. I couldn't just stay and see her off all hopeful and positive and shit. I all but knew she was walking out to her death, and taking my other two sisters with her. As the youngest and the only male sibling, I was woefully outnumbered in this fight.

There was one more thing I had to do for her, but she couldn't know about it. I left my aunt and uncle's house without another word, hopped on my bike, and headed straight for the Steel Demons compound, which was just an abandoned hotel we took over.

Angie was right about that, at least.

I crashed through the front doors, heading to the bar where Reaper was parked. "Yo, Reap." I smacked his shoulder to pull his attention away from the girl dancing on the stripper pole off to the side of the bar. "I need to run an errand, it'll take a few days. I'll take Shadow with me, that should be enough."

Reaper's green eyes narrowed at me through the haze of cigarette smoke surrounding him. "What's going on?"

"Angie," I admitted with a sigh, scrubbing a hand down my face. "She's finally had it and she's taking off."

He straightened in his seat, looking more alert as he turned to me. "You sure you don't want more of us?" Reaper had a brief fling with my sister a few years ago that went nowhere, but it wasn't even about that. She was my family, and by extension, his too. The whole club would rally to protect her if he said the word.

"Nah." I shook my head. "We're gonna hang back so she won't know we're tailing."

"Why?"

"She's taking off with that guy she's been penpalling," I grumbled. "Can't get in the way of her fucking prince rescuing her. I'm just gonna make sure she gets to Oregon like she believes she is and not straight to a trafficker's compound."

"So you're not stopping her?" Reaper looked curious.

"She's a grown-ass adult, what am I gonna do?" I

leaned on the barstool next to him. "Would you get in Noelle's way if she pulled this shit?"

"Huh, no." He took a drag on his smoke and said loudly, "Those psychopaths can have her."

"I can hear you, asshat!" Noelle called from somewhere behind the bar.

"Whatever. D'you find that bottle of Beam yet?"

I tapped Reaper's shoulder again to get his attention. "Back in a few days. Me and Shadow."

He waved an arm to dismiss me, his attention returning to the girl on the stripper pole. "I hope Angie's guy is alright. But if he's not, put an extra bullet in him for me."

"Oh, I was planning on it," I said, heading to Shadow's room. A dim light spilled out through the crack under his door, where I rapped my knuckles twice. "Hey man, it's Jandro."

I barely heard his footsteps as he approached the door and it still baffled me how such a big dude could be so silent. He didn't open the door for me, but the deadbolt sliding out from its locked position was my cue to come in. When I entered, Shadow had already returned to his desk, hunched over his sketchpad with his hand sweeping over the page.

"Hey." I closed the door softly behind me. "You've been cooped up in here a while. Let's go for a ride, get you some fresh air."

"Where?" he grunted out, not even looking up from his page.

"To Oregon and back. I gotta watch over someone heading out that way."

Shadow paused in his drawing, turning his head to look at me suspiciously. "Who?"

"My sister," I said, then swallowed. "Three of my sisters, actually."

"No—"

I raised a hand to calm him before he started freaking out. "You won't have to talk to them or be near them. They'll be in a car. We'll be on our bikes, just following to make sure they get there safe."

Shadow's hand clenched around his pen. I could hear the agitated breaths rushing in and out of his lungs.

"You won't interact with anyone but me," I continued to placate him. "Come on, man. You need to get out of these four walls, and I need some backup."

He took a long time to respond, and I could see the internal battle as he spun the pen in his hand. The big dude loved having freedom—the open road and flying sensation of riding, even just the ability to come and go as he pleased. But that kind of freedom was still unnatural to him, even spiking his anxiety sometimes. Shadow always picked the smallest rooms when we moved around, and I figured the cramped space was comforting to him, if only because it was familiar. Once he retreated to his hiding place, it was always a battle to coax him out again.

On the upside, winning that battle got a little bit easier every time.

"Promise?" he asked finally. "Just you and me?"

"I promise," I said with a sigh. We had come a long way as far as him trusting me, but sometimes Shadow fell back into thinking I was trying to trick or deceive him.

"We're going through Nevada, right?"

"Yeah, so?"

"No women," he said, teeth clenched. "I mean it, Jandro."

"You sure?" I couldn't help but tease him, grinning as I leaned against his door. "I could've sworn I heard you say you wanted to swing by the bunny ranch."

"No," Shadow repeated. "Maybe another time, but I'm not in the mood for…*that*."

"Fine, be a cock block," I sighed in mock disappointment. In all honesty, I wasn't in the best of moods for fucking some random woman either, definitely not with my sisters on my mind. "We'll just go there and back, crash when we need to. Cool?"

"Okay," Shadow relented. "I'll get dressed."

"Meet you in the garage." I turned to leave, closing his door again behind me as I stalked down the long, dark hallway.

My mind was elsewhere as I checked the tire pressure and fluids on Shadow's bike, my movements on autopilot. All I could think about was Angie, how I was just going to watch and hover until she was gone for good.

Sure, this Drew guy *might* be okay. She could end up safe and happy with him for all I knew. I had to hope for a good outcome.

The Collapse last year was still fresh on everyone's minds, the lingering effects of it continuing to ripple out across the country. We no longer had a national currency, no more government agencies to help people in need. Everyone was wondering about the economy, infrastructure, and if we would unify and rebuild.

No one talked about this—families splitting apart because they had no other options. This world made people cling to fantasies, like Angie did with this guy. It drove people to seek out anything better than their current situation, even in people and places completely unknown.

"At least she's going for something," I muttered to myself. "At least she still believes in something better."

I opened the garage door and went to sit on my bike to wait for Shadow.

ONE

MARIPOSA

PRESENT DAY

I held onto Jandro's arm, squeezing around his bicep as we watched the men drill the commemorative plaques into the wall. He placed his fingers over mine, a deep breath filling his lungs. On the other side of him, Slick leaned on his crutch and bowed his head when the final bolt secured the plaque into the concrete.

A small crowd had gathered while the plaques were being installed, curious onlookers between me, my men, and the Sons of Odin, who got their own plaque for the loss of their own people.

Silence filled the City Hall foyer once the drilling was done, only the soft echoes of footsteps filling the open building.

"Thank you for doing this," Jandro said softly, turning to Governor Vance. "Honoring our fallen is so important to us."

"It's both my pleasure to do this for you, and a

regret for your men and their families," Vance said, his face full of sympathy. His daughter Kyrie stood next to him, hands clasped demurely in front of her.

"We apologize for the delay in commemorating your fallen people," she added, inclining her head toward the Sons of Odin, standing across from her in our small semicircle. "The Sons too deserve remembrance in Four Corners' history."

T-Bone nodded politely, a thick swallow working in his throat. "Thank you, Miss Vance."

His reply was stiff, formal. Kyrie looked briefly taken aback but smoothed out her features quickly.

Not wanting to dwell on the tension between them, I released Jandro's arm and stepped forward to lay my bouquet of flowers at the wall under the plaques. My guys and other club members who came to pay their respects stepped up after me. Cigars, patches, silver rings and pendants, lighters, more flowers, and even small glasses of whiskey were laid down for Brick, his nephew Wells, the other Steel Demons we lost, and for the fallen Sons of Odin.

Jandro and Slick's faces were the most somber I'd ever seen them. The bodies of the men they'd lost on that mission were never recovered, hence the plaques. A recovery mission had been shot down because it was deemed too dangerous. Secretly, I was glad that it hadn't been approved. It could have been Jandro and Slick commemorated on a plaque too, a poor replacement for the men at my side. I slid an arm around Jandro's waist, his arm coming to rest on my shoulders as he pressed a kiss to my temple.

"I would never rush any of you through your grief," Governor Vance said slowly as the crowd began to disperse. "But this war is not waiting for us to be ready." His eyes scanned over my men and the Sons. "If you're able, please meet us in the conference room. We have much to discuss."

Gunner walked up to my opposite side, fingers twining gently with mine. "Coming, baby girl?"

I glanced at him in surprise. "You think I should?"

He nodded insistently. "They need to hear about what you and Shadow ran into on your way back. And honestly," he blew out a long breath, "we need all the fresh ideas we can get."

"Then I'll be there."

He smiled roguishly at me, then leaned down to brush a quick kiss on my lips. Under the guiding weight of Jandro's arm, I turned to follow the others down the hall to the conference room. Reaper and Shadow were already ahead of us, walking side-by-side as they spoke to each other in low voices. Those two had grown closer since we got back, more like friends than a president and his foot soldier.

Reaper reached up and swatted Shadow on the back at one point, his palm slapping the freshly printed Steel Demons patch on Shadow's cut. The grinning skull stretched wide and menacingly across the expanse of his back. Shadow's already-imposing figure was amplified now that he was decked out in a cut and patches again. People walking past us steered clear, taking one look at him before jerking their gaze away and hurrying their steps.

I almost wanted to laugh. It was such a contrast to how he was with me privately—arguably the most loving, gentle man in existence. I couldn't lie to myself, it was hot as hell that he came off as so intimidating, but was truly anything but. Like he could hear my thoughts, Shadow glanced at me over his shoulder, a smile pulling at his lips.

"You guys talking about me?" I demanded.

"Never." The sarcastic reply came from Reaper, who tossed me a charming smile over his shoulder.

My stomach did flips at the sight of those green eyes. I felt like I did when I first met Reaper, so inexplicably attracted to him but also completely unsure of where we stood. Only this time, the power was in my hands and it was him waiting for me to make things clear.

For every urge to run up and kiss him, to erase all the uncertainty of him being mine, there was an equally strong force pulling me back. It was like reaching out to touch a stove after I'd already been burned, trusting that it wouldn't hurt me again. I *wanted* to move on—Shadow clearly had. I wanted to forgive and have my first husband back.

But the hurt wasn't gone. It still cut through me when I thought about what Shadow had endured, how he must have felt when he was made to leave Four Corners and travel across the country alone.

It was getting a little easier every day. Shadow was back home and happy. Reaper and I were talking now, even flirting from time to time. He never pushed for anything physical, though he looked at me with such longing and I wanted so badly to give in. The wall between us was slowly crumbling, but it was still there, an invisible barrier.

"Slick." I turned my attention to Jandro's apprentice, the young Demon who had saved Jandro's life. "How's the leg?"

He shot me a good-natured smile as he walked tirelessly alongside us on his crutches. "Better, thank you, Mari. Rhonda's whipping my ass in physical therapy. She said I should be off these in another week."

"That's great news!" I looked down just in time to see a small black blur walking along Slick's other side.

Freyja's tail was in the air, large eyes fixed on him. Slick made soft clicking sounds at her and she meowed in reply. Jandro and I laughed softly, exchanging a knowing glance. Slick's recovery from his gunshot had taken longer than any of ours since the gods came into our lives, but I was hopeful that Freyja's presence would speed things up for him.

"I told him he's not a real Demon 'til he takes a gunshot," Jandro told me smugly.

"Don't say that," I grumbled with a smack on his arm. "Just because you've been shot a dozen times."

"It builds character," Jandro insisted with a straight face. "Puts hair on your chest."

"Huh." I looked down while tugging the collar of my shirt. "Where are my chest hairs then?"

Jandro chuckled and wrapped both arms around me in a protective embrace. "You're the exception, *Mariposita*. You're a Demon because you save all our dumb asses. I'd never in a million years wish for you to get shot."

"I know." I lifted on tiptoes to kiss his cheek. "You're not entirely wrong, though. Getting shot…changed things."

I had never come so close to death, nor had been in so much pain in my entire life. The aftermath still came to me in flashes—blinding pain, Doc digging into my leg, the worn leather of Shadow's belt between my teeth.

And Shadow, holding and soothing me. The solidness of his chest like an anchor, the sound of his voice keeping me from losing my mind to the terror running through me.

As painful and horrifying as that experience was, it was also moving. A shift had occurred that day, one that brought us back together. It gave Shadow the chance to see for himself that he was capable of so much more than killing. That he was a deserving partner of me, from the moment he beat my shooter to death, to holding me during the bullet extraction, and then the aftermath and my recovery.

I had a feeling he'd never believed himself worthy of caring for someone until circumstances forced him into doing so. And for that alone, I'd do it all over again.

Governor Vance's assistant, Josh, held a heavy door open as we filed into the conference room. Reaper's father, General Finn Bray, was already seated at the head of the long table, surrounded by a few of his lieutenants. Reaper and Gunner took their seats to the general's left, knowing instantly where to go, like they'd done this hundreds of times before. Jandro led me to the general's right, pulling a chair back for me before he sat down next to my father-in-law.

Finn leaned over the table, smiling at me and mouthing a *hi, sweetheart.* I smiled and mouthed hello back as Shadow sat on my opposite side, the table quickly filling up with people. I hadn't seen much of my in-laws since Shadow and I returned, and while I missed them, I was grateful for the space. The fewer people digging into my and Reaper's relationship, the better.

"Thank you all for coming," Finn addressed the room once everyone had been seated. His fingers drummed on top of a manila folder in front of him. "I'll start with the good news. Andrea has made contact once again, which means she is still alive and her position has not been compromised."

The whole room seemed to let out a sigh of relief. I couldn't wait to tell Tessa when I had the chance.

"I'm afraid the good news ends there," Finn continued in a grave voice, flipping open the folder. "The information she gives does not bode well for us." His eyes scanned the document as if making sure it hadn't magically changed to better news. "Two-thousand of General Tash's troops have mobilized as of a week ago, heading directly west." *Straight toward us*, were the unspoken words hanging in the air. "Most of them are foot soldiers, but she estimates sizable motorized and aerial units as well."

"Aerial?" Reaper barked, his face drawn in a scowl. "Does that mean drones or…?"

"Yes," his father confirmed. "Andrea has also made note of at least five attack helicopters as well."

No one made a sound in response to that, but Reaper dropping his head into his hands must have summed up everyone's thoughts.

"And that's just their first wave," Finn added, leaning back and folding his hands. "Who knows what Tash is still holding back?"

"Meanwhile, we've got Blakeworth creating decoys and hiding in the grass like ninjas to the north," Jandro chimed in. "After that first skirmish, they're keeping their soldiers *very* close."

"I wonder if they're hoping Tash flushes us to the north, then they can pick us off, like shooting fish in a barrel." Gunner rubbed his jaw. "It makes sense. We can't exactly flee in any other direction."

"We're not fleeing," Reaper growled. "We're fighting."

"I don't disagree, son. But we're at a huge disadvantage," Finn said.

"There is still Jerriton," I piped up.

All eyes in the room turned to me, and I felt Shadow give an encouraging touch of my thigh under the table.

"Jerriton is Tash's territory now," one of Bray's lieutenants informed me.

"It's under his control, yes," I said. "But the people of Jerriton are not loyal to him. They're organizing a resistance."

"I'm sorry, but how does that affect anything? The citizens don't have any—"

"Let her speak," Shadow snarled to the lieutenant across the table.

The man in question shut right up, and the entire

row of soldiers seemed to shrink in their seats. I allowed myself a small, smug moment to squeeze Shadow's hand on my leg before continuing.

"Tash had citizens imprisoned. We," I tilted my head toward Shadow, "freed them, at first to create a distraction so we could get back to Four Corners undetected. Tash's border patrol caught up to us, but the citizens saved our asses."

"How?" another soldier blurted out before withering under Shadow's glare again.

"We killed a few prison guards," I said. "It was chaos, so the prisoners were able to arm themselves and steal vehicles. Knowing their territory, they knew exactly where we'd be blockaded and came to our aid. Their leader, Samson, told us himself that they stood with Four Corners."

"Did they inform you of any specific plan?" The question came from Finn, who was looking at me intently. "Or any way to keep in contact, at least?"

That was where my confidence faltered, and I wanted to shrink down in my seat. "No, General. I invited them here but they wanted to continue helping others in their own territory. I wanted you to know we have someone else supporting us, but as far as specifics to help us in battle? I'm afraid I don't have anything."

Finn smiled kindly at me, but I noticed the downturn in his lips. He was disappointed I didn't have anything substantial to offer, and I was kicking myself for not thinking of it when I had the chance. At the time, all I wanted was for me and Shadow to get home.

"Maybe we could send a bird out," T-Bone

suggested. "See if there's a secure way we can exchange messages."

"If we can get a direct line to their leader, that would be the best," Finn agreed. "But in the meantime," he sighed, "we need to decide how to split up defenses to the north and the east." His fingers dragged across the map in the center of the table. "I will not let us be corralled and herded like livestock for General Tash. So what do we do?"

Gunner leaned over the map, his eyes sharp and calculating. "Send heavy artillery toward Tash. It'll do the most amount of damage."

"But will it be enough?" the general challenged.

Gunner steepled his fingers, holding them to his lips as he stared at the table. I knew dozens of scenarios were playing out in his mind and like a true tactician, he was filtering down to the most effective ones.

"If we act fast enough," my golden man said, "I think so." His eyes shifted toward Reaper, and I knew he was considering the president's newfound ability to see through the eyes of the dead. Something we didn't want made known to this packed room.

"Heavy artillery with the fewest possible amount of people," Gunner decided. "I'm talking going all-out, like planting IEDs in their direct path and picking the rest off in the chaos. But we have to act fast, before they get too close to us."

"What about Blakeworth?" someone else asked.

Gunner snapped his fingers, turning toward the speaker. "The exact opposite. Large numbers but sleek weapons. Just rifles and handguns. We'll comb the landscape and flush those sneaky fuckers out of their hiding places. Now that my boy's back," he paused to pet Horus' chest feathers while shooting a grin at me, "I can survey the area better. We'll be able to spot more of them before they spot us."

"Sounds viable," General Bray mused, rubbing his palms together.

"We can set up field hospitals outside of the northern and eastern borders," I chimed in, eager to be useful. "Just let me know where."

"Excellent." The general beamed at me. "Steel Demons officers," his eyes swept over my four men, "Sons," he nodded at T-Bone across the table. "Stick around to discuss the logistics of this and receive your unit assignments. The rest of you are dismissed."

I started to get up when Finn clicked his tongue. "Sit down, Mrs. President."

All of my guys were grinning when I plopped back down into my chair. "Never thought I'd get a seat at the big boys' table."

"Honestly." Jandro leaned in to kiss my cheek. "You should have been here since the beginning."

TWO

MARIPOSA

———————

T he meeting went on for most of the day, long into the afternoon. Finn sent for several meals and beverages to be brought up to us. No alcohol, much to my men's disappointment. They were planning to strike Blakeworth and General Tash that very night.

"I can have emergency medics on-site with you guys right away," I said. "But it will take a few hours for a full-on field hospital to get set up at both locations."

"We'll take whatever you can support us with," Finn said. "As long as we have some medics there once things get ugly."

"I can definitely do that." I nodded. "You want people who can ride bikes?"

"Reaper's team should have the experienced riders." Gunner jerked his chin across the table to the president. "Your guys will need to move fast, since you don't have the big numbers covering you."

"Makes sense," Reaper agreed.

"I'll be with Gunner's team then," I decided. "To even things out, since he'll have less medics on his side."

"Good idea." Finn smiled warmly at me. "You've got a good mind for this, Mari."

I lowered my eyes to the table bashfully, still feeling slightly out of place despite being among friends and family. "Thank you, I'm trying."

"Alright." The general's eyes scanned over everyone in the room. "Does everyone know where they're going?" When no one said otherwise, he rose from the table. "Good. Inform your units, then spend the last few hours of daylight with your loved ones. Eat a good dinner, but don't get shitfaced." He looked pointedly at Reaper. "We start moving at nightfall."

The Sons of Odin stood abruptly after the general finished speaking. "We'll inform the soldiers and the medics," T-Bone announced. "Don't worry about it, Demons. Steal a bit of extra time together."

"You guys don't have to do that," Jandro protested. "You're fighting with us, you're not our messengers."

T-Bone shrugged, sending quick looks to Dyno and Grudge with a smirk. "Y'all have been separated long enough, and while we're optimistic about the battles, none of us know how it's gonna go. Spend the time together now," his voice softened, "while you know you still have it."

"If it's gonna be that way then," I huffed, making my way around the table with my arms out. "Gimme hugs now. I won't see you guys until after it's over."

T-Bone chuckled, his gaze watching the men behind

me before wrapping his broad, tattooed arms around my back and crushing me in a tight squeeze.

"Be safe," I whispered in his ear, hugging tightly around his neck. "Come back to us, all of you."

"You too, little lady." He kissed my cheek. "Bring yourself and all your bastards back home in one piece."

We released each other and I moved on to hug Grudge and Dyno. After my men said their goodbye-for-now's, the Sons left to inform the troops of their assignments, and it was only my men and my father-in-law in the room with me.

"I'll leave you all to it," Finn said, taking his cue to leave next. "See you in a few hours."

And then there were five.

Jandro came up to me first, locking his hands around my waist as he pulled me closer. "Anything you want to do in our free time, *Mariposita*?" He lowered a kiss to my neck and heat filled my skin, like a match had been lit.

Over his shoulder, I saw Reaper pull his gaze away to shuffle papers on the table. Shadow watched us with a kind of cool curiosity. He didn't look *not* interested, but it wasn't the clear desire I saw when we were alone. I realized we'd never really discussed group bedroom situations. Of course he knew he wasn't my only husband, but he might feel differently about sex. So far our time together had only been with each other, and always so intensely intimate.

Reaper and I still hadn't done anything sexual since I came back. I wanted more one-on-one time with him too, when I came to that point in healing those stubborn past wounds. With everyone here now, I wasn't about to leave Reaper out. Nor was I about to potentially make Shadow feel uncomfortable.

The only one who looked at Jandro and I with clear interest was Gunner, teeth sinking into his lower lip as he grinned at us. For all his initial hesitancy about this relationship, lately he seemed to love sharing me the most. Gunner's main priority in the bedroom was having fun. He and Jandro together ensured that I would be laughing just as much as I'd be having orgasms.

"Honestly." I pressed lightly on Jandro's chest. "I just want to relax at home with all of you. *Actually* relax, like cuddling," I clarified.

Reaper's eyes lifted to me, relief in his gaze. Shadow's face relaxed too, and I knew quality non-sex time was the right decision. We'd all been so busy since Shadow and I returned, it was rare for us all to be together at once. With just a few hours, I sure as hell didn't want to waste it.

"Home, it is." Gunner pet Horus on his shoulder as he whirled toward the door. "Jandro, can we have tacos?"

"Make 'em yourself." Jandro released me to grumble after him.

I walked up to Shadow first, hugging around his waist as I propped my chin on his chest. "See you at home."

He smiled knowingly, swiping his thumb over my cheek in a quick caress as he bent to kiss me. "See you there, my love."

Reaper was already following Gunner and Jandro out to the parking spaces when I untangled from

Shadow. I jogged to catch up to his long strides, slipping my hand into his. "Can I get a ride with you?"

Reaper smoothed over his surprise quickly with a cocky grin. "You sure can, sugar."

This was another baby step forward for us. I didn't know when riding behind one of my men became something intimate. Maybe it always had been.

On the ride home, the memory of Reaper fucking me on his bike drove my thighs to squeeze tighter against his. That felt like an eternity ago, when my feelings for him were at an all-time high. When I thought nothing could shatter the bond between us.

He'd always be groping me, grabbing me, and whispering sweet, filthy things in my ear. Now, he kept his hands to himself. And my hands, resting on his stomach, couldn't seem to stroke his chest, nor dip under his shirt to tease and touch him like I used to. I *wanted* to. More than anything, I wanted to break this wall between us and go back to being happy together. But the thought of doing so made my heart race with anxiety.

To let myself love him wholly again opened up the possibility of being heartbroken again. The one thing I wanted most also terrified me beyond words. So my hands never moved, and neither did his. Every day that he was patient and accepting of my coldness only made me feel worse about it.

Reaper braked slowly as we pulled up our driveway, the others falling in behind us. "You good?" he asked, pausing while I climbed out of the seat.

"Yeah, thanks." I dusted myself off, mentally kicking myself. He probably wanted to help me off the bike, and have another excuse to touch me. Another baby step forward.

I hated that this all felt so awkward. He was my *husband*, not some guy I started dating yesterday. Still, Reaper didn't seem bothered as he shut off the bike and headed for the front door. Everyone left their steeds in the driveway, since they'd be back on them soon anyway.

Once I kicked off my shoes by the front door, a large arm wrapped around my waist from behind and lifted me off the ground.

"Shadow!" I shrieked with laughter as he swung an arm under my knees to carry me. "Where are you taking me?"

"The couch," he answered flatly. "To cuddle."

I let my head flop against his chest with a smile, just curling up smaller as he sat down with me across his lap. My legs stretched out to find another lap, Jandro's. The VP placed my feet on top of his thighs and immediately set to work rubbing them. The other two were rummaging in the kitchen, by the sounds of it. I shifted and scooted between my two men, making myself comfortable to the sounds of cabinet doors closing and murmured voices.

"Whatever you guys get, bring some for us," Jandro called, running his thumbs up my arches.

"There's not much, besides eggs and liquor. And we have orders *not* to drink," Reaper scoffed.

"We can drink, your old man just said don't get shit-faced," Jandro reminded him.

"There should be ice cream," I yelled. "Unless one

of you dicks ate it all."

"I could go for some ice cream," Shadow mused, his fingers making delicious circles of pressure on my back.

I heard the refrigerator doors open, and then Gunner's voice over the machine's hum. "I kinda want scrambled eggs. Easy comfort food."

"Make me some!" Jandro called, his hands still doing wonders to my feet. "And don't forget to season that shit with salt and pepper. We should have cheese too."

"Yeah, whatever. Baby girl, you want eggs?"

"No thank you, just ice cream."

Not twenty minutes later, we were all piled around the couch with our very grown-up dinners of scrambled eggs, ice cream, and whiskey. I held the tub of cookie dough ice cream in my lap and fed hearty spoonfuls to Shadow, which he chased with small sips of whiskey.

"I'm tellin' you, bro." Jandro scraped his plate of eggs clean. "You gotta cook it on really low heat, folding it the entire time. You want perfect scrambled eggs, you gotta cook 'em for like forty-five minutes."

"Fuck that," Gunner scoffed from the armchair across from us. "I like my eggs crispy anyway."

"See, I don't understand that." Reaper, in another armchair, set his whiskey on his knee as he looked at Gunner. "You grew up with butlers and chefs and shit, and you eat like a garbage disposal. If it was anyone who demanded perfect eggs, I figured it'd be you."

"Nah, food is food. If it doesn't poison me or taste like Satan's asshole, I'll eat it."

"Food is not *just* food, it's culture," Jandro protested. "It's love. It's bringing a family together. It's an experience brought on by a chain of events, leading to what's on your plate." He pointed at Gunner. "You ate those eggs because I rescued—"

"You mean stole?" Shadow interjected with a chuckle.

"Fine, whatever. I *stole* my girls from the Sandia outpost and trekked across the desert with them. They miraculously survived the attack from Razor Wire, then got transported again to this place, where they'll finally live happily ever after. Those aren't *just* eggs, man. My girls went through hell to reach paradise, so you could have deliciousness on a plate."

"I get it man, I'm just saying," Gunner laughed, raising his palms in the air in mock surrender. "That I've never discriminated against what's been on my plate, whether it came from a personal chef or a dumpster."

"It is really sweet that you love those chickens so much," I said, digging my toes into Jandro's thigh.

"Sometimes I do, and then there's days like yesterday," he sighed. "Where those little dumbasses chase and peck the shit out of me for no good reason." Jandro lifted his chin. "Cream me, babe."

"Excuse me?"

"Ice cream, let me get some."

"What's the strangest thing you've ever eaten, sugar?" Reaper was relaxed and leaned back in his chair, eyes following me as I fed Jandro a spoonful of ice cream.

"Hmm." I spooned some of my healthy dinner into my mouth while I thought. "You heard of calf fries?"

Reaper took a pensive sip of whiskey, looking all too sexy while doing so. "Don't think so."

"That's what we called them in Texas. You might know them as Rocky Mountain oysters."

He nearly spat out that sip he just took, as did Gunner who was already red-faced and laughing. Jandro cackled at Reaper's reaction while Shadow just looked at me curiously. "What is that?"

"We-ell…" I purposely drew out the word while scratching the rough beard on his jaw. "You take a bull's testicles, deep-fry them——"

And then Shadow was choking on his drink, trying not to spit it all over me, which only made the other guys laugh harder. Gunner and Reaper were sliding down to the floor, clutching their stomachs. Jandro would have done the same if it weren't for my feet in his lap.

Those few hours passed by too quickly—talking, laughing, and just relaxing with my loves like we had all the time in the world. My ice cream ended up getting passed around until it was finished. The sun was less than an hour away from setting by the time Gunner was scraping the last of it out of the tub.

"We should head out," Reaper voiced what everyone else was reluctant to acknowledge.

I had shifted directions on the couch and slowly lifted my head from Jandro's lap, pulling my feet out of Shadow's hands as I came to a sitting position.

"Be careful," I managed to whisper to the VP before he pulled me in for a deep kiss with a hand on my neck.

"Don't worry," he murmured against my lips. "I promise I won't get shot more than once."

"*Jandro*," I growled as low and threateningly as I could manage.

"I mean I'll *try* not to get hit at all, but you never know." His mouth pulled into a wider grin, still teasing me.

"No getting shot," I insisted. "Not even once."

He kissed me again, slow and lingering, while holding the sides of my face. "I'll be careful, *Mariposita*."

Knowing I wouldn't get more of a promise than that, I slid across the couch to Shadow. Those massive, solid arms wrapped around my back while my arms braced against his chest.

"Come back to me." I ghosted a kiss over his lips.

"I'll never leave you." The promise rumbled from deep in his chest before his mouth pressed solidly to mine.

It was hell to stop kissing him and pull away, both because of how physically addicting he was, and the simple fact that I was seeing my men off to battle. A *real* battle.

I rose from the couch and went to Gunner, who was already up and strapping on a bunch of weapons.

"Be careful," I repeated, the sentiment sounding lame and empty at this point.

"Always, baby girl." He placed his hands on my waist and pulled me closer, the easygoing smile never leaving his face. "I'll have you and Horus watching over me. How can we lose?"

"Don't tempt fate like that," I warned. "But I know you'll be smart."

"You know me well, then." We shared sweet and playful parting kisses, then I turned to Reaper.

Except he was already gone.

"What?" I spun around the living room, a quick flash of panic rising.

Jandro cleared his throat. "He, uh, went outside while you and Shadow were making out."

I headed out the front door without wasting another moment, finding the Steel Demons president checking the tires on his bike.

"You were *not* about to leave without saying good-bye," I accused, folding my arms as I approached him.

Reaper stood up and shrugged sheepishly. "Didn't want to, uh, ruin any of your goodbyes with them." Meaning he didn't want to stand around awkwardly and watch me kiss and whisper promises to everyone but him.

"Come on." I opened my arms and approached him for a hug like I had with the Sons earlier.

But when his arms came around me, there was nothing platonic about that hug. Chemistry fired between us from his hands on my back, to my breasts against his chest, to the breath of air tickling my neck from his mouth.

I found myself clutching hard to his back, fingers digging in, while I buried my face in his shoulder, inhaling his signature scent of clove cigarettes and leather. I wanted to linger there, to pull the shirt away and taste the heat of his skin again.

It took all my resolve to pull back, and I immediately hated losing the solidness of his body against mine.

"You need to come back too," I said, stepping further out of the embrace. "You're just as important. Just as needed."

Reaper's hands fell away, dropping to his sides with a small smile. "To Four Corners or to you?"

"Both." I rubbed my arms and hugged myself against the cold, fighting the urge to burrow into his chest again. "You're still my husband."

His smile brightened at that. "As long as you keep telling me that, sugar, I'll keep coming back home to you."

THREE

REAPER

It didn't seem feasible at first glance, taking on a couple thousand troops with just a few hundred of us, some howitzers, and some strategically placed IEDs. But Gunner obviously put a lot of thought into it, covering all angles to maximize an effective attack while putting a minimal amount of bodies at risk. That same night as the meeting, when we started putting the plan into action, I wasn't exactly feeling *optimistic*, but certainly better about this war than I had in previous weeks.

Gunner and Dad split up units between the northern and eastern fronts to best utilize the skills of those involved. Those dealing with Tash specialized in stealth and scouting, with a select few heavy artillery experts manning the howitzers. The Blakeworth front consisted of nearly everyone else, specialized or not. They needed numbers to keep their advantage, while we needed tight coordination and precision.

I was heading east no matter what Gun or Dad told

me. I knew it wasn't likely to happen in *this* battle, but I wanted the chance to hurt Tash myself regardless.

Shadow and I were leading the eastern units together, with his sight giving us an advantage in the dead of night.

"Where did Mari see the line of soldiers when you all were out there?" I double-checked all the straps and tie-downs on my bike, ensuring nothing explosive would fall off on the ride.

"Hm." Shadow tilted his head, looking skyward as he thought. "Two, maybe three hundred miles from our border."

"And it was all on foot? One long, unbroken line, she said?"

"Yes," he confirmed gravely. "And that was days ago, so I don't suspect we have to go far. They might be right on our doorstep, with vehicles and attack helicopters not far behind."

"Let's go greet our neighbors, then."

Shadow started up his bike with a roar, with mine and a chorus of hundreds of others filling the air after him. With his night vision as our guide, he'd lead us to the first site to plant a bomb. Gunner was using Horus on the northern side, so we didn't have an exact location on Tash's movement until there were some dead folks for me to see through.

We just had to pray that we didn't run into Tash before we were ready.

I mentally scoffed at the idea of prayer, then shifted the thought immediately. I knew gods existed. Maybe praying wasn't so far-fetched after all.

Yeah, right. It's not like the gods have answered half of the things you've prayed for.

Hades offered no comment as I kicked my feet up and followed Shadow out of the army base's lot and onto the road. We kept our headlights on low power, and the dog nearly turned invisible in the dark landscape. In the corner of my eye I only saw flashes of white teeth as he ran alongside me.

Despite my cynical thoughts about prayer, I couldn't completely write off the gods as cruel puppet masters. I had my parents back. I had Mari back. Who knew how much the gods played a part in those events, but they had certainly been out of *my* control. And having Shadow back too…

I hit the throttle, speeding to catch up to his tail light on the road ahead of me. So many times I replayed that confrontation with Hades in my head, before I attempted to kill Shadow. The big guy was still needed for something, either in this war or something else. It had to be bigger than just him and Mari getting back together. No god would step in to prevent his death for only that, would they?

After roughly an hour's ride, Shadow pulled over to the side of the road, with the procession of bikes filing in after him.

"We start planting them here," he called out. "Moving further up and covering until someone has a visual. If you do, you know the signal."

"Look at you giving orders," I chuckled, sliding out of my seat to begin unloading.

"Heh," Shadow said dismissively. "It's getting easier,

I guess."

"You're good at it," I told him.

He paused, seemingly taken aback by the compliment. "Thank you, president."

We and our units fanned out in a wide zig-zag pattern to plant the bombs a quarter-mile apart from each other. The landscape was mostly flat with only gently sloping hills, which wasn't great for our ground cover. Canyons or rock formations would be ideal, but Tash wouldn't be stupid enough to lead his troops where they could be easily sniped from above.

Planting the explosives took most of the night. We set them up at very specific coordinates so everyone knew not to accidentally drive over them. Dawn was peeking over the horizon when the radio call came.

"This is Stealth Unit 2, we've got a visual at 3-o'clock. Roughly two miles out."

I couldn't grab my receiver fast enough. "Y'all heard him, get into your positions. Unit 2, can you confirm it's Tash's army?" I released the button and waited for a reply while my heart jammed against my ribs.

The radio hissed for a few seconds that felt like an eternity before the answer came. "It's definitely an army marching on foot. I see no insignia or flags to indicate any allegiance. Do you want me to wait until I can see better, president?"

"No, proceed," I answered. "That's exactly who we're supposed to be fighting. Get into positions and stand ready, everyone."

"Coming from three-o'clock means they'll hit these

first." Shadow pointed at the map marking all of our bomb placements.

"Should've concentrated 'em all there," I mused.

"We had no way of knowing," he reminded me. "And anyway, they'll scatter in a panic and set the others off."

"I hope you're right." I went to lean against my bike and idly scratched Hades' head before setting up a long-range automatic rifle against my seat. Shadow got to working on setting up his own gun, and all there was left to do was wait for the boom.

About twenty minutes later, the first boom came.

The earth shook beneath our feet at the explosion, and I gave a quick tug at the straps holding my gun to my bike seat. "Shadow, you got that for me if it starts to slip?"

"Yes, president. I have no visuals yet, so go ahead."

The act of leaving my own body never stopped feeling strange. I couldn't even explain how I did it, aside from closing my eyes and simply stepping out of my own skin. It was nothing like what Gunner had with Horus, from when we tried to compare experiences. I wasn't sharing consciousness with another living thing, but temporarily filling a space where consciousness once existed.

The time between being in my own body and into the dead person I'd be seeing through felt like zipping through a dark tunnel. And when I emerged on the other side, I could see, hear, and feel the movement of my surroundings, but all other senses were simply not there. I had no heartbeat, no breath in my lungs, and of course, I couldn't move. It was eerie, especially now when I still felt the warmth of a body that had just been killed.

The first dead man I slipped into was face down on the ground. Panicked shouts and running footsteps surrounded me, but I couldn't see for shit, so I went through the dark tunnel again before finding another host. This next one was facing straight up at the sky. I saw quick flashes of people running, but because I couldn't move my eyes, I missed the directions in which they were going.

This ability sucks. I'd much rather see through a bird.

The third time was the charm, the deceased bastard was lying on his side and giving me a front row view of our work. It was just the panic and chaos we were hoping to create, people running around wildly and unaware of the dangers right under their feet.

Another boom went off to my right, sending a small cluster of people flying.

"It's a minefield, stop moving!" Someone was smart enough to figure it out, but no one paid him any attention. The more explosives set off, the more heightened their panic became.

I surveyed what I could before returning to my own body, jolting up from sitting against my bike.

"You back?" Shadow asked.

"Yeah." I blinked several times and came slowly to my feet—the vertigo always lingered for a bit. "Let me see the map."

Shadow handed it to me and I was quickly able to triangulate where my dead body host had been. Grabbing the radio, I barked out firing and movement orders to the units nearest where the body had been.

"Like shooting fish in a barrel, boys, but stay covered," I said into the radio. "Remember, this only works if they don't get the upper hand and figure out our positions."

"We've got incoming," Shadow warned, swinging his assault rifle to aim between his handlebars.

I looked in that direction, at first only seeing a dust cloud, but the shape of several Jeeps became clearer as they got closer.

"Their backup is hauling ass," I noted. "Easy, man. Don't shoot yet."

"I know, just waiting for the…"

BOOM!

The explosion went off louder than any of the previous ones, the affected Jeep rolling to its side and quickly becoming engulfed in flames.

"Oh shit," I remarked. "That's gonna—"

BOOOOM!

Shadow and I both ducked on instinct, the force of the blast rocking the ground beneath our feet. Despite being over half a mile away, I still felt the heat of the blaze scorch my skin. The other Jeeps were blown off their wheels, two of them still rolling across the landscape like children's toys.

"Damn, that might have done most of the work for us." There was too much dust and smoke in the air to see bodies, but no one close to that blast could have survived it.

"You going back out there to see the damage?"

Shadow leaned down to peer through the scope on his rifle.

"Fuck no. I'm not about to find out what it's like to be cooked alive."

A corner of his mouth quirked up. "It's not like you're *technically* alive."

"Yeah, yeah, man. You don't need to tell me how smart you are."

My radio stopped hissing as calls started coming in.

"Holy shit, did you *see* that explosion?!"

"Ugh, bro, I was taking a piss and it made me fall in it!"

"All units come in," I said into the receiver. "Give me numbers, any casualties or major injuries from that blast?"

"Nothing major here, President. Medics are standing by."

"Scared the piss and shit out of us, but we're good."

One by one, everyone reported that they were fine and damn if my heart didn't soar a little. *We're okay*, I realized. It was too soon to feel like we might actually win, but not being utterly fucked from the start was damn better than the luck we'd been having.

"Keep to the plan and stay calm," I ordered. "All the dust and smoke puts us at an advantage. The less they see us, the better."

"I hear helicopters, can't see 'em yet," someone reported. "Sounds directly overhead, but hard to tell. This is Unit 5."

"Howitzers, that's you," I answered. "Take your shot when you see 'em."

Another boom sent the earth shaking not five minutes later. Tash's soldiers scattered madly as a dark form hurtled down from the sky. The falling helicopter only sent more smoke into the air, obscuring everyone's vision too much to get away. It hit the ground and started rolling, then must have hit another one of our bombs, setting off another explosion that knocked us off our feet.

"Feels like goddamn Fourth of July!" I yelled, my ears ringing. "All units, how we doing?"

They all reported in positively again, with only minor burns and shrapnel injuries to treat. But we were still alive and kicking ass. I clipped the radio to my belt and returned to watching the horizon with Shadow.

"I got a few clear shots," he reported, one eye squinting shut while the other looked through the scope.

"Take 'em." I knew he wouldn't miss.

Tash's units on foot were still advancing, the majority of them still unaffected by our bombs due to their sheer numbers. They were definitely nervous though, their marching all out of step and their tight formations breaking. And the closer they got, the thinner their numbers would become.

The unit heading straight for us had to be one of Tash's best. They never broke formation once, their marching steady and robotic. They were clad in black and wore masks and hoods—not unusual for trekking through a dusty desert, but the sight of them coming remained unsettling. They had missed all the previous detonations without breaking a sweat, but if they continued marching in a straight line they'd walk right over one.

My finger hovered over the trigger on my rifle. They knew what was going on by now, their defenses had to be up. But they were laser-focused, and I didn't want them alerted to my position yet. By the time they got close enough to see us, they'd hopefully be blasted sky-high.

I stalked them from my position, checking my scope and pulling away to gauge their distance. They were heading directly for the IED and would be stepping on it within the next twenty feet.

Closer, closer, and closer they came. I no longer needed a scope to see them for a clear shot.

"Come on, come on…" My trigger finger was cramping from how badly I wanted to squeeze. Shadow was next to me, taking people out from a distance like a true assassin, and I just wanted to mow down some Tash followers.

The masked soldiers kept marching closer and then my heart started to race with panic. Why wasn't it deto-nating? They were walking right over it! I couldn't take on the whole unit myself and everyone else was spread out too far to help.

"Fuck, Shadow, I'm gonna need—"

BOOM!

Shock and relief hit me in equal measure, the blast raining down pebbles and dirt as I ducked under my arm. Something must have been fucked with the deto-nating mechanism for such a delay, but fucking finally! I went to re-aim my gun, and what I saw made me freeze.

They were *still* marching.

The soldiers toward the center and back of the formation had been hit, their bodies scattered around with either mortal injuries or dead. But the unit leader and the ones in the front carried on like nothing had happened.

No panic. Not a single sign of being shaken or afraid. It wasn't even like they acted *determined* to keep going, but more like they were machines with a single purpose. Human beings didn't act like this. Something was very, very wrong with these men.

"Reaper, shoot them!"

Shadow's command brought me out of my stupor, and I squeezed that trigger with all the fucking strength in my hand.

My initial shots went wild—I was unfocused and thrown off my axis. But thankfully with an automatic rifle, I didn't need to be all that accurate. Some of my shots hit the soldiers in the lower legs. When they fell, the men behind walked on top of them to continue marching.

"Reaper, the leader—"

"I see him," I assured Shadow.

The soldier front and center, the only one with some kind of gold insignia pinned on his all-black uniform, drew his gun and aimed the short barrel at me. Thank all the gods I was faster.

My rapid fire never stopped, all I had to do was aim the rifle at the man's chest to see him go down. His guys kept marching, stepping on him like all the others, and drawing their weapons as soon as they caught sight of us. My ears rang painfully from all the blasts and gunfire. My hands were burning up and cramped with my constant, rapid-fire shooting. But fuck no, I wasn't about to stop until they were all dead.

With Shadow's help, the whole unit fell, until no more men marched like creepy zombies toward us.

"I want that unit searched when it's safe, especially the leader." My hands were surprisingly steady as I checked my gun and reloaded, especially considering how fast my heart was hammering.

"Yes, president. How are the others doing?"

"I think all of our bombs have detonated." I picked up the radio. "All units come in, give me a status update."

The replies came a few agonizingly long seconds later.

"We've got minor injuries, just some debris from the blasts but medics are on it."

"All good here, president."

"Minor injuries here, couple bullet grazes and a twisted ankle but no casualties."

"Same shit here, Pres. It's like target practice."

I looked at Shadow with disbelief as the calls came in. "Are you hearing what I'm hearing?"

"No casualties." He sounded just as awed as I felt. "Despite being massively outnumbered."

"Holy shit, Shadow." I lowered the radio to my bike seat and turned around in a slow circle. "I think…I think we actually won this one."

"It looks that way."

The world surrounding us was hazy, thanks to all the

dirt, smoke, and gunpowder being thrown in the air. I heard shouts and pops of gunfire but no longer felt the dread of wondering how many men we'd lose. At the end of the day we might still lose a handful and it would be tragic, but that was war.

Our losses could have been so much worse. Just one soldier panicking and forgetting the plan, allowing his unit to get overwhelmed—that was all it would take. But everything was perfect, seamless.

"President." My radio crackled from one of our unit leaders. "They're surrendering. Your orders?"

"Call in the vans and have them brought back to Four Corners," I answered. "They'll be questioned and tried." If there was anything these people knew about Tash, I wanted it at any cost. After giving my orders, I looked to Shadow. "Shall we search them?"

"Yes, president." He sounded pleased.

We kept our guns on us—in case of any surprises— as we walked out to the battlefield. The landscape was riddled with craters now, thanks to our explosions. Surviving members of Tash's units were on their knees as our guys searched them and bound their wrists while waiting for the army transport vans.

Shadow was already searching through the bodies of the unit that came straight toward us, while I took a moment to just look around and marvel.

We did it.

It may have been just one battle of many, but this victory was *ours*.

"Anything interesting?" I asked Shadow, kneeling

next to the unit leader. Hades had been searching with him, sniffing out the bodies.

"No." He almost sounded disappointed. "No photos, letters, jewelry, or anything personal on them at all. Not even tattoos, although…"

He shoved back the sleeve of one man to expose an extensively scarred forearm. Nothing like Shadow's scars, but the man's entire arm had been severely burned at one point.

"This guy *had* tattoos," Shadow remarked. "I can still see ink spots where his skin wasn't burned as badly." He placed the man's arm down at his side. "A couple others have burn scars too."

"So they've had all unique identifying markers taken away." I scanned the dead men's faces, all of them individuals that had acted as mindless drones.

They are now free and at rest.

One glance at Hades told me the answer to the question I didn't know I had. These men may have died just minutes ago, but they certainly hadn't been alive before.

"What do you make of them marching over each other like that?" I asked Shadow. "Not responding to any of their surroundings."

Shadow's hands paused in his quick, efficient search of the soldiers' clothing. "It reminded me of when I'd been hypnotized but…different."

"Different how?"

"It's like…" He cocked his head as he searched for the words. "Hypnosis is not control. It's like being guided through a dream. I was aware the whole time and could stop or wake up at any point. But on the surface, it looked like Doc could control me." He glanced down at the man he'd been searching. "I don't think any of these guys could have stopped if they wanted to."

"So something *was* controlling them."

"I think so, yes." Shadow's mouth hardened as he gazed at each of the dead men. "And erased their individuality in the process."

I reached for the pin on the unit leader's jacket, ripping the fabric as I yanked the gold thing off—it wasn't like he needed it anymore. The more I stared at the golden brooch thing, the more confused and unsettled I got. Whatever the thing was, it wasn't *right*.

"You ever seen this?" I held it up for Shadow to see.

"No. Actually, well," he squinted, "it looks kind of familiar, but I can't recall ever seeing it anywhere."

"Same here." I laid the pin flat in my palm, as though looking at it from a different perspective would jog my memory.

It was little more than a stick figure of an animal, but nothing I could place for sure. The animal looked roughly like a dog, it had four legs, a head, and a tail. But the tail was forked—splitting in two halfway down the length. The ears were triangular like a wolf's, but in reverse, so the thinner ends attached to the head and widened at the tops. The head itself had a long snout like a canine, but the nose and overall head shape was wrong.

I closed my hand around the pin and slid it into my pocket. Looking at it was disorienting in a way, like I was staring at some paradoxical thing that should not have existed, but did. I'd make sure to give it to my dad and his lieutenants later.

"You ready to get out of here?" I rose to my feet and started back toward our bikes.

"Yes." Shadow followed after me. "Can we check in on how the northern battle is going?"

"Excellent idea." I picked up my radio. "Let's hope they've had as good a day as we have."

FOUR

GUNNER

"Listen up, fuckers!"

"Jesus, Gunner, do you *have* to call them that?"

I couldn't see Mari behind me, but had the image with crystal clarity in my mind—hand rubbing her forehead, groaning but trying not to laugh at how I addressed the soldiers.

"Yes, it's protocol," I whispered under my breath. Then to all the unit leaders in front of me, "You should all know the plan by now. I want no stone unturned, no blade of grass uninspected, between here and Blakeworth. Is that understood?"

"Yes, Captain!" came the chorus of replies.

"Killing blows are only to be made in self-defense. If your unit finds a Blakeworth scout, I want them detained and brought back to me alive. Anyone with injuries should be brought immediately to the field hospital, whether Blakeworth or our own. Any questions?"

T-Bone cupped his hands around his mouth and hollered, "When you gonna come sit in Daddy's lap, pretty boy?"

"You can fuck right off." I grinned as I waved my middle finger at him. The other soldiers allowed themselves a tittering of nervous laughter when they realized we were just fucking around.

"Mari said we could borrow you," T-Bone egged on, draping his arms over Grudge and Dyno's shoulders. The two of them just shook their heads at his antics. T-Bone was clearly the flirt of the trio, although who knew how successful he was with lines like that.

"Shut up, you have your own," Mari fired back.

"Man, I *hope* Blakeworth captures your ass," I laughed before waving my hand to everyone at attention. "Dismissed. All of you to your posts. We head out in thirty."

T-Bone's hounding certainly lightened the mood, if nothing else. Everyone had been serious, if downright somber, about the two battles going on today. Now everyone seemed a little more relaxed, a little more confident as they filed out of the meeting tent.

We were just outside the Four Corners northern border already, gearing up in massive numbers to take out Blakeworth spies and scouts in neutral territory. Mari's field hospital was the tent next door, and she'd use this one for overflow if the medics needed it, although we were hoping it wouldn't be necessary. Our large numbers were meant to flush Blakeworth's spies out from hiding, cut off communication to their territory, and question them for more information. Just on sheer numbers alone, the odds were stacked heavily in our favor.

My thoughts turned to Reaper and Shadow, heading east to confront Tash. They were in the much riskier battle, relying on more complex tactics to balance out their smaller units. But if anyone could pull it off, I knew it was them. I just hoped that whenever these battles were over and I got to go home, that my family would still be intact.

The sky was still dark, but the sun would be rising soon. No one knew exactly where Tash's line was, so they could have been engaging with the enemy already.

Slender hands ran around my waist while my thoughts were on the others. I returned Mari's hug with a squeeze around her shoulders, soaking up the last little bits of warmth and love before a day full of carnage.

"You ready, captain?" She propped her chin on my chest to look up at me.

"Keep calling me *that*," I sighed. "And I never will be. I'll ditch the whole thing to stay here with you."

She laughed lightly and turned her head to place her cheek on my chest. "Be careful out there."

"I will". Horus clicked his beak from his perch on my shoulder. "*We* will," I amended. "You be careful back here too. We shouldn't have much to worry about, but we keep underestimating how sneaky these fuckers are."

"We'll be fine. Jandro's hanging back and I've told all the medics to stay sharp."

"Good." I cupped her face, allowing myself a long gaze at her beautiful features before I lowered a kiss to that mouth. She returned it, holding on to the edges of my cut to keep me in place. I closed my eyes to savor her, to really feel the accelerated pounding in my chest when she kissed me.

Weeks ago she probably would have watched me ride into battle and hoped I never came back. Never again would I take this woman and the family we created for granted.

"Captain."

Some lieutenant calling me from outside the tent jolted me out of the moment. "What?" I growled.

"They're ready for you."

"I'll be right there." My touch slid down Mari's arms, our bodies separating with slow reluctance. "I'll see you when it's done, baby girl," I sighed out, my forehead heavy on hers.

"You better." Her face was tense but a smirk pulled at her lips. "Or Horus is gonna get an earful from me."

The falcon chirped from my shoulder, fluffing up his feathers once before smoothing them down again.

"Let's get this over with then." I headed for the tent flaps, my hand still connected to hers. "So we can move on and finally start our lives."

Mari followed me, her hands squeezing mine as we exited the tent together. Before we could separate, she drew up next to me and kissed me again for all the units to see.

"I love you," she said as she pulled away, untangling our fingers at the last possible moment. "Come back to me."

"I love you more," I called back, not giving a damn

about our audience. "And you're the only thing worth coming back to."

————

OH YEAH. I see you, Blakeworth fuckwads.

Horus soared over miles of rolling hills and endless plains. Our units were still a couple miles south, moving in while T-Bone and I scouted through our birds up ahead.

From up here, it was easy to see how the spies snuck up on us so quickly. They used flashlights with colored film taped over the lenses to communicate messages without making a sound. Most of them were positioned at various points in elevation so they had eyes from every possible vantage point. These fuckers must have seen Jandro and Slick from miles out, and tracked their movement by relaying the coordinates to each other through their lights.

It was genius in its simplicity, really. I was a little annoyed that I never thought of something similar.

Sending my focus back to my own body, I felt heavier and a little disoriented. Next to me on his bike, T-Bone blinked rapidly and gripped his handlebars as he also got his bearings.

"D'you see 'em?" I asked when he came to.

"Oh yeah," he chuckled, flexing his wrists. "We got this in the bag, pretty boy."

Now that we knew where the Blakeworth spies were, it should be a slam-dunk to round them up. I wasn't about to go tempting fate by speaking it out loud, though.

"Take your units around to the east and west to surround them," I said, marking the locations on a map. "We'll come up the middle."

"Yes, sir." He turned his bike around, grinning as he went to relay the orders to Dyno and Grudge.

I hit the receiver on my radio and told my unit leaders all the points we'd be hitting. "If a target isn't at one of those points, let me know and my falcon will find them. We don't want any of them getting back to Blakeworth."

"Roger that, captain. We're on the move."

I stuck the radio in my cut and revved up with a loud roar before tearing across the landscape. My units' Jeeps picked up speed too, racing to give our hiding enemies a rude awakening.

The first ones heard us coming as we got closer, but running on foot and their little dirt bikes had nothing on us. We hunted them down like it was a sport. One of my lieutenants swung his Jeep around, cutting off a couple of runners so close that they bounced off his doors. They weren't badly injured but were quickly surrounded, dropping to their knees with their hands in the air.

I drove on, heading right for another small group trying to zig-zag through some tall weeds. One of the ballsier ones turned around and fired shots at me, all of them going wide in his panic. I rode right up to his ankles, laughing directly in his ear.

"Do you know who the fuck you're shooting at?"

I eased off the throttle, letting him get ahead of me while I pulled out one of my smaller handguns. He looked over his shoulder as he ran, relief in his eyes as he thought he was losing me. But I just wanted some target practice.

I aimed low, where the weeds were the most dense and his legs were barely visible as he ran. I popped off three shots before the grass stilled and a scream rose up.

One of my lieutenants, Gonzalez, walked up as I leisurely drove forward to check my target.

"Four scouting units captured so far," he reported. "We've lost track of a few."

"Gotcha, I'll find your hidden ones in a sec." I was in a good mood, and in no hurry. None of them would be able to escape Horus' sight.

My target was lying on his back, gripping his leg and wincing when we approached. I grabbed his arm and turned him over roughly, patting him down for weapons while inspecting his leg wound.

"Only one shot out of three?" Gonzalez clicked his tongue at me. "You're losing your touch, captain."

"I know, just haven't been practicing." I started searching through my pockets, finally settling on a spare rifle strap. The injured Blakeworth man started crawling away as I approached him with it.

"No, no! Don't kill me."

"Quit squirming and calm down." I pushed him to the ground with a boot on his back, then turned to face his legs as I sat on top of him. "I'm tying this around your leg so you don't bleed out. But feel free to untie it any time if you do prefer to die."

"Wha...what? You're not gonna kill me?"

"Nope. We're not gonna torture you either," I said cheerfully with a pat on his butt. "We will detain you and ask questions, though. Cooperate and you'll be fine."

The man stilled, dumbfounded as Gonzalez and I hauled him up to stand on his good leg.

"I'll track down your escape artists if you're good here."

"Go ahead." Gonzalez bound up the man's wrists and started guiding him toward the other soldiers. "Holler if you need back up."

He had just disappeared through the tall weeds when I planted my feet wide and turned my face toward the sky. "Show me, Horus."

My eyes closed and I was weightless, with the sun on my back and air lifting through my feathers. When my eyes opened, I could count every blade of grass from three hundred feet in the air. Our army swarmed the landscape, just as we intended, but a few had broken past the line we tried to corral them in.

Three Blakeworth scouts ran on foot, their camouflage no match for my falcon's binocular vision. I could count their eyelashes from here. They were fast, I'd give them that. And with the distance they were clearing, they had great endurance. But no human could outrun a motorcycle.

I dove through the air, not to get a closer look, but to touch base with another being who had eyes on them.

Munin waited for me on the branch of a tree in the runners' direct path. I landed next to the glossy black raven just as the humans ran underneath. T-Bone's bird stared at me with its dark eyes and cawed once. Horus screeched back.

In the next moment, my awareness was hurtling through space back into my human body. I caught my footing after a quick stumble and ran back toward my bike. I had that machine between my legs and drove her hard straight north, flattening the tall weeds in my path until they gave way to the rockier terrain.

Not a minute later, I saw T-Bone cutting across the landscape until he fell in next to me. He shot me a maniacal grin, accelerating hard to pull up ahead. His bike was fucking loud, the roar reverberating off of every rock and tree for miles. The runners definitely heard him, and I hoped they were pissing themselves knowing they were being hunted.

The two of us stayed in tandem as we gave chase, following on the heels of the sneaky fuckers we saw through our birds. We could see them with our human eyes now, their forms growing bigger as we kept closer.

"Feel like playing with fire, pretty boy?" T-Bone yelled over our engines.

"What do you mean?" I glanced over to see him flicking a lighter on and off with one hand.

"It's all dry brush up there." He nodded ahead toward the runners, the distance between us and them shrinking with every second. "It'd be a mighty shame if a little brushfire was their last obstacle before making it home."

"You crazy fuck," I laughed, patting at my cut in search of my own lighter. "Let's do it!"

The runners would have to go up another hill before they were technically back in the Blakeworth territory. The city was still miles further up ahead, but we had agreed to fight in neutral territory only.

"Let's split up," T-Bone yelled. "Make a wall of fire they'll need brass balls to jump through."

"Fuck yeah." I was already veering to the right, going around the runners to head them off. T-Bone did the same on the left side of them.

The runners skidded to a stop, grabbing hold of each other's arms and panting with exertion as they watched us pass in front.

"Keep running, little cowards! You're so fucking close," T-Bone taunted. He held his lighter out to the side as he drove, the flame instantly catching the dry bushes like kindling.

The scouts started backing away, darting to the right in an attempt to go around the flames, but we headed them off that way too.

"Ah-ah-ah." T-Bone shook his index finger at them. "That way's not gonna work either."

My brushfire was already bonfire-sized, the flames licking six feet up in the air. The scouts tried darting for an opening between T-Bone's fire and mine, but he quickly blocked them with his bike.

"You want to run home so bad?" he continued taunting them. "Where your governor sits high on the corpses of those who built his city for him?"

"Come on, T. Let's just grab them." I pulled out zip-ties to bind their wrists, but he apparently wasn't done.

"You want to run to a territory that kidnaps women and forces them into marriage?" he went on. "Go ahead!" He gestured toward the fire. "Run through it, jump over it. Let's see how important your home is to you."

Holy shit, he was making this fucking personal for some reason.

"T-Bone," I yelled louder. "These fires could get out of control. Let's just grab them and go."

"Let them get out of control!" he roared at the top of his lungs. "Let these people see what it's like to have everything they love go up in smoke!"

"T-Bone, dude!" I rode up next to him and clapped my hand around the back of his neck, forcing his head to turn until he faced me. His gaze was wild and unfocused, with pupils like pin pricks. "You're not with me right now, man." I slapped his cheek. "Get it together! I need you to focus."

He blinked rapidly, eyes dilating as he focused on me. "Gunner?"

"Help me tie them up and let's get the fuck out before we choke to death." The smoke was already stinging my eyes and throat, our visibility getting hazy. Maybe I shouldn't have been so quick to jump on the fire idea.

"Go!" T-Bone pointed at the Blakeworth runners making a break for it up the last hill. I didn't blame the guy for still grieving those he lost, but he had cost us valuable time.

We spun our bikes around in a cloud of dust and exhaust as we took off after them. The incline grew steeper and I grit my teeth hard as I fought gravity, the rocky terrain, and now the smoke in my throat and eyes. We could still catch them, but were right on Blakeworth's doorstep. We could not afford to dally anymore.

My bike was more lightweight than T-Bone's and I pulled ahead of him, closing the distance on our runners just as they began cresting the hill. If they made it to the bottom, they'd be firmly across the Blakeworth border, and we could not capture them without nullifying our original agreement and causing a much bigger problem.

Steering the bike with one hand, I pulled out my handgun and took aim. A couple of non-lethal shots would end this chase quickly, and we could go home before sundown. I curled my index finger around the trigger as the runners reached the top and started running down the other side. Only by the grace of Horus or some other god watching did I have the sense to look beyond my targets at what awaited us just a few hundred yards away.

"Oh fuck, fuck!" I swerved and braked hard, struggling against my momentum and all the force now carrying me downhill. "T-Bone, turn around! Fucking go back!"

But he couldn't hear me over both of our vehicles running on such a high gear. We nearly crashed into each other as I started my way back up, and he began his way down.

"What are you doing?" he roared before looking

past me, his determined expression falling to stunned disbelief. "Oh no…"

"Go! Gooo!"

We started back down the way we came up, and with a confirming glance over my shoulder, I saw my worst fear coming true.

Blakeworth's army was hot on our heels.

FIVE

GUNNER

A fucking trap.

We should have known.

T-Bone yelled something like, "They're catching up!" but I couldn't make it out over the *hundreds* of vehicles hot on our tails now. Mostly motorcycles, but I saw some Jeeps and Hummers too. And knowing Blakeworth, these vehicles were souped up, powerful and fast.

In essence, T-Bone was right. We couldn't outrun them.

Fuck it all, this was *not* how this battle was supposed to go.

We pushed our bikes to their limit, but riders on some kind of crotch rocket-dirt bike hybrids zipped around us like it was nothing. Two long lines of riders converged ahead of us to surround us and cut us off.

T-Bone glanced at me and I gave the tiniest shake of my head. We could plow right through them, probably killing a couple people and hurting ourselves in the process. But that would also lead them straight to Four

Corners. We were miles ahead of our army, and most of them were probably heading back to base at this point.

No, I'd rather let myself be captured before bringing an army right to our doorstep when our people were unprepared. I began to slow down and T-Bone did the same, his face hard-set and determined. At least we were of one mind about this.

The riders ahead of us already had guns drawn, pointing them directly at us when we came to a stop.

"Off the bikes," someone yelled through an opaque black helmet.

T-Bone and I dismounted with our hands in the air, the two of us getting immediately shoved to our knees and patted down aggressively for weapons.

"At least buy me a drink first," the Son muttered. He got a punch to the stomach for that, doubling over with a groan.

I tensed under my own rough patting and groping, fighting the instinct to rush to his aid. My heart drummed wildly as Blakeworth soldiers closed in tighter around us, and I tried to force calming breaths through my chest.

Captured doesn't mean dead, I thought. *And it doesn't mean you'll never get back home again.*

Oh fuck. I promised Mari I would come back.

Sorry, baby girl. Looks like it won't be happening today.

"Why do you look so familiar?" A looming figure stood over me, the uniform decorated with war medals and an opaque black helmet blocking out the sun.

"I dunno. If you used to be a woman, we probably had a good time at some point—ugh!" Apparently it was my turn for a punch in the gut. I didn't see the hit coming and it knocked the wind out of me. "You hit hard for a Blakeworth pussy," I wheezed.

"Ah, I've always wanted to punch a Youngblood." After shaking out his fist, the figure removed his helmet. The face underneath belonged to a middle-aged man with blue eyes and grey hair at his temples. I stared at him for a few moments but the recognition never came.

"Haven't had the pleasure of meeting you before but," I coughed, "I would love to punch you as well." Sadly, my hands were now zip-tied behind my back.

"Your father and I have some…history," the man sneered down at me.

"Yeah, well, join the club, dude. Oof!"

I earned a fist to my cheek for that one, his ring cutting across my face with a stinging pain.

"I knew you were his the instant I saw your pretty fucking face," he went on. "I gotta say, it's such a joy to see how far Youngblood's golden boy has fallen."

"I haven't fallen," I hissed, spitting blood on his shoe. Like I cared if he kicked me in the face with it. "I've risen."

"Huh." The man looked around at his army, now completely closed in on T-Bone and me. "Doesn't look that way to me, kid."

"You'll never get it." I shook my head at him. "Dogs like you will never understand."

"Understand what?" he humored me.

"Let me guess. You hate my old man because he burned you on a deal. Either that or you're jealous of him. You wanted his life—the contracts, the money, a different mistress for every day of the week." I shook my head, ready to welcome whatever hit came next. "Just another sad little man who wanted everything Jon Youngblood had."

"And look at his sorry shithead for a son." The man, who I figured was a general, regarded me with disgust. "Born into the best possible life and he threw it all away."

"And I'd do it again." I leaned forward, a thrill running through me at his retreating steps and the flash of fear in his eyes. Hands clapped down on my shoulders to hold me in place, but I paid them no attention. "I traded my life and my name for freedom, general. For the open road and the sky. For integrity. Things you can't even imagine."

"What an ungrateful child," the general scoffed.

I grinned at him, knowing my teeth were stained red with blood. "No argument there."

"And to think I almost promised my daughter to you."

"I hope she finds her freedom too." I didn't know where this conversation was going anymore, if I was stalling or just pushing his buttons for the hell of it. This guy wanted to gloat, so I wanted to knock him down. Adrenaline was still riding me hard and I was just spouting jabs at him without thinking. "I hope she finds a man you'll never approve of. One who loves her deeply and worships her pussy with his tongue every —oof!"

There came the second punch across my other

cheek, pain ringing through my teeth and up to my skull.

"She's thirteen, you fucking brute!"

I spat out more blood before peering up at him. "Are you fucking joking?"

"Do I look like I am?"

"Think about this for a minute." I paused to spit out more blood. "You'd marry her off as a child bride to someone she doesn't even know. Who do you think is the bigger piece of shit between the two of us?"

"I would have secured her future with the Young-blood name! Set up my legacy for life, if only your father had kept *you* under control!"

"Yeah, that's the thing." My grin grew wider. "No one controls me."

This general was getting hot under the collar, but managed to calm himself after taking a few steps back from me. "Some control will do you good," he promised with the creepiest fucking smile.

All his posturing was getting boring, so I slid my gaze over to T-Bone, who was not having riveting conversations like me. His head was tipped back, eyelids heavy and twitching. I hissed in a breath of shock. Was he really seeing through Munin *now?* That was some risky shit. I knew I was vulnerable out of my own body, so I'd never look through Horus while in a compromising position, much less in the hands of the enemy.

But the soldiers posted on T-Bone paid him no mind, apparently waiting on orders from their general who was obsessed with riding my dad's coattails. He had his back turned to me at the moment, talking in low voices with his unit leaders when T-Bone finally came to. The other biker slid a glance and an amused smirk in my direction.

"No worries, pretty boy," he muttered under his breath.

That phrase could have meant anything, but he didn't elaborate. He did seem calmer though, taking a deep breath that puffed his chest out. His zip-tied hands stretched out behind him like he was waking from a nap.

"You okay, dude?" I asked him.

"Peachy," he grunted back. After a few beats of silence he added, "Sorry about that."

"It's alright," I said. "That stuff sneaks up on you."

"When you least expect it," he murmured.

One of the men speaking with the general whipped around right then. "Do I have to cut your fucking tongue out?"

T-Bone's expression morphed into a rage I'd never seen on his face before. "You think that's funny? Come and try, Blakeworth pussy."

The memory hit me right then—Grudge couldn't speak because his tongue had been removed. And T-Bone took that threat *very* personally.

Everyone had stopped talking and turned to look at us now. The man who threatened T-Bone laughed lightly as he pulled a knife from his belt, the small, silver blade flicking open and closed. "I'll find you much funnier when you can't talk anymore."

"Come get it, then." T-Bone stuck his tongue out and wagged it, taunting him. "Take it from me. You take everything else from people tied up and on their knees!"

"T-Bone, shut up!" I hated how he flipped on and off like a light switch. Grudge and Dyno must have kept him even-keeled, because he was a fucking maniac without them.

"I recognize him too," the general mused, narrowing his eyes. "He's one of the thugs who stole the governor's daughter-in-law."

"She was never his!" T-Bone roared, face red and veins popping in his neck. "She never belonged to your fucked-up territory."

The general was the epitome of calm compared to my friend foaming at the mouth like a rabid dog. "Captain, go ahead and remove his tongue." His eyes drifted to me. "Make sure Youngblood Junior is watching."

"No, no, no, no." They turned my body toward T-Bone as the captain approached him, brandishing the knife. "Stop this. He won't talk anymore."

"He sure won't," the general said with a quiet sort of glee.

"Take it from me!" T-Bone goaded, not helping his own case at all while pulling against his restraints. "Show me what a big man you are to silence me, tied up and on my knees with all these fuckers holding me back."

"Stop it, T! He's not fucking around."

"Oh I know, pretty boy." T-Bone's gaze slid toward me, and I was stunned to see his eyes were sharp and fully aware. He wasn't somewhere else like with the runners and the fire. He was all there, and he actually *wanted* this. "I told you, it's alright."

He refocused on the captain in front of him, the

man flipping the knife in the air like a taunt. With a lurch of his body, T-Bone somehow got a leg underneath him and started pushing himself to stand.

"Hold him! Fucking hold him!" the captain ordered.

More soldiers rushed in to push T-Bone back down to his knees. One person wrapped an arm around his neck in a triangle choke hold. Someone else started binding his ankles together. Altogether, there were five people restraining him. He just grinned at the captain, not at all disturbed by the knife now hovering inches in front of his face.

"Can't make it too easy for you now," T-Bone goaded. "Otherwise you'll still look like a pussy to all of your men."

The captain only scowled. Everyone was watching to see what he would do. I couldn't help but wonder how the soldiers would feel if he actually went through with it. Some men could be intimidated into falling in line, while in others, the same act could spark a rebellion.

"Hold him still." The captain stepped closer. "Hold his head and open his mouth."

"That's it. Gimme a kiss, captain," T-Bone said before a soldier grabbed his jaw and forced it open.

"Don't!" I struggled against my own bonds, the zip-ties just digging tighter into my wrists while more soldiers came to hold me in place. "Don't, please. Take my tongue instead."

"No, we can use Youngblood," the general said in response to his captain's questioning glance. "This scum," he jerked his chin at T-Bone, "we don't need for shit."

"I'm useless too!" I insisted, desperate enough to say anything at this point. "My father wants nothing to do with me. You'll never get access to his fortune through me. I'm just a fucking biker like T-Bone."

"We'll see," the general said dismissively. "Get on with it, captain."

"No!" I fought and wiggled a shoulder loose, only to have a foot crash into my back. I landed facedown in the dirt and then felt the punishing weight of a boot on my head.

I could only see the captain's shoes a few feet in front of me, and T-Bone's knees. Any second now I expected to hear his screams and watch the blood drip down his body. God, why the fuck would he ask for that? So Grudge wouldn't be the only one?

Someone yelled from a distance, but I couldn't make out the words with a rubber sole crushing my ear. The shoe on my head was gone in the next second, and all the boots in front of my face started running around, people shouting in a panic.

T-Bone had been shoved down and was now lying in the same position as me. He coughed out a mouthful of dirt and grinned at me, his tongue still very much intact.

"What's happening?" I grunted out, trying to push myself up, but I was too hogtied.

"These fuckers were so focused on cutting off my tongue, they didn't see the cavalry come to our rescue," he chuckled, then winked at me. "Told ya, it would all be alright."

SIX

MARIPOSA

"Is that smoke?" I shielded my eyes, squinting far across the landscape. There was definitely a plume of gray smoke rising up in the distance. "Was making a fire part of the plan?"

Lieutenant Gonzalez shrugged, his eyes never leaving the Blakeworth prisoner I was treating. "It's dry as hell out there. Even just hot ammunition could spark something."

"It looks big," I noted. "Could it be a signal of some kind?"

"Maybe. I'll check-in with Gunner when the POWs are secure."

I waved a hand over the man on the hospital bed, who was now firmly under general anesthesia. "He's not going anywhere, lieutenant. Can you check-in with him now, please?"

Gonzalez ducked his head with a sheepish grin. "I'll be right over there." He pointed outside the hospital tent flap.

"I'll scream if I need you," I promised. I also had my little handgun in a holster and one of Shadow's daggers strapped to my calf under my scrub pants. Chances were I could take this drugged up gunshot victim by myself, but I didn't want Gonzalez to feel inadequate.

He stepped outside and spoke with a low voice into his radio as I cleaned up my station. Like Gunner had expected, we only had a few injured come through the field hospital. Most of them were the Blakeworth scouts they'd been sent to capture, primarily minor injuries but some gunshot wounds. So far nothing had been fatal, which was a huge relief to me.

I looked toward the battlefield again with crossed arms, frowning at the smoke reaching higher. The day was nearing its end and some of the soldiers were coming back already, their assignments complete. But there was no sign of my husband and his falcon.

"Captain Gunner I repeat, do you copy?" Gonzalez said into his radio. His voice sounded tense and my heartbeat began to accelerate.

I hurried out of the tent. "What's going on?" The lieutenant turned to face me but said nothing, his lips pressed into a tight frown. "Gonzalez, please don't even *think* about keeping information about my husband from me."

"He's not answering," he admitted. "My unit met up with him about an hour ago. He was going to fetch a couple of runners. They were on foot and he was riding. It should have been easy, but we haven't heard from or seen him since."

"We have to find him." My feet started moving, instinct taking over, but Gonzalez grabbed my arm, halting my movement.

"We will, Mari, but *you* can't go out there."

"I have been in battles before. Let go of me!" I yanked my arm from his grip.

"I'm sorry, but your husbands would never approve of me letting you out into that field."

"Well, they never approve of a lot of the shit I do. They're used to it."

"Mari." Gonzalez's jaw ticked. "General Bray will come down on *me* if you do this."

"No he won't, I'll explain it to him. But we're wasting time here arguing. Which units are heading back out? I'll join them."

"You will *not*!"

"What's going on?"

I whipped around to see Shadow and Reaper walking up, my hope soaring. "You guys are back!"

"We nailed it, sugar," Reaper grinned, opening his arms in a subtle motion for a hug.

I went to squeeze around him briefly, then pulled back. "I'm so glad! But no one has heard from Gunner and I'm worried."

"Is that smoke?" Shadow squinted at the horizon much like I had.

"Give us the rundown, lieutenant," Reaper said to Gonzalez, who repeated the same information he gave me.

"You're right, Mari should stay here." Shadow

glanced at his president with a cool, neutral gaze. His assassin's gaze, I realized.

"Why?" I demanded. "I can help. What if he's injured out there?"

"If it's anywhere near that smoke, it's not that far. It's better if you're here, with all the tools you might need." Reaper reached out and brushed his fingers against my hand. "If he's in bad shape, we know how to keep him stable until we bring him back here."

"What if you don't, though? What if Blakeworth ambushed him and you guys are walking into a trap?"

"All the better that you stay here." Shadow approached me, all imposing and predatory to the point that Gonzalez took a step back. But I stayed put and allowed him to tower over me, his hand coming out to rest on my hip with a comforting weight. "Let us ride into danger while you stay safe, for once."

"I don't like it," I said with a shake of my head.

"Yeah, well, we don't like you running off either," Reaper chuckled. "Stay, sugar. We'll keep you updated over the radio."

"Hey, guys?"

We all spun to find Jandro walking up with a grim-faced Dyno and Grudge. My heart sank as I silently wondered, *Oh no, what now?*

"T-Bone's units are back, but no sign of the man himself," Dyno reported. "He didn't rendezvous with us at the agreed-upon spot."

"Gunner is missing too," I said.

"Well, shit. What are we waiting for then?" Jandro

spread his hands. "We're taking prisoners, Blakeworth probably is too."

"Not if we can help it," Reaper growled. "Let's go."

Everyone followed his lead and my frustrated groan mostly fell on deaf ears. But Jandro hung back, wrapping me in a warm embrace and tilting my face up to press insistent kisses to my mouth.

"We still outnumber them," he whispered, forehead against mine. "We'll be fine, and back before you know it."

"I know I'm more useful back here," I admitted. "I just hate that all of you are going. I can't lose you all in one swoop!"

"Not gonna happen, *Mariposita*." He cupped my face sweetly, but his smile was devilish. "You softened us up, but the Demons are still crafty bastards when we fight. With two of the Sons with us, we can't lose."

"Stop tempting fate and just get them back." I shoved him away roughly. "The sooner the better."

"We will." His promise was solemn, sealed with a final kiss before he hurried away to join the others.

DUSK CAME. And then nightfall, with no signs of my men.

I was exhausted but knew I couldn't sleep a wink. Most of my time was spent pacing around the hospital tent, listening to the static of the radio in my hands.

As promised, Reaper had given regular updates until

roughly three miles out. Last I heard, they still hadn't spotted Gunner or T-Bone. One lieutenant speculated that Blakeworth had put some interference out that messed with radio waves. Whatever the case, the silence made the hours pass by torturously slow.

Nightfall eventually turned to early morning, with no news and no sight of them. At four AM, I said, "Fuck it," and marched out to where my dirt bike was parked. Unfortunately, it was near the officer's meeting tent, and I hoped I could take off quickly enough before any lieutenants spotted me.

No sooner had I grabbed my handlebars and started walking it out toward the battlefield when I heard a distinct rumbling fill the once-quiet air. Headlights turned on in the distance, which would have looked remarkably like fireflies if I wasn't so desperately hoping.

It wasn't just a few lights, or even a dozen. More and more switched on, creating a festive line that shined upon our camp. There were at least a hundred of them, motorcycles and Jeeps from the looks of it. People started coming out of their tents to look, and I stiffened for a moment. Were these our people returning to us? Or was it Blakeworth invading? It was too dark to tell, the headlights too bright to make out anything on the vehicles they shone from.

Somehow, over the rumbling growing louder, I heard, "We got him, *Mariposita*!"

My knees buckled, threatening to give out from under me as I sagged from relief. They found him, and they were coming back!

I returned my bike to its parking spot and went back to the hospital tent, setting up sutures, forceps, scalpels, local anesthesia—whatever Gunner might need for the shape he was in. I had just scrubbed my hands and pulled on gloves when my men burst through the tent flaps.

"Gunner!" I choked out a sob at the sight of him.

He was filthy, covered in dirt with dried blood on his cheeks, lips, and chin. But he was standing there, on his own, smiling easily like it was just another day.

"Sorry to keep you waiting, baby girl," he rasped. "But I told you I'd come back, didn't I?"

"Y-you asshole," I hiccuped through my sobs, rushing over to him. "What happened?"

"Runners lured us to the waiting Blakeworth army just outside their border." His arms came around my back, rubbing up and down soothingly. "They had me and T-Bone captured for a hot minute but—"

"Captured?!" I cried.

"We were okay, honestly." He cupped my face, bright blue eyes staring down at me before glancing at the others over his shoulder. "They were chatty fuckers, so we kept stalling. T-Bone distracted their attention enough so they didn't even see anyone running up on them."

"It was still a hell of a battle," Reaper huffed. "But we made it through, and captured ourselves a general and a captain."

I looked at the rest of my men for the first time since they arrived. They did look worn out and dirty, like they'd been scuffling for hours. "Are any of you hurt?"

"Nah, sugar. We're fine."

I sagged with relief against Gunner's chest. "And T-Bone?"

Gunner frowned. "We got separated in the chaos. I sure as fuck hope he's okay."

"I saw him riding back with Dyno," Shadow confirmed.

"Thank fuck."

"So what was the smoke? Some kind of signal?" I asked.

Gunner shook his head with a soft laugh. "A total fucking accident that ended up saving our bacon. If you guys hadn't seen it, T-Bone and I would be in a Blakeworth cell right now."

"But you're not." I untangled from him to grab alcohol wipes for the blood on his face. "None of you are, and that's what matters."

"So I'm not a super smart math guy or anything but," Jandro scratched the back of his head. "Did we win *two* battles today?"

There was a beat of silence before Reaper answered softly, "Yeah. We sure as fuck did."

I paused in cleaning Gunner's face so he could turn and face the others, his grin infectious and bright. "Holy shit, guys. We did it."

"We can't afford to celebrate yet," Reaper said. "Tash has a lot more in store for us, and I'm sure Blakeworth does too. But for now?" He looked at the dust covering his arms, then at his fellow men. "We deserve a fucking shower at least."

"I need some fucking sleep," Shadow grunted out.

Reaper laughed and thumped Shadow's chest. "Go on and get a solid few hours. We'll need to brief my dad on everything later today."

"We'll be right after you guys," I said. "I want to make sure this one is medically cleared before we head home." I returned to dabbing at the cuts on Gunner's cheek.

"I won't say no to a beautiful medic fussing over me." Gunner smirked.

"We'll see you at home then." Reaper nodded curtly, then quickly stepped out of the tent.

The sudden departure had me staring at the tent flap for a few seconds. A familiar discomfort coiled in my gut. He was doing that moody, hot and cold thing. Again.

Don't read into it, I told myself. *We've all been up for over twenty-four hours. He's exhausted.*

But Jandro and Shadow came over to give me quick kisses goodbye before heading out after Reaper. I sighed before returning my attention to Gunner's wounds. Reaper and I were still complicated, messy. I couldn't get upset over every little thing when I hadn't fully allowed him back in yet.

"You okay, baby girl?" Gunner's eyes were watchful as I cleaned his face. He had deep scrapes on both cheeks that had bled, but they didn't appear to need stitches. His lower jaw was bruised and swelling on both sides, but nothing appeared broken.

"All things considered, yeah." I dabbed ointment on his cheek. "What happened here?"

"The Blakeworth general popped me a couple times," he grunted out. "He had rings on."

"Who wears gaudy rings out to a battlefield?" I grumbled.

"Someone who doesn't actually fight," Gunner scoffed, then went quiet for a few moments. "He knew my dad."

"Oh?" I paused, watching his expression. "Is that… bad? Good?"

He shrugged and let out an indignant huff. "Doesn't matter to me. Never has. My old man's just a sperm donor as far as I care."

"Something about it is bothering you enough to mention it," I noted, returning to treating the cuts on his cheeks.

"He was going to cut out T-Bone's tongue and then beat him to death, most likely. He only wanted to keep me alive because he thought he could use me," Gunner sighed out tiredly. "My whole life used to revolve around strengthening my dad's power. Or people using me as a stepping stone to access my dad for their own gain. It just," he raised a hand and let it flop back down to his thigh, "sucked to be reminded of that. I thought I got away from that life." Gunner used the heels of his palms to rub his eyes. "Sorry, I'm whining like a little bitch while you've been worried about me. Sorry about—"

"Hey, stop." I grabbed his wrists to pull them away from his eyes. "You were almost captured by the enemy today. That's going to bring up a lot of upsetting shit. You don't have to apologize for anything."

"Yes, I do." He freed his wrists from my hands and laced his long fingers with mine. "I'm not done apologizing for failing you as a husband."

My breath stuttered in my chest for a moment. "Tonight, you *are* done. Believe it or not, I'm not mad at you today."

Gunner let out a soft chuckle, lowering his forehead to mine. "How was I lucky enough to end up with you?"

"Because I know you're more than your name and your family's wealth," I said. "I've never met your father, but I know you're a hundred times the man he is."

His grin grew. "It wasn't until you that I really felt like I could be."

"You are." Finished with his face, I lowered my hands. "Did you get hit anywhere else?"

"No."

"Good." I peeled my gloves off with a triumphant snap. "You're cleared to go home. Might want some ice and painkillers for your jaw soon."

"Okay," he said absently, reaching for my hands again. "Hey, can I take you somewhere before we go home?"

I raised a brow at him. "Take me where?"

"A place I used to stop at on supply runs. It's not far from here. I've been meaning to take you out there, just," he lifted one shoulder, "we never got the time."

"I'd love to, Gun, but I'm exhausted. I need a shower and—"

"This is a great place to rest. And we can uh, wash up." He smirked. "It's totally secluded. There won't be anyone else but us, promise."

My eyes narrowed. "Okay, really. What is this place?"

"You'll see." His eyes lit up. "I don't want to ruin the surprise."

SEVEN

MARIPOSA

T he ride was cold, even for how early in the morning it was. The sun wasn't even up as Gunner drove us roughly a half hour through a small, winding canyon, and I shivered as I clung to his waist.

"How did you even find this place?" I asked at one point. I'd lost all sense of direction miles ago. There was no trail here, we drove over completely wild terrain. The twists and turns through the rocky formations seemed endless.

"Had to hide some contraband a couple years back," he answered. "I figured if *I* got lost the first few times up here, thieving MCs definitely wouldn't find our stuff."

"Mm-hm." I lifted off the seat and leaned forward to stick my tongue in his ear. "What kind of contraband?"

"Weapons, mostly."

"Mostly."

"And a certain green herb, occasionally." He smirked at me over his shoulder. "Never anything harder than that, though."

"Amateur," I teased him, kissing his cheek as I settled back down in the seat. The guys and Noelle loved to joke about me about trading prescription drugs, like I was the most hardcore dealer ever to join the Demons.

A few more twists and turns later, I saw what looked like fog in the distance, hanging thick and heavy, only in this section of the canyon. Gunner slowed as we approached it, warm air brushing my cheeks the closer we got. It was a shocking contrast to the cold on the entire ride here, and took me a moment to figure it out.

"Is that steam?"

"Damn right it is." Gunner stopped the bike a few feet away from where the steam cloud hung in the air. "This is a natural hot spring, baby girl."

"Oh my god!" I couldn't scramble off the bike fast enough. Gunner laughed as I ran directly toward the steam cloud, the warmth now coating my skin in dew like I was in a fancy spa. There was a gentle slope and more rocks to climb over but sure enough, the steam rose from a small pool filled with glassy, crystal-clear water.

"Told you it'd be great for relaxing." Gunner came up behind me, already shrugging off his cut and pulling apart his belt buckle. "And washing up," he added with a lascivious grin.

"Is it safe?" I asked him.

"Oh yeah. I've been up here dozens of times. It's

pretty hot, but you get used to it after a few minutes." He pulled his shirt over his head and gave me an intent look. "It's shallow, and you're a fine swimmer now anyway."

I didn't have to say anything and he assuaged my worries anyway, coming up to me and wrapping me in a hug. "I won't let anything happen to you regardless," he added with a kiss on my forehead.

"Fine, you've convinced me." I smacked his abs once and started shedding my own clothes.

"Just think of it like a hot bath." He bent over to unlace his boots and remove them, then shoved his pants down his legs. "From nature."

Once both down to our birthday suits, Gunner took my hand and started leading me down to the pool.

"Watch your step. Some of these rocks are sharp," he cautioned. He let out a hiss as he stepped one foot into the water and then the other. "Been a while. Feels like it's gotten hotter."

"Probably 'cause the air is colder," I mused. My skin erupted in goosebumps the moment my clothes came off, and my hand that wasn't holding Gunner's was clenched in a fist against the cold.

"Whenever you're ready, baby girl. Try a foot. Take it slow."

I pointed my toes and reached, skimming across the surface of the water. "Yeesh, that's hot!"

"My feet feel okay now." The water was so clear, I could see Gunner's toes wiggling a few inches below the surface. "Just let your body acclimate."

I nodded and, tightening my grip on his hand,

lowered my foot into the scorching water next to his, making the same hissing sound as he did.

"Just a few degrees below being cooked alive," he laughed, wrapping both arms around my waist.

"Sure feels that way." I wrapped an arm around his shoulders and waited until the water felt pleasantly warm enough before dipping my other foot in.

Together we eased in slowly. He was right about it being shallow—the water only came up to waist-height while standing. Working our way down to sitting, I finally let out a satisfied sigh once the water rose past my shoulders.

It was ten times better than a hot bath. The constant heat soaked into all my tired muscles and made me utterly relaxed, languid. Gunner splashed water over his face and shoulders, then dipped his head back to wash the rest of the battle out of his hair. I did the same and oh, that heat felt incredible on my scalp too.

"This is amazing," I told him, sitting sideways in his lap once we finished rinsing the past day away. "Thank you for bringing me."

"I didn't want to wait," he admitted, fingers dipping in and out of the water as they traced patterns on my back. "Who knows when the next battle will be? Or how long this war will drag on for? I want to make time for things like this whenever we can."

"Me too." I nuzzled his neck and kissed him there, lacing my hands on his opposite shoulder.

"I want you and Shadow to come up here," Gunner went on. "I've always thought of this place as mine, but I want it to be a refuge for you." His arms circled my waist under the water. "A place you can run away to when some of your husbands are driving you crazy."

"Gunner." I lifted my head from his shoulder and pressed my forehead to his temple. "I don't need apology gifts from you. Or sacrifices or whatever. This place *is* yours, and I'm grateful you shared it with me."

"Well there's not much else I can give." He chewed his lip. "And I owe you. Because I contributed to taking him away from you."

I wrapped tighter around his neck and kissed his cheek. "All I want is for you to be honest with me, love me, and love the other guys."

"Loving you is easy, baby girl."

"And the rest?"

"Of course, but loving you is easiest." He turned his head, nudging his nose against mine. "You ask so little of us."

"Well at the end of the day, you're all pretty great men."

"Huh." Gunner let out a small breath of laughter as his hand slid up my back to grip the back of my neck. "At the end of the day, we're a pack of outlaws who found ourselves a queen."

His mouth came down on mine with demand and heat that rivaled the water we sat in. Our tongues dove and crashed, lips sliding against each other with a friction that lit me up even hotter. I turned in his lap to straddle him, his thickening cock stroking my lower belly as our kisses stoked the fire that always burned bright within us.

In fact, I was getting a little *too* hot.

"Gunner," I gasped, breaking off a kiss, then forgetting what I was going to say as his tongue teased the spot below my earlobe.

"Mari," he groaned back, nipping me before dragging his mouth down the side of my neck.

"Gun, can we, um, get out?" My hips rolled forward despite the request, my core seeking the solidness of his cock between us.

"Yeah, if you want." His tongue laved my collarbone, hands lifting me higher out of the water so he could kiss the swells of my breasts.

"Yes, please!" The cooler air was a shocking relief from the hot spring, which had started to get overwhelming. "It's too hot now."

"Hold on." Gun's face remained firmly in my chest as he lifted us out, my arms and legs clasped around him.

It was such a sensory delight, the cool air caressing my overheated body, and still having the heat of Gunner's bare skin on mine.

"Careful," I told him as he walked us out of the pool.

"I know where I'm goin'." The skin of my chest was reddening where he kissed and teased me, his fully engorged cock now pulsing between us.

I glanced over my shoulder to see that he was heading straight for his bike, and a thrill bolted through me. Gunner went for the back end of the motorcycle, perching me on the edge of his seat, and returned to kissing my mouth with a ferocity that had me aching between my legs.

Mid-kiss, he reached behind him and forcibly unlocked my ankles from each other. Holding my thighs apart, Gunner ignored my whimpers and pleas to be fucked as he began to descend down my body. He went back and forth between each breast, sucking and running his teeth along my nipples until I begged for more. That wicked tongue dragged down my body until he finally devoured my pussy in a long, succulent kiss.

"Fuck!" My screams echoed off the canyon walls as Gunner probed me with his tongue, running it from my opening to my clit and back down again. My thigh muscles were no match for his hands splaying me apart, no matter how badly I resisted his grip in an effort to clamp my legs around his head.

"Gunner, Gunner…" I reached for him, fingers sinking into the wet, golden strands of his hair. "Gunner, please…"

His eyes met mine and he shook his head no, dragging that scorching hot tongue across my clit in a way that made my head fall back on the bike seat. I must have sounded like a wounded animal with how much I whined and begged. My core closing around nothing was pure torture.

He dragged my orgasm out for as long as he could with that tongue, finally giving my poor clit some relief with some fast, flicking magic that I never felt another man replicate. But even as the release swept over me, shooting out through my limbs, I still felt too hollow and empty.

Gunner stood upright, towering over me as he licked

his glossy lips and fisted his cock. "You want this, baby girl?"

I was almost afraid to say yes, out of fear that he would deny me. My lips parted as I watched him stroke up and down that thick, beautiful length. Jesus, he could have been a porn star just with how pretty his cock was, never mind his actual bedroom skills.

Apparently impatient for an answer, Gunner released himself, letting the dense weight of his cock fall onto my clit with a soft slap. I was still incredibly sensitive from my orgasm and squirmed with a groan. He grinned, held around his base again and repeated the motion. That one was more of a direct hit and it sent sparks through me.

"Yes!" I cried out, almost in tears. "Yes, I want it. Please, please fuck me, Gunner."

"That's my sweet girl," he praised, drawing his hips back until his blunt head slid through my folds.

When he pressed forward it was the sweetest relief, almost better than an orgasm. The ache inside me was replaced by such a satisfying fullness that my head fell back with a reverent moan.

"Fuck…" It was Gunner's turn to bite out curses, his eyes locked on where our bodies connected as he dragged slowly out of me. "I can never get over how fucking incredible you feel."

"More, don't stop," I breathed, rocking my hips as he returned to sheathe himself in me.

"Not a chance, baby girl." His voice was always lower, rougher during sex. I loved how being together this way brought out a growly, possessive side to my sweet, always-smiling husband. He anchored one hand on my hip as he picked up the pace, using the other to grip one of the compartments next to the seat. "I can't believe it's taken this long to fuck my woman on a bike."

"Better late than never," I grinned up at him. Only Reaper and I had sex directly on a bike before. A passing thought of doing it with all my guys, like filling up a punch card, made me giggle.

"Something funny?" Gunner arched a brow and he slammed into me harder, that cocky smirk showing how much he enjoyed my attempt to reply—words turned into moans and curses and babbling that made no sense because *holy shit*, I was going to come again.

His skilled fingers went to my clit and he never fell out of rhythm with his thrusts, sending me hurtling over the edge with a few quick swipes that turned me into a quivering mess.

I didn't even feel the cold anymore. The heat of our fucking, our connection, our love, roared like a bonfire.

Gunner pulled completely out of me when my aftershocks dulled to hot pulses and I whined at the loss of the delicious fullness. In the next moment he grabbed me and flipped me over onto my stomach, my arms and legs now straddling the back of the bike as he re-entered me from behind with a deep thrust.

"Holy fuck, that's so fucking sexy," he grunted, hips crashing into my ass while his hands dug into my waist. "I need a picture of this, or for Shadow to draw it at least."

"Yeah? Ahh…" I held on to the edge of the seat,

taking and relishing in all of Gunner's hard crashes into me.

"I love this view," he panted. "My gorgeous woman with these hips and her sexy tattoo. My bike's pretty sexy too," he added with a laugh. "And fuck me, I just love watching your sweet pussy take my cock." His thrusts slowed as he moaned loudly and I looked back to see his head thrown back, eyes shut as his grip tightened on my flesh. "You look so fucking amazing, it's gonna make me come too fast."

"Don't stop, I'm getting close again…"

Gunner's growl was primal as his hips slowed, his grip tightening on my waist as he forced himself to take long drags of his length through me. I trembled around him, my release so close but just out of reach. His breaths were labored, ragged as he fought for his own control.

"I want to make this last," he rasped, running his palm up my back. "I don't want to go back to war and meetings so soon."

"Then fuck me again after this."

He laughed breathlessly and leaned over to brush a kiss along the back of my shoulder. "I think I just might."

Gunner stilled inside me as his lips teased the back of my neck, my earlobes, wherever he could reach. I arched up to kiss him, and his hands swept underneath to my breasts, plucking my nipples to aching peaks in the cold air.

With his hands and mouth occupied, I did the

moving for him—pressing back on his length so I could feel that delicious stroke inside me.

"Oh fuck," he groaned, forehead heavy on mine. "That's, fuck, that's gonna do it."

"Me too," I whined, holding the edges of the seat while my lower body rocked back and forth. The dull roar from our short breather fired up into a demanding blaze again, the need too great for me to stop or slow down.

"Oh fuck yeah, use me," Gunner growled, his arms tense and straight on either side of the bike as he held himself still for me. "Take what you need from me, baby girl."

"I need all of you," I whimpered, my backward thrusts desperate and frenzied on his stiff length. He swelled inside me, the pressure making me breathless with need.

Gunner reached around and between my legs, finding my clit and keeping his fingers pressed there so I could rock onto his cock and his hand with every move- ment. I didn't even have time to take a breath and shout *yes* before my pleasure reached its peak. My limbs shook with the release, Gunner's hand remaining firmly in place as he finished with a last few stuttered thrusts through my aftershocks.

His forehead came to my back with a heavy moan, panting breaths making my skin shiver. We remained locked together, our bodies pulsing gently where we connected. Gunner's hand eventually trailed up my arm, his fingers curling through mine.

"Wish we could stay here," he murmured, stirring gently as he dragged lazy kisses on my back.

I brought our joined hands to my lips and kissed his palm. "One day we can."

"One day," he agreed before carefully sliding out of my body.

EIGHT

SHADOW

I woke up to a soft weight resting along the length of my back. Warm skin covered me like a heated blanket, and the smell of some floral lotion filled my senses. And then kisses rained down lightly on my shoulder blades.

"Mm, morning," I murmured into the pillow, unwilling to move and disrupt the sweetness I'd woken up to.

"It's afternoon," Mari informed me, her lips on my spine and hands running down my sides. Strands of her hair dragged lightly over me, cool and damp in contrast to the warmth of her skin. She must have just gotten out of the shower.

"Huh, napped longer than I thought."

"Good dreams?" She kissed the back of my neck before laying her cheek down on my shoulder blade.

"Better than that." I reached a hand back to touch her leg straddling my waist. "No dreams at all."

Mari made a soft humming noise before returning to

her task of kissing my back. A smile pulled at my lips. Did she see me sleeping and decide to come in and lay on top of me? Just because she wanted to?

"Did you just get home?" I circled my fingers around her knee, tracing the scar tissue from where she'd been shot.

"Gunner and I got back a couple hours ago. We took a detour to a little hot spring in one of the canyons."

"Oh, his secret place."

"You know it?"

"Know of it, but never been there."

I waited for the jealousy that never came. It used to cut through me, sharp and biting when I saw her with the others, when they would talk within earshot about being with her. Now I realized that feeling came from wanting what I never thought I'd have—the love and attention of this woman right here.

"He wants us to go there," Mari said. "You and me." She paused in the middle of a kiss. "He still feels guilty about what happened."

"He'll get over it," I murmured, not wanting to dwell on negativity during such a sweet moment. "Let's take him up on his offer when we have a free day. I've never been to a hot spring."

"Neither had I, before today." I felt her smile against my skin. "It's a date."

Mari's mouth lingered on me sensually, indulgently, in the same places where blades had sliced me and my mother's bullwhip had ripped my flesh away. All the while, her hands ran leisurely up and down my back, pausing to rub tighter areas. In some places, her fingers curled up as she lightly scratched me, the feeling sending a pleasant buzzing up into my scalp. She was in no hurry, lips placing kisses instead of telling me urgent, worrying news like this morning on the battlefield. A rare moment that I wanted to last forever.

I still had to get used to the fact that, with what little free time she had, she *chose* to spend it with me.

"You're really enjoying this?" My words slurred as though I were drunk. Her touch had lulled me into utter relaxation.

She laughed softly, the air from her mouth blowing softly over my skin. "What do you mean by *this*?"

"This right now. Touching me like you are. Kissing all of…*that.*"

Mari slid off me then, crawling up the bed to lie on her stomach next to me. She was topless, wearing nothing but a pair of panties. No wonder I felt so much of her beautiful skin on mine.

"You're mine and I love you," she said. "Of course I enjoy kissing you and touching you." She reached out again, smiling as if she couldn't help herself, and ran a hand from my shoulder down the length of my back. "I can never get enough of you."

I rolled to my side, freeing an arm from under my pillow so I could wrap it around her. "So does that mean I've been…satisfying you?"

Mari looked confused and then started laughing. "You really need to ask?"

"Yes," I admitted, glancing away from her face.

"You always seem happy with me, but for my own peace of mind, tell me honestly if you are?"

"I'll answer your question with a question." She scratched lightly at my jaw, fingers trailing over my beard as she scooted closer to me. "Is water wet?"

My gaze found hers again. "Yes."

"Does a bear shit in the woods?"

Her smile was so contagious, I couldn't stop myself from mirroring it. "Yes."

"Does Freyja snore when she sleeps upside down?"

I started laughing then. "Yes."

"Does a rooster—"

I leaned in to cut her off with a kiss, which she returned eagerly before her lips pulled back with another smile.

"You're perfect for me," Mari whispered before planting another kiss on my lips. "Don't ever question that."

"I won't anymore," I promised, stroking down her back. "I just want to make sure I'm doing this right. That I'm keeping you happy."

"You are." She kissed me again, her mouth warm and succulent on mine, before moving on to my neck, the spot she knew drove me wild with wanting her. "You are, you are…" The whispered words became a chant, soothing and repetitive, punctuated by kisses. "Am I satisfying *you*?"

Her question took me by surprise, making me pull back slightly to see more of her face.

"Of course you are." I slid my hand up her back until I cupped the nape of her neck. "You make me happy beyond what I thought was ever possible. Have I made you doubt that?" A knot of anxiety tightened in my chest while I waited for her answer.

"No my love, never," she assured me with more kisses, warm hands stroking my chest and relaxing me again. "But your needs are important too. If you're checking in with me, it's only fair that I do the same with you." Her nose nudged against mine. "This is a partnership, Shadow. We take and give to each other."

"I just want to give you everything." I cupped her face with one hand and dragged the other to her hip, pulling her flush to me. "I love you."

"I love you," she answered in a quick breath before I swallowed her mouth in another kiss.

Our hands roamed each other lazily, our kisses long and indulgent. The world might have been a war zone outside this room, but everything about this moment with her was perfect. I knew she'd been with Gunner recently, so I was in no rush for sex. To know she wanted me, *loved* me, was more than enough.

My fingers traced her necklace at one point, running along the small links in the chain to the colored glass on the butterfly pendant.

"I should get you something like this," I mused, kissing the space between her collarbones.

"You don't have to get me anything." Mari scratched over my scalp in long, luxurious strokes that felt like pure heaven.

"I can't be the only one of your men that doesn't give you a gift."

"It's just stuff. It's a nice gesture, but I don't need it."

Her palms swept forward, cupping my jaw for another kiss. "I have everything I need right here."

Determined now, I shook my head. "No. I'll think of something."

Mari groaned, a playful, exasperated sound. "You've already given me tattoos."

"I've given lots of people tattoos," I scoffed. "No, I want to give you something unique to us."

An idea did strike me then of what I could give her. Finding it in a jewelry piece would be nearly impossible, unless I had it custom-made. But the only decent jeweler I knew was Reaper's mother, and I didn't want to risk Mari finding out about it before I could surprise her.

If I tattooed it on her, however…

I ran a hand down Mari's side, picturing the design in my head and imagining it transferred to her skin. Oh, it would be beautiful. Perfect, even. And doing it myself would ensure it looked exactly as I wanted it to. The only catch would be the element of surprise.

"Question for you," I murmured after lying quietly for a few moments in each other's arms.

"The answer is yes." Mari kissed my forehead and returned to stroking her fingers through my hair.

I laughed, pushing up to my elbow. "Don't be so quick to answer before you know."

She just smiled, dragging a gentle touch along my ribs and abdomen. "What's your question?"

"Would you let me tattoo you without seeing the design until it's done?" I rested my hand on the side of her hip. "Or choosing where it goes?"

Mari's eyebrows lifted. "Oh, interesting." She pursed

her lips for a moment, then came to a decision quickly. "Yes. I trust you."

I knew she did, in all the ways that mattered. But hearing her say it sparked all kinds of emotions in my chest. *She trusts me.* It felt like such a gift.

"I take it back about the tattoo." My hand slid up to hold the beautiful, dipping curve of her waist. "I just thought of something, but I want to surprise you with it."

"Ooh, color me intrigued." She grinned. "I like that idea. And it is still unique to us."

"Yes, it will be." My hand slid back down to rest on her thigh as I pictured it on her skin. Already, I was itching to sketch it out. Next to the drawing of her I put on my arm, it just might end up being my favorite piece of artwork.

"Can you tell me where you'll put it?" she asked, watching me drink in her skin.

"I'm thinking here." I returned my hand to the top of her hip, and slid it back down to her upper thigh. "About this big."

"That's pretty big," she mused.

"Mm-hm. Some of it might go here." I slid my touch behind her, helping myself to a squeeze of her ass.

Mari groaned as if annoyed but she was laughing. "I'd expect nothing less."

"You're really okay with not seeing it until the end?"

"I'm already dying to know what it is, but I know it'll be worth the wait." She scooted closer, nuzzling her head into my chest. "I know it'll look amazing. And knowing you, it'll be so meaningful and unique."

"I hope so." I wrapped both arms around her back, holding her tightly to me. "I hope you'll like it."

"I'll love it." Mari lifted her head and kissed under my chin. "You could get drunk and tattoo a bunch of squiggly lines on my ass and I'd like it."

"Don't let Jandro hear you say that," I scoffed. "He'll think it's a great idea and try everything to make it happen."

Mari laughed into my chest again, then went quiet for a few moments while she touched and kissed me some more.

"I have a question for you now," she said.

"The answer is yes." I leaned in to nip at her ear.

She chuckled, a bit of nervousness lacing the sound as she held the sides of my neck and kissed my mouth once. "How would you feel about Jandro coming to bed with us?" Before I had a chance to think, she quickly added, "If you don't want to, that's okay. I'm just wondering."

I paused to study her expression. "You mean sharing you with him during sex?"

Mari nodded, a dark flush running up her neck.

I shrugged, playing absently with the ends of her hair. "I figured it would happen at some point since we're all with you."

"That doesn't mean it *has* to happen," she said. "If you wouldn't like it, if you prefer our time together being just me and you, we can absolutely do that."

"Hmm." I rolled to my back to look at the ceiling, keeping her close to me with one arm. "I didn't know I had a choice in the matter."

"You always have a choice." Mari leaned over me, brushing another kiss against my chest. "Always."

This woman was so perfect, how could I not share her? This blissful, sparking feeling in my chest—she made *three* other men feel this way. She deserved more than I alone would ever be able to give her. And still, she gave me the option of being selfish enough to keep her to myself in the bedroom.

"You don't sound thrilled." Mari smiled lightly at my silence, trying to hide her disappointment. "Forget I brought it up."

She slid down, moving to place her head on my chest, but I pulled her back up, my mouth landing on hers with a rough crash.

"I told you," I growled, heat and want lighting me up like a bonfire. "I want to give you *everything*."

Mari's lips pulsed against my own, her breath coming in soft puffs from the harshness of my kiss.

"If my wife wants more pleasure in bed," I continued, dragging my thumb along her swollen bottom lip. "She can bring a hundred men into the bedroom."

Mari laughed a bit breathlessly. "We don't have to go *that* far."

"Yeah, that's probably too many." I chuckled and kissed her again, more lightheartedly. "But yes, Jandro or any of them are fine with me."

"You're sure?"

"Yes." I banded my arms tightly around her again, feeling beyond touched and loved that she would be so considerate of my feelings. "I knew what I was getting into, Mari."

"I just don't ever want you to feel neglected or… unimportant." Her brows knitted together with concern.

"You could never make me feel that way." I brushed my knuckles against her cheek, just utterly in love with this woman and marveling at the fact that she was mine.

"Still, I want you to tell me if I do." Mari opened my fingers and leaned her cheek into my palm. "If I make you unhappy in any way, I want to know so I can correct it."

"There is nothing to correct." I tipped her chin forward until her lips just barely grazed mine. "You are perfect."

She traced my mouth with a smile. "The rest of our lives is a long time, hopefully."

"Hopefully," I agreed.

"There's bound to be some moments where not everything is perfect."

"I'm sure there will be." I used my other hand to brush the hair off of her shoulder. "But that's not right now."

"No." Mari smiled wider, keeping her lips connected to mine. "Everything about this, right now, is…"

"Perfect," we said together.

NINE

MARIPOSA

My stiff legs were happy to see our home at the end of the long, winding driveway, but the rest of me wished the ride could be longer. I just loved being wrapped around Shadow, flying down the road with him with the wind whipping past us—even if I must have looked like a child-sized jetpack strapped to his back.

I squeezed around his waist once when we came to a stop, then groaned as I threw my sore leg over the seat to hop off.

Shadow reached for my waist, pulling me close once I was steady on my feet. "Thanks for coming with me," he murmured, nudging his forehead against mine. "I think having you there made me feel a lot better."

I grinned, running my hands up his broad shoulders to wrap around his neck. "Of course. I'm always here when you need me."

He drew me against him, winding both arms around me like a shield of muscle at my back. "I'm actually starting to believe it when you tell me that."

"Good." I planted a quick peck on his mouth. "You should."

We had a free morning the day after the battle and decided to take a day trip to visit Doc's colleague, Dr. Ellis. She was far enough away in neutral territory that it was deemed safe by the other guys. Blakeworth was no longer spying on us, and Dr. Ellis' practice was well out of their sphere of influence.

Shadow had been nervous when we arrived, but Dr. Ellis immediately put us both at ease. She had served us tea, was barely five feet tall even with her mane of white frizzy hair, and made it feel like a social visit with a grandma rather than a therapy session.

"Sorry to waste your time, but there's nothing you need from me, dear," she'd told Shadow with a smirk. "It seems old Bill Harman worked you through the most difficult part. You're in fine shape to continue the work yourself." Dr. Ellis then beamed at me. "A loving, patient, supportive environment is so important for continued progress, and it seems you have that in spades."

We spent another hour small-talking with her before we took off for the hot springs. Gunner had written down directions for us, and we were lucky enough to run into a taco truck before winding through the canyon. Shadow and I had lunch, made love, and soaked in the spring. I couldn't imagine a more perfect day with him.

Now at home, Shadow's smile, full of genuine happiness and warmth, was so beautiful to see. He leaned in to pull a longer kiss from me—slow, delicious, and lingering. I indulged him for the first few, loving how the gentle pulls of his mouth contrasted with the roughness of his beard.

When we parted for a breath and he leaned in for more, I patted his chest to pause him. "Get off that bike and come inside."

"Inside the house or…?"

"Shadow!"

He grinned at my peals of laughter, thoroughly pleased with his joke as he dismounted his steed and grabbed my hand as we headed for the front porch.

"Jandro is a bad influence on you," I teased.

"I think I stole that one from Gunner, actually."

"Oh yeah?" I widened my eyes dramatically. "And who was Gunner offering to *come inside*?"

Shadow tried to put on a serious face, but he was still smirking. "Oh, no one important. Some random woman long before you came along."

"Oh *really*?"

"I don't think she took him up on the offer, if that's any consolation."

"Hmph. I'm not sure it is." I flipped my hair over my shoulder, maintaining my sass as we walked up the porch and through the front door. The sight in the living room made me stop in my tracks, and Shadow nearly crashed into me.

"What happened?" I demanded right away.

T-Bone and Dyno were sitting next to each other on the loveseat, their arms intertwined and clasped together. Jandro and Gunner sat across from them, and Reaper stood next to the couch. All of them wore grim, worried expressions.

"Grudge is missing," T-Bone said with a hard swallow.

"Missing?" I cried.

"Grudge?" Shadow gasped at the same time, moving out from behind me. "Since when, the battle?"

Dyno nodded, his thumb stroking over T-Bone's hand. "When he didn't report back afterward, we thought he might have been laying low. We all technically went behind enemy lines, so we figured he'd take his time getting back to us, to not alert anyone from Blakeworth. But it's been almost two days."

"I couldn't find him with Munin," T-Bone choked out. "I even went out to the battlefield and called for him with our distress signal. He didn't answer."

"I just searched the area over the past few hours with Horus too," Gunner added softly. "And nothing."

"Well that's…that means he's still alive right?" I babbled out, my heart already hurting for Grudge. "If he's not out there…"

"Then he's been captured," T-Bone spat out, confirming my fear. "By fucking *Blakeworth*."

A heavy silence filled the room. So much implied meaning was held in the name of that territory, the place that built an elite class on slave labor and whose scumbag governor approved the kidnapping of Kyrie Vance. Blakeworth's working-class had few rights, and harsh punishments were inflicted for the most menial of crimes. I didn't dare imagine how such a territory would treat a prisoner of war.

But that wasn't the worst of it. If anyone in the military recognized Grudge from when we took Kyrie back months ago, stealing a piece of Blakeworth property as they saw it, Grudge would be more than just a war prisoner.

He would be a political prisoner, someone who directly undermined the authority of Governor Blake. I had no doubt in my mind he would be made an example of, tortured beyond any lines that would be considered ethical.

From the expressions on everyone's faces, it was clear they had already been thinking of all this.

"What can we do?" I asked the room helplessly as Shadow made his way to the couch, his shoulders tight and brows drawn tightly together. He and Grudge were brothers, likely by blood as well as their bond in friendship, and my chest ached for my husband too.

"I think a hostage exchange is the only way we can do this without more bloodshed," Gunner said. "We have some of their people too—important people. Members of their elite class."

Frowning, I went to sit next to Shadow and started rubbing his back. "I thought Blakeworth only sent their 'disposable' people into battle."

"We have one of their generals," Reaper said. "And a captain, both of which have made clear they're *very* loyal to their governor. They haven't said a peep to us in their interviews."

"Blakeworth will probably want goods too," Jandro added. "Isn't that why everyone wants a piece of Four Corners in the first place? They might want lumber and sheet metal. Tools and vehicles too, probably."

"I can negotiate with 'em," Gunner said. "We can—"

"There is no price for Grudge," T-Bone growled out between his teeth. "He's *our* man, and a brother-in-arms to you. He's not just fucking livestock you can trade goods for."

"Of course he's not, I didn't mean it like—"

"T-Bone's right," Shadow cut in, his hands clenching. "Give them their general, their captain, and any goods they want. No price is too high for getting Grudge back."

Silence filled the room again, but it was a more hopeful, determined silence. T-Bone nodded his agreement with Shadow, jaw clenched hard and red eyes blinking rapidly. Dyno held onto T-Bone's arm and kissed his shoulder, their intimacy and vulnerability clear and out in the open. This was someone they loved, after all. I couldn't even imagine the pain if it was one of my men captured by the enemy.

"I'll ride over and tell Dad." Reaper was already pulling on his cut and heading for the front door. "Gun?"

"Yeah, coming." Gunner sprang up from his seat, gave T-Bone a brotherly pat on the shoulder as he passed him, and then a quick kiss to me before joining Reaper in putting his boots on.

"Ride safe," I said to both of them, my hand still moving over Shadow's stiff back.

"We'll be back soon," Reaper promised. "And let you all know what happens next." He looked at me for a long moment, like he was trying to decide if he wanted to kiss me goodbye too or not. He ended up not, instead following Gunner out to the garage with a quick slam of the door. Their motorcycles started up moments later.

"You guys are welcome to stay here," I said to the two distraught Sons.

"In fact, you should stay," Jandro added, rising from the couch. "For dinner, at least. You guys should be surrounded by family right now." He headed into the kitchen like a man on a mission.

"Thank you," Dyno said, sounding grateful but weary. T-Bone still looked too choked up to say anything. "We'd really like that, actually."

"Take the guest bedroom," I said. "Stay as long as you'd like."

T-Bone only nodded gratefully with a small glance at me, the two of them wrapped up in each other. I wrapped a hand around Shadow's bicep and planted a kiss on his shoulder. "I'm going to help Jandro cook, okay?"

"Okay." He brushed a kiss along my forehead. "I'll stay with them."

Reluctantly unwrapping from him, I stood and headed to the kitchen. "What can I do, *guapito?*"

"Enchilada sauce, please," he answered immediately, carving a raw chicken with experienced precision.

"Got it."

We worked around each other in quiet collaboration, anything to get our mind off of the situation at hand. Grudge wasn't a Demon, but the Sons of Odin had become something of a sister club to us. Him being captured was like one of our own missing. I could only hope he was just being held for the time being and not suffering.

While Jandro and I cooked, Shadow came into the kitchen briefly to grab drinks for himself and the Sons, his expression downturned and grave.

"Come here," I said to him, my fingers coated in enchilada sauce from dipping tortillas in the mixing bowl.

"Hm?" Shadow paused, clearly distracted.

"Kiss." I leaned up and across the counter toward him.

The smallest smile twitched on his lips as he leaned to meet my lips. We sipped at each other lightly, a few brief moments of comfort for both of us before he pulled away to serve drinks to our guests.

"Yo, where's my kiss?" Jandro called after him.

Shadow didn't answer, but T-Bone's throaty chuckle floated in from the living room.

"He's a whole new person," Jandro remarked in a softer voice, carefully laying out enchiladas in a baking tray.

"He is," I agreed, a note of pride in my voice. "As much as I hate to say it, I think that time in exile was good for him. He was forced to grow and make new connections. And Doc's therapy was nothing short of amazing."

"I would've liked to see it." Jandro washed his hands in the sink, then dried them on the dish towel over his shoulder. "But I'm glad you got to."

"I don't know if you would've wanted to, honestly." My throat tightened at the memory of Shadow confined to Doc's metal chair, confessions and memories pouring out from the deep recesses of his mind. "It was so hard to listen to, Jandro. I knew he'd suffered but couldn't fathom how much. I've seen suffering, but nothing could have prepared me for that."

A warm, strong hand squeezed my shoulder, followed by a kiss on the back of my neck. "He had the right people listening to him, helping him without any judgment. That's the important thing."

"You're right." I placed a kiss on his knuckles resting on my shoulder.

The food was ready a half hour later, and we called T-Bone and Dyno to our table. They didn't have hearty appetites, understandably, and Jandro thankfully bit his tongue, not making any cracks when they only picked at their food. Normally we'd be going for seconds and thirds of Jandro's enchiladas, but all of us seemed to have trouble just with our single portions.

Reaper and Gunner came home just as the table was being cleared. The Sons practically sprinted to the door, the most energetic I'd seen them today.

"What did your father say?" T-Bone demanded, well up in Reaper's personal space.

"He met with Vance and together they drafted a message for Governor Blake." Reaper shrugged off his cut and placed it over the back of an armchair. "It's being sent by a secure courier tonight."

"And?" T-Bone pressed. "What did the message say?"

Reaper hesitated in answering, allowing Gunner to jump in. "He's offering to exchange just the captain for

Grudge, first. And wait to see what Governor Blake says."

"Wait to see?" T-Bone's eyes narrowed. "The longer we wait, the more opportunity they have to torture him."

"When they see we're offering a hostage exchange, they'll know he's valuable to us," Gunner explained. "They know now that we can take them in battle, so they won't hurt him too badly. And by offering a high-ranking officer in exchange, Blakeworth knows we're reasonable, if even generous."

T-Bone let out a frustrated groan, walking several paces away from the two men before spinning back aggressively. "Grudge is *not* a bargaining chip for these fucking war games. We already established that no price is too high to get him back, so why the fuck is Vance playing like this?"

"Easy, T." Reaper held his hands up in a defensive gesture. "You know I agree with you. If it was me, I'd offer up all of Four Corners on a platter to get Mari back."

My eyes locked on Reaper with shock, my heart rate doubling the moment those words registered in my brain.

"But we can't do that and still expect to win this," Gunner said cautiously, earning T-Bone's murderous glare. "If we offer the keys to the kingdom for one man, Blakeworth will gladly take it all and come at us again when we have nothing left."

"Do you *know* what we've done for Vance? What Grudge has done?" T-Bone roared in his face. "We've protected this territory for a decade. We marched right into enemy territory and rescued his precious fucking daughter! Grudge has bled and sacrificed for Four Corners, and Vance doesn't see him as valuable enough to offer a bigger prize? Fuck him, fuck you—"

"Trav, come here." Dyno wrapped his arms around T-Bone's waist and forcibly pulled him away from my men. "Sit down, take a breath."

The fight seemed to go out of T-Bone then as he sank into the couch cushions, hands cradling his head. Dyno remained wrapped around him, murmuring something private and intimate to his ear.

"For what it's worth," Gunner said after several moments of tense silence. "Reaper and I fought with them for thirty minutes, trying to make them offer the captain *and* general for Grudge, but they wouldn't budge."

He threw a glance to Reaper who nodded, chewing his lip in grim agreement. "Dad and Vance insisted on negotiating this way. Depending on what Blake says, they'll offer more. But what Gunner said is right—we can't show Blakeworth we're willing to do anything to get one man back. Even if it is the truth."

"We know," Dyno sighed, his hand making long, sweeping passes over T-Bone's back. "It's war. It's bigger than us. It's just hard when…"

"You've lost so much already," Shadow filled in quietly.

"Yes." Dyno continued to hold T-Bone with an arm around the distraught man's back, rocking him gently from side to side.

"We will get him back," Reaper insisted. "Dad and Vance *do* understand how important he is. They want to handle this a certain way, and we have to trust them."

"If we don't," T-Bone muttered, his head still bent low. "So help me Odin, if they fuck this up—"

"Travis." Dyno squeezed tighter around his partner. The affection and calling T-Bone by his given name seemed to have a calming effect on him. Dyno's voice was low and soothing. "Don't let your thoughts go that way, not yet. Let Vance and Bray carry out their plan." He looked up from comforting his partner. "When do they expect a reply from Blake?"

"Any time tomorrow," Reaper said.

"Blake will likely wait until the end of the day to send a reply. They'll want to make us sweat and panic," Gunner added.

T-Bone let out another pained groan, and everyone looked at him in sympathy.

"I think we'll lie down in your spare room if you don't mind." Dyno's dark eyes were tired, but his posture remained protective and supportive of T-Bone. "Not that we'll get any sleep."

"Of course, go ahead," I told them. "The bedding's just been cleaned. You can use the restroom in the hall."

"Thank you, Mari." Dyno stood, gently pulling T-Bone along with him.

My guys mumbled goodnight to them as they crossed the living room, and I reached out to rub T-Bone's arm when he passed me. He didn't acknowledge the contact, his mind off somewhere else as he blindly followed Dyno's lead.

Once the guest bedroom door shut quietly, Jandro turned to Reaper and Gunner. "There's plenty of enchiladas left if you guys want any."

"Thanks, man. I might have a small plate, but my appetite is shit today." Reaper rubbed his forehead. "It's early, but I might go to bed soon too."

"Yeah, same." Gunner raked his hands back through his hair. "We should head to City Hall early tomorrow, so we're there once the reply comes."

While the two of them lumbered into the kitchen, I grabbed Shadow's hand and pulled him back to talk privately. "Do you want me to spend the night with you tonight?" Lately, I usually cycled between his, Jandro's, and Gunner's beds, but tonight was different. I didn't want to leave Shadow's side for a single moment.

His large palm found purchase on my waist, the thumb of his other hand tracing my cheekbone. "If you want to."

"I'm asking you if you need me." I wrapped both arms around his waist, propping my chin on his chest as I stared up at him.

Shadow bent to kiss me, forearm sliding around me until it hooked around my lower back. "I love when you're in bed with me. I...just..."

"It's okay." I reached on tiptoes to kiss him again, smiling to make sure he knew I wasn't offended by his reluctance. "I didn't know if you'd rather be alone after today or—"

"No, I don't," he protested quickly. "I *do* want you with me, I just don't think I'm in the mood for..."

"Oh, sex?" I blinked. "Of course we don't have to. I wasn't even thinking of that."

He huffed out a sheepish laugh and smiled back at me briefly before the expression died on his face. "I'm sorry, I just can't stop thinking about Grudge."

"You have nothing to apologize for." I pushed a lock of hair out of his face and kissed him once more. "We're all worried about him. I just want to be there for you."

Shadow wrapped both arms around my lower back and lifted me off the ground to give me a deeper, longer kiss. "You're the most amazing woman, and I love you."

"You're amazing." My fingers raked through his hair as I returned every warm press of his mouth. "And I love you."

He lowered me slowly to the floor after a few more kisses, the sounds of low conversation and glasses clinking filtering through to remind us of our surroundings.

"A drink with the guys and then bed?" Shadow suggested.

"Sounds good," I agreed, then followed his lead into the kitchen.

My three other men were around the breakfast bar, talking quietly among themselves. Jandro started pouring me a small tumbler of *anejo* tequila before I even had to ask. As I took my first sip, my eyes caught Reaper's.

That smoldering green gaze was just like the first time I ever saw it the moment he walked into the service center at Old Phoenix. The difference was now, I *knew* the danger and ruthlessness behind that gaze—I didn't have to speculate based on legends. When Reaper said he'd give up all of Four Corners for me, I knew he wasn't exaggerating. Recalling those words now lit up a fire in my belly that had nothing to do with the alcohol.

He might have taken me and tied me to his bike that day, but I was captured the moment he laid those eyes on me.

TEN

GUNNER

R eaper was already up and pouring coffee by the time I came down from my room. "Mornin'," I greeted, earning a noncommittal grunt in reply. "Thanks," I added, reaching for the mug he poured me.

He was looking better since Mari and Shadow got back, but still not *great* by any means. He still wasn't sleeping much, that was clear from a single look at him, but he wasn't as cantankerous either, which was some improvement.

"Will your dad be up this early?" I brought a tentative sip of coffee to my lips.

"Mm-hm. Hardly anyone is sleeping well." He shot a joking accusatory look at me.

"Don't look at me like that. I was tossing and turning all night." I set the coffee down and rubbed my face once with a groan. "Everyone else still down?"

He nodded after a long pull of coffee. "Jandro will be up soon. He's still got a long day of repairs ahead of him."

"Shadow and Mari?"

Reaper shrugged, the motion tight in his shoulders at the sound of her name. "She'll be making rounds at the hospital, I assume. Shadow might stay with the Sons, I dunno. I'm not keeping tabs on them." He drained the rest of his coffee before meeting my eyes again over the rim. "What?"

"You don't have to avoid her, you know," I said. "She's taking steps. She *wants* things to work out."

"I know, I just," he rubbed his face with a groan. "I've been too overbearing in the past and I don't want to do that again. I don't want to make demands of her. She doesn't owe me anything, so I just…don't want to be in her way."

"The timing of it all fucking sucks right now," I sympathized with him. "Trying to fix what went wrong between us in the middle of a fucking war."

"Yeah," he agreed. "She's got a lot on her plate, and I don't want to put any pressure on her. The last thing I want to do is drive her away again."

"There's a middle ground between pressuring and avoiding," I reminded him. "It's not like you gotta leave the room when she pays attention to us. Unless it bothers you," I added quickly. I never knew Reaper to be jealous, but maybe that had something to do with it. He was the one all about sharing and got *me* roped into it, so jealousy wasn't something I'd considered in him. But maybe he was just better at hiding it.

"It doesn't bother me," he answered. "I'm not entitled to anything from her, and I'm glad she has all of you." He looked toward the backyard where Foghorn was stretching his wings and getting ready to crow his ass off. "It's just, I dunno. I can see she's happy as fuck with the three of you, even when things are really shitty right now. Maybe…maybe I overestimated how much she really needed me."

"Reap, dude. Come on—"

"I've always just hurt her," he cut me off, eyes hardening. "Ever since the beginning, I've been a fucking dick to her. I've lashed out at her, made her cry for no fucking reason. It's always been you guys that pick up the pieces."

A long silence stretched between us. "What are you saying?"

"The truth. You know it's true, Gun."

"I mean yeah, you're kind of an asshole but you're a…" My hands gesticulated wildly as I grasped for words. I was no good at this shit. "You have your reasons. You're a good person underneath that asshole exterior. You own up to it when you fuck up. You love her, man. And she loves you."

"I do," he sighed, eyes closing for a moment. "More than anything. But after everything that's happened…I wonder if that might not be enough to keep us together."

"So I'm gonna ask again, and I want a real fuckin' answer this time." I leaned closer to him, my forearms on the kitchen counter, and lowered my voice. "What *exactly* are you saying?"

"I'm not making any decisions about this right now." Of course he would fucking backpedal when push came to shove. "But when all this shit is over and everyone's heads can clear, I think Mari and I need to decide once and for all what's going to happen between us."

"Dude, she just needs time—"

"And I'm giving her that," he growled. "But I've also been thinking back on *everything* I've done wrong, and it's quite the fucking list. I'm not holding my breath for a mediocre-husband award, or even…" he trailed off, but I kept staring at him hard, daring him to say it out loud. "Or even if she wants to keep me around as a husband at all."

"Jesus fucking Christ, Reap." I rubbed the heels of my palms into my eyes.

"You know it's a possibility," he said. "If some woman did to me everything I've done to her, I sure as fuck wouldn't stay. Would you?"

"Fucking hell, dude. Just stop for a second." I held a palm up. "This is the same shit you always do. You get ahead of yourself, you build up this whole plan and all its justifications in your head, then you carry it out without a thought as to how it's gonna affect other people."

Reaper opened his mouth to protest then promptly slammed it shut, his gaze turning away with the realization that I was right.

"You *have* to talk to Mari if you're feeling this way," I said. "And listen to what *she* says, don't just unload everything running through your mind and steamroll over her."

"I know." He rubbed his forehead with a groan. "Fuck. Yeah I know, Gun."

"If you just drop this on her like a bomb, I guarantee you she's gonna be blindsided and get hurt even more. She's trying to have a relationship with you again. You gotta at least meet her halfway."

"You're right." He blew out a long sigh. "I know you're right." He fiddled with the coffee mug, still not looking at me. "I guess this is my way of trying to prepare for the worst."

"Making you obsess with that outcome, more like."

"I know. It's not good."

I reached across the counter and slapped his shoulder. "One thing at a time, man. Let's get Grudge back first, alright?"

"Yeah." He seemed relieved at the change of subject, sliding off of his stool. "Hades." He whistled on the way to grab his cut, and the dog came trotting to wait by the door.

I only had to look up to the perch near the ceiling before feeling Horus' talons in my shoulder. The weight of him there felt grounding, if even comforting. He guided Mari back to Shadow, and then the two of them back home. I could only hope his eyes would let us check on Grudge today.

I stroked his chest feathers. "Gonna show us some good news today, buddy?"

A soft chirp and a nip to my ear was my answer.

———

"YOU'RE IN EARLY, BOYS." General Bray regarded us curiously from across the conference room table. Ever the general, he looked refreshed and polished in his pressed uniform, his hair still a little wet from his shower. He had a steaming cup of coffee in one hand and some documents spread out in front him.

"Wanted to be here when the answer came." Reaper went to the side table to get a second cup of joe, and I followed after him.

"You might be hanging around a while." My father-in-law flipped idly through the papers in front of him. "Blakeworth is in no hurry to respond to our request."

"Are those intake forms for our prisoners?" I asked, seating myself across from him.

"Yes." The general flipped a few sheets around and slid them across the table to me.

"Got any from our battle?" Reaper asked, and I heard the shuffle of papers as his father handed him a few to read.

"Bunch of normal folks, from the looks of it," I mused while skimming through my stack. "Most of them seem to be open to renouncing their Blakeworth citizenship, which is good."

"We'll need more extensive interviews to be sure," Bray said. "The last thing we need is more Blakeworth loyalists trying to stab us from within our own ranks." His head tilted toward Reaper. "What do you make of your stack, son?"

Reaper flipped through several more pages before answering, his brow furrowing deeper with every page. "You pranking me, Dad? These are all fucking blank."

"Not a prank. Those have all the information Tash's soldiers gave us when we checked them in."

"Which is nothing."

"Correct." General Bray folded his hands on the tabletop. "Read the notes at the bottom of each page."

I scooted closer to Reaper and read over his shoulder. "P.O.W-number-19 refuses to give his name or rank. He seemed willing to at one point, but started screaming and grabbing his head. The fit passed, and he returned to silence. Medics are calling it a catatonic state."

Reaper and I looked at each other, then back at his dad.

"Medics have noted blood coming from the ears of roughly twenty percent of those captured from Tash's army," Bray reported, looking at us pointedly. "They seem to correlate with the ones that scream like they're in pain."

"And the ones that don't?" I asked.

"Catatonic state, like the notes at the bottom. They say nothing, do nothing, just stare blankly forward. They don't even respond to stimuli. The medics are pretty certain they don't even sleep."

"What the fuck are we dealing with?" Reaper stared down at the sheets as if they had all the answers.

"A zombie apocalypse," I muttered.

"Boys, I hate to even ask this but…" General Bray's hands curled into fists on the table, his neutral expression turning distressed. "The symptoms that correlate with yours from last week, the pain and the ear bleeding. Do you think it means…you've been compromised?"

"No," Reaper and I answered together.

"How can you be sure?" The general kept up his pressing stare. "If Tash's soldiers are being controlled and that thing that was in your head is how they're kept to heel—"

"I do believe you're right about that," Reaper admitted. "It felt like something was trying to crack open my brain and shove something inside. I'll bet you anything that's how they turn them from normal people to zombies. They comply just to stop the pain, then it's a gradual shift until they're puppets with no sense of individuality."

He looked at me and I nodded my agreement. "But we have our own gods," I reminded Bray. "I don't know how, but I think they're some kind of shield against what's controlling those soldiers. My head hasn't felt like that since the first time."

"Mine either. Mari and the other guys seem fine too," Reaper nodded.

"That might have been an attempt to control us. But he, it, whatever it is, didn't succeed."

"I sure as fuck hope you boys are right." General Bray still looked grim across the table. "'Cause as soon as I saw those symptoms in the reports, I *knew* it was something related to what happened to you."

"We're good, Dad," Reaper assured him. "If it turns out we're not, you'll be the first to know."

"We have to carry out certain protocols in case something like that happens," the general said uneasily. "For the good of the territory."

"Understood." Reaper glanced at me and I jerked my chin down in a sharp nod. Being family made it harder, but we would have to be removed from our duties if we became compromised, and likely imprisoned like Tash's men. That was just war, and one of the first things I learned at the academy.

"Did you find out anything about that gold pin I gave you?" Reaper asked, setting his papers aside.

"No, we haven't yet." The general frowned pensively as he took a sip of coffee. "Which is strange. We've reached out to historians, archaeologists, experts of all kinds. They've never seen anything like it."

Reaper slumped in his seat. "How is that possible? Shadow and I found Hades, Horus, and Freyja in a book."

"Maybe it's a trait of the god, entity, whatever, that we're dealing with," I suggested. "We're talking chaos, right? Maybe it's something made up just to fuck with us."

"These things tend to be archetypal, if I'm understanding correctly," Bray said. "So there must be something that already exists to draw from."

"Well, there's gods of chaos, right?" Reaper piped up.

"Several," his father nodded. "But even if we narrow it down to the right one, how does that help us beat it?"

"I don't know that it does," I mused. "I think we just have to keep winning battles. Reduce its power and its influence so it doesn't run rampant and turn all of us into zombies."

"I hope you're right." The general's gaze rested on me. "We have good momentum now. If we don't lose focus and keep winning, we can turn the tide on this. With our combined experience and brains, the battles are in our hands. But when it comes to fighting gods?" He leaned back in his chair. "I'm out of my element there."

"So are we, really." Reaper shrugged. "We're just doing the best we can."

"Let's keep doing what we're doing, then," I said.

That seemed to settle the matter. Bray gathered up the papers to stack them neatly in his folder. "So while we're waiting on this response to the hostage exchange," he ventured, peering at Reaper. "How are things at home?"

I wanted to jump in, brush things off or smooth them over, but the question wasn't directed at me.

"Things are fine." Reaper shrugged again.

"Just 'fine'?" his father repeated.

"Fine enough," Reaper answered with more hardness to his voice. "I don't need to discuss everything in my marriage with you, Dad."

"You're right," Bray relented, backing off. "It's just been a while since I've seen Mari in any unofficial capacity. I miss my daughter-in-law."

"I know, she's just busy."

"We all are. But making time for family is—"

"Can we drop the subject, please?" Reaper barked.

The general's eyes slid over to me and I gave him a sympathetic look. I wasn't about to air out what Reaper told me privately. While I didn't know Bray well, I had a feeling he'd dropkick his son for even considering splitting from Mari. My gut churned at the thought of her finding out. If she knew, there would be no coming back from that.

But Reaper and Mari both deserved the time to sort out their feelings, to get clarity and start anew, whether that was together or going their separate ways. This war hanging over our heads certainly wasn't helping with stressful decisions.

We spent the next several hours planning the next battle. Bray's lieutenants and advisers cycled in and out of the conference room until all their faces blurred together in my brain.

It was the middle of the afternoon, not as late as I expected, when Blakeworth's reply to our message finally came.

A young private stumbled in with the letter and then quickly made himself scarce, apparently taking *don't shoot the messenger* very seriously. General Bray opened it first, scanned the contents, then dropped it on the table for us to read. Reaper and I both grabbed for it, but I was quicker.

The answer was brief, only half a page of typed, double-spaced sentences. It had Governor Blake's official crest at the top, despite the unlikelihood that he wrote it himself.

"He doesn't even want the captain back?" I handed the letter to Reaper as I looked up at Bray.

"That's what he says." Bray rubbed the stubble on his jaw as he stared out the window. "I wonder if he's bluffing and trying to see if we'll call it."

"He wants his general instead." Reaper peered up at both of us. "And says we can just kill the captain? His *own* man?"

"Keep reading," I said, rubbing my temple.

Reaper's eyes returned to the letter. "Feel free to send me a souvenir. Captain Lance's finger bones will make a nice addition to the collection in my office. He'll be far more useful as a decoration than a leader of my army." Reaper's head jolted up abruptly. "What the fuck?"

"He's got to be bluffing." I shook my head, turning back to face Bray. "We beat his ass, so he's just talking a bunch of shit to make himself sound like a super villain."

"Regardless, we're not killing anyone in our custody, nor are we sending pieces of them as souvenirs," General Bray growled. "It's a fair enough trade. He can have his general back in exchange for Grudge."

"He doesn't list any other terms or when it should happen." Reaper scanned the letter again.

"Good, that means we set the terms. Is tomorrow evening soon enough?" I glanced between the two of them.

"Not soon enough for the Sons," Reaper muttered. "You think we could get him back tonight?"

"Tonight doesn't give Blakeworth enough time to prepare for whatever charade they'll want to put on for the exchange." Bray turned back to face us.

"And?" Reaper snarled. "Who gives a fuck if we rush them? They lost. Those fuckers jump when *we* say it's time."

"We still have to look like the bigger person," I reminded him. "The reasonable side. It's what the soldiers and civilians are gonna remember when all this is over."

134

"How we treat hostages is going to be another," Bray pointed out. "Everyone knows Blakeworth doesn't deserve an ounce of courtesy from us, but we still have to show that we're better than them."

"And what if they show up with their whole cavalry?" Reaper asked. "'Cause we all know they're not above doing that either."

"We should prepare for that," I agreed. "Giving them time to prepare for a hostage exchange doesn't mean we trust them."

"The exchange means nothing in the grand scheme of things," Bray said. "We're still enemies. All it really does is show that we care about our people enough to get one of our men back."

"I don't like it either," I said, noting Reaper's scowl. "It's politics and it's shitty that Grudge is in the middle of it. But we have to play it a certain way, because *this* is the shit people will remember generations from now— how two warring territories handled the exchange of prisoners."

"Whatever, I get it." Reaper dropped the letter dismissively to the table. "Just don't ever let T-Bone hear you say that."

ELEVEN

MARIPOSA

T he wind howled and whipped through the canyon walls. It had been warm not long ago, but the sun hadn't touched the rocky terrain down here for hours. I kept my focus straight ahead on the slow procession lumbering toward us.

Four Corners soldiers looked over us from the ridges above, every one of them holding assault rifles. Not long after we settled at the meeting place and waited, drones approached the canyon from the north, humming and hovering over our heads. Several people looked up at the small, sleek aircraft with disgust. What an arrogant display of wealth from Blakeworth before the VIPs even bothered to show up.

The general from Blakeworth, General Arroyo, stood handcuffed between two of our lieutenants to my right. I had checked the man over for a final exam before we came to make the exchange. Arroyo hadn't been happy in our custody but was otherwise in fine health. I didn't appreciate how he leered at me while I examined him, but at this point it was nothing I hadn't experienced before.

My four men stood off to my left, primarily serving as bodyguards for me. Once the exchange happened, I was to examine Grudge as well. If he hadn't been treated well, Blakeworth would have a bigger problem on its hands.

The Sons of Odin were the only major players absent for this exchange. General Bray advised them to stay back in the city, and after much yelling and swearing, T-Bone and Dyno relented. This meeting was expected to be tense at the very best. The last thing we needed was either of them losing their cool and starting an impromptu skirmish when we were trying to put on a display of diplomacy.

I could feel Shadow vibrating at my side with barely contained anger. He would keep calm but I knew how much he wanted to explode, to take Grudge back by any means necessary. On his other side, Gunner squinted down the length of the canyon as we waited. Occasionally his eyes rolled back for a few seconds at a time, sneaking peeks through Horus while there was still a bit of sunlight left.

"They're coming," Gunner muttered. "But they're in no hurry." He looked more annoyed than anything else, and I could see why. Blakeworth was taking their sweet time and making us wait. On purpose.

It was all a game, and I hated that part most of all. Each side was trying to show they were better, more powerful. They made pokes and jabs at each other, trying to provoke a reaction while the people caught in the middle were the ones who suffered.

An extensive motorcade rolled slowly toward us— first, riders on sleek black motorcycles, then matching Hummers with shiny chrome rims on their off-road tires.

"Unbelievable," Jandro muttered.

I wanted to rub his arm in sympathy, but remained stoically facing forward. The Hummers were followed by four massive SUVs, then more Hummers and motorcycles brought up the rear.

When the entire entourage came to a stop, the passenger door of the first SUV opened. A smiling, middle-aged man stepped out casually, like he was showing up for a family barbecue. His uniform was perfectly fitted and pressed, an assortment of military stripes and medals pinned to his jacket—clear markings of a decorated general.

"Good evening!" he called cheerfully. "I'm General Rolf Larson, Chairman of the Blakeworth Military Council."

"General Finn Bray. Head of the Four Corners Army," my father-in-law replied stiffly.

"My deepest apologies for our lateness." An insincere smirk crossed Larson's lips. "Our vehicles are not well-fitted to this terrain, so we had to drive slowly."

One of my men pulled in a sharp breath. Gunner had told me all about how they set the terms to be reasonable and accommodating, and here they rolled up with the underhanded remark that we still weren't accommodating enough.

Fuck everything about Blakeworth.

Finn stepped forward, his face a stern mask. "Where is the hostage?" He ignored the other general's first remark.

"Where is ours?" Larson countered.

My father-in-law turned his body, keeping his eyes on the enemy in front of him as he gestured to the cuffed man between his lieutenants. Larson started walking forward, prompting all the Four Corners soldiers and Steel Demons in attendance to draw their guns. My heart jammed up into my throat when the Blakeworth motorcyclists drew their weapons in response. Fuck, no. This was getting too fucking tense already.

"Hold, everyone." General Bray was the epitome of calm as he extended his arms forward and back. "You can see your hostage, general," he said to Larson. "Not another step forward until we see ours. That is what you agreed to by coming here."

"Arroyo!" Larson called to our prisoner, ignoring Bray completely. "Are you alright?" He waved as if they were neighbors across the street. Bray's jaw ticked but he otherwise didn't react to the blatant antagonism.

Arroyo grunted out an affirmative, wrists pulling slightly at his cuffs.

"Very good, glad to hear it!" his colleague called out cheerfully across the line. I'd never wanted to punch someone so badly. "Bring out the prisoner," Larson called, turning to face the motorcade behind him.

The rear passenger door in the last SUV opened, and everyone on our side seemed to hold their breath.

Nobody came out for a few seconds, and then a bound man was shoved roughly out of the car, sprawling face-down in the dirt.

"Grudge!" Shadow hissed under his breath.

My hand shot out to the side to stop him and for once, I was faster. Shadow's stomach connected hard with my palm as he stepped forward, the impulse to save his friend riding him hard. He was strong enough to crash right through the flimsy barrier I'd thrown up, but thankfully he didn't. He froze mid-step, eyes fixed on the man the Blakeworth soldiers were now manhandling to his feet.

It took all my strength to swallow my cry at the first sight of Grudge's face. His hair and beard were matted with dried blood, his left eye swollen shut, lips split open and still bleeding. He was still wearing his cut, with only a thin white T-shirt underneath, also stained with blood. The difference between our two hostages could not be more obvious.

The only thing I was grateful for was T-Bone and Dyno not being there to see him like this. It would have become a bloodbath the moment Grudge got shoved out of the car.

General Bray sucked in a harsh breath as Larson stepped aside so Grudge could be brought forward.

"Hand him over." Bray extended an open palm toward the beaten man, choosing not to comment on the state he was in.

"No, pull him back. Remove him from my sight," the other general sneered.

"Larson," Bray hissed in warning. "This is not what we agreed upon."

"I didn't agree to send this scum back to your loving arms with no repercussions," argued the other man. "Give us General Arroyo first, as a sign of your goodwill."

"Our man needs medical attention," my father-in-law said. "We have a medic right here." He gestured toward me. "If he dies because of your carelessness, that'll only further increase the bad blood between us."

Larson's eyes landed on me with a leering kind of curiosity. I returned his gaze with a hard stare of my own, refusing to look meek and submissive. *I* was the one who stole Kyrie out from under his governor's nose. He hurt one of my friends, and I wasn't about to play nice. My men stiffened at my side, their protective natures and simmering anger palpable on the breeze.

Grudge sagged against the two men holding him up by his arms, his breaths coming in painful wheezes. I had to clench my hands at the sound, holding back the urge to fight my way through the soldiers to give him aid.

Completely oblivious to his suffering prisoner, General Larson grew bored of looking at me and returned his attention to Bray. "Give us General Arroyo first," he repeated. "You may have claimed one victory, but you are the ones desperate to have this prisoner back." He threw a disdainful glance at Grudge over his shoulder. "I can't imagine why. The idiot can't even talk."

Shadow's breathing labored with angry huffs at my

side, like a bull. I didn't have to look at him to know he looked shit-your-pants terrifying right then. I'd never seen him, the *real* him, this eager to kill for personal reasons. A couple of the Blakeworth soldiers tightened their grips on their weapons.

"General Arroyo is clearly the more valuable of the two hostages," Larson prattled on.

"No one human life is more valuable than another," Finn shot back.

"Oh please." Larson rolled eyes. "Now is not the time to get sanctimonious. I don't want to be out here any more than you do, Bray. Just hand over the general so I can get back to cigars and cocktails."

My father-in-law held firm with a shake of his head. "I don't trust you. We exchange at the same time."

"You think I *want* to keep this waste of air?" Larson snorted. "Please, I'm eager to be rid of him. He's useless as far as extracting intel, not to mention there's blood all over my seats. The only reason I'm holding on to him is because he means so much to *you*, Bray."

"Every citizen of Four Corners is worth rescuing to us." Bray amazed me with his calm. I and everyone surrounding me seemed a hair's breadth away from tearing into these people. But my father-in-law remained ever the diplomat in tone and posture. "We'll make the exchange at the same time," he repeated. "Let the soldiers hand them off to each other."

General Larson squirmed a little. It was a reasonable request, but he didn't want to look like he was giving in to our demands. Everyone seemed to hold their breath while waiting for his response.

"Fine," he relented, stepping aside to make room for his soldiers to step forward. "Let's get this over with."

Bray copied his movements, moving aside so his lieutenants could march General Arroyo forward.

The escorting soldiers of both sides halted a few feet in front of each other, Grudge struggling to get his feet under him between his two, while General Arroyo stood proud and proper.

"Uncuff him," snapped Larson.

"You don't give orders to *my* men." Finn's jaw ticked, the only sign of tension beneath his calm facade. "Have your men untie Grudge."

"You first," sneered the other man.

"I'm gonna fucking lose it," Jandro growled under his breath.

Me too. Every word from Blakeworth was just to show-up or antagonize us to provoke a reaction. They were the playground bullies enjoying our torment and dragging it out for as long as they could get away with it.

My father-in-law sucked in a sharp breath, but otherwise nodded to his soldiers. "Remove General Arroyo's cuffs." He stared down at Larson until he ordered his men to do the same.

Each prisoner was now held only by his arms, and a few heavy seconds passed without anyone moving. It felt like a game of chicken, both of them waiting for the other to move first.

"Shall we count their steps forward together?" Finn asked finally. "And then order the release at the same time?"

General Larson rolled his eyes again. "I'm flattered, Bray, but I didn't come here to dance with you."

"You're the one unwilling to make the first step in good faith," Finn retorted, an impatient growl entering his voice. "We have accommodated your every request, even when we do not need to. Handing off at the same time seems to be the only way we get this done without more blood shed."

"How precious, I'm so touched." The general mockingly touched his hands to his chest. "Fine. We'll do this together, like a little tango."

It was a painstakingly slow process, the tension only ramping up as the soldiers approached each other with the captives in tow. Finn and Larson negotiated over every single footstep and the release of the men. But when Grudge finally collapsed into Finn's arms, we all breathed a massive sigh of relief.

"Make room, bring the gurney," I instructed the soldiers behind me. "Lay him down on his back, slowly," I said to Finn.

Our enemies standing not twenty feet away were the last thing on my mind as I prepared to examine Grudge. While Finn lowered him gingerly to his back, I snapped on a pair of gloves, then clicked on a small flashlight and handed it to a nearby soldier. "Hold that steady for me."

Grudge groaned and writhed when I started cutting away his shirt, his fists swinging up as if to defend himself.

"No, no, it's okay," I said to one of the soldiers grabbing his arms to restrain them at his sides. Grudge was so weak and disoriented, it was no issue to bat his hands away. It was hard to believe he'd only been captive for a few days. He looked like he'd been suffering for weeks.

I smoothed a hand back through his hair and leaned down to speak to him. "Grudge, sweetie? It's Mari. You're home now. We got you back, and I'm gonna make you all better, okay?"

He stopped his swinging immediately, opening his fists. "Mah?" he asked in a raspy croak.

I grabbed his nearest hand and gave it a light squeeze. "Yes, it's me. Shadow's here too. You'll probably need a hospital stay, but we'll get you back to your guys as soon as we can."

Grudge gave a weak nod and reluctantly let go of my hand.

"Hold that light up higher," I instructed the soldier and lifted my head to look around. "Shadow?"

"I'm here, love." My assassin's footsteps brought him soundlessly to Grudge's side in the next moment. "What can I do?"

"Just sit with him. Hold his hand and talk to him while I work."

If Shadow felt any hesitation about comforting another person, he didn't show it. He took Grudge's hand carefully as he sat on the ground next to the gurney. "Hey brother. You're safe now. Mari's going to fix you up."

"You might feel some stinging," I warned, clearing the blood around Grudge's head first. Then to Shadow I muttered, "What's going on now?"

"Nothing. Blakeworth's leaving." His mismatched eyes glanced up and behind me, glaring at the spot where the motorcade had pulled up. "I was so close to killing him."

"You weren't the only one," I sighed.

Grudge's head and neck looked okay. He'd obviously been punched a few times, but the swelling and lacerations weren't life-threatening. He would need plenty of stitches though, and I wouldn't rule out a concussion. I moved on to feel around his torso and he immediately thrashed in pain. "Sorry! I'm sorry, Grudge. Does it hurt to breathe?"

He nodded, his face a tight grimace of agony.

"Bruised ribs for sure, possible breaks," I noted. His chest and ribs were covered in dark tattoos, so it was hard to tell where exactly he was injured without examining him, and thus hurting him more. "He needs a hospital right away."

"I'll take him. Fold down the seats in my car and put him in there," Finn ordered. "You all can jump in and hold him steady on the way."

"We'll follow," Reaper added, his gaze rising to the tops of the canyon walls. The motorcade had already left and the drones were just now starting to fly off in the same direction. "We'll make sure you don't get any surprises along the way."

"I'll stop at home and tell the Sons we got him back," Shadow said.

"The Sons are gonna want blood," Gunner remarked with a tone of worry. "There's no excuse for treating a hostage this way."

"They have every right to want it," Finn said bitterly.

"I know we all felt like ticking time bombs out there, but we have to be smart about our next move."

"Guys!" I clapped my hands once. "Talking can wait. Get this man into the general's car *now*."

The rest of my men hurried around Grudge's gurney and carefully lifted him. I stood back and out of their way, feeling a mixture of relief and wrung-out exhaustion as I watched them secure him in Finn's SUV.

No one would say that exchange went *well*, but it certainly could have gone a lot worse.

TWELVE

MARIPOSA

"That hostage exchange was an absolute shitshow."

Governor Vance frowned at Finn's declaration from across the conference table. Next to him, Josh paused in his note-taking as if wondering if he should include the word *shitshow* in the meeting's minutes.

"But it *was* successful," Vance broached cautiously.

"They got their man back safe and sound, we got ours barely alive." My father-in-law was restless in his seat, clasping and releasing his hands, only to ball them into fists before clasping them again. His usually clean-cut appearance was the most disheveled I'd seen him, with his shirt collar unbuttoned and his hair sticking out in places like he'd been tearing his fingers through it. I even noticed a five-o'clock shadow on his jaw.

It was like seeing Reaper aged by twenty years. Their expressions of stress were exactly the same. Finn's military career seemed to contribute to his calm, controlled facade—something my husband never quite developed. But now, three days after the hostage exchange, even the stoic general was cracking.

"The Sons of Odin, who have supported this territory and your administration for years, don't just want blood." Finn leaned back in his seat, lifting his chin to the governor across from him. "They want the whole territory of Blakeworth razed to the ground, and frankly, after seeing the condition Grudge was in, they're justified in wanting that."

Vance shifted a nervous gaze to me and cleared his throat. "How is Grudge holding up?"

"He's stable," I reported. "But the damage is extensive and he'll have a long recovery. His two broken ribs led to some organ damage. He also received some blunt force trauma to his back, which has caused some damaged nerves and balance issues."

I had never seen anyone look so heartbroken as T-Bone when Dr. Brooks read him the full diagnostic report. At first, it was crushing sadness and disbelief, then came the anger in full force. Thankfully, the only casualties were some filing cabinets, but our biggest concern was T-Bone doing harm to himself. It took all four of my guys plus Dyno to calm him down and remove him from the hospital. Poor T-Bone fought every step of the way because he didn't want to leave Grudge's side.

It almost reminded me of Shadow's violent outbursts, except that T-Bone was conscious the whole time, and his pain was for someone else. But he still felt helpless and lashed out because there was no other way to express his pain.

"We will support the Sons in any way we can, of course," Governor Vance said.

Something about that statement rubbed me the wrong way. It sounded like lip service to me.

"Give them a home of their own, to start."

All eyes in the room swiveled toward me, most of them wide. I was probably breaching some kind of protocol but didn't care at that point. Grudge had nearly died. He probably would have if we had waited another day. "Honestly governor, they should have gotten one after their clubhouse burned down with everyone they loved in it. They're not your polished military officers, sir, but it's shameful how little they've received after all they've done for Four Corners."

"We had contracts with them, Mari. They were well-compensated for the tasks they carried out—"

"They saved *your* daughter!" I blurted out. "They're staying at our house—which you had no issue giving us —because they still live in a room above a bar!"

"The Sons never wanted a permanent home here," Josh spoke up timidly. "We offered them housing but they refused—"

"Gee, I wonder why!"

"Thank you, Mari." Finn didn't yell, but his voice filled the room with a sharp command. It was General Bray speaking, not my father-in-law. But I noticed the small smile he tossed my way down the length of the table. "I believe what our medic is trying to say is that the Sons of Odin deserve not only support, but retribution for their suffering."

Governor Vance paled. "How?"

"We need to strike harder against Blakeworth. I think it's past time we go to them directly."

"But we've won a battle. We successfully exchanged hostages. Wouldn't a negotiation be—"

"Did you read my report, Governor?" Finn's pulse throbbed in his neck. His patience wasn't only wearing thin dealing with enemy territories, but also his own.

"Yes, General. I did."

"Then you understand that Blakeworth did everything in their power to provoke a reaction out of us without a direct attack. And that says nothing of the state Grudge was in when we received him." My father-in-law leaned across the table like he wanted to get into the governor's face. "They won't attack us first, but they will needle us, harass us, kidnap our citizens, and disrespect us to our faces until we're forced to retaliate. I say, fuck giving them that chance. Fuck being diplomatic with these people. We're smarter and stronger, so let's just fucking crush them."

My guys, who had been silent throughout this whole exchange, appeared to be sharing hidden smiles amongst each other. Reaper was the first to speak.

"I'm with my old man on this one." He slapped his father on the arm.

"We can do it," Gunner agreed. "And we should. They're scared of us now."

"Grudge's captors deserve nothing less," Shadow weighed in, an icy ruthlessness in his voice.

All eyes turned to Jandro, who just shrugged. "I'll follow these boys anywhere. Fuck yeah, let's rock and roll."

"What about General Tash?" one lieutenant piped up. "If we focus a hard hit to the north, that'll leave us vulnerable to the east."

"We need to keep eyes out that way for sure," Gunner nodded. "They've got the numbers and the artillery. But if we can eliminate Blakeworth as a problem for good, it'll be a lot easier then to focus on one opponent, rather than splitting up the army."

"Andrea is still in their base," I reminded everyone in the room. "At some point, we'll also have to get her out safely."

"That's correct." Finn smiled openly at me before returning his attention to the governor across the table. "I'm suggesting we be aggressive, Vance, not stupid. Our enemies expected to crush us, and we've proven to them that we can hold our own. Now they have to rethink their attacks, which also buys us some time." He clapped Gunner's shoulder and shook him affectionately. "We have the best strategic minds on our side. It was Gunner's tactics that won us those battles. If we keep planning our moves wisely, we can't lose."

Gunner blushed redder than I'd ever seen him before, and he looked bashful for once, instead of cocky.

Governor Vance still looked apprehensive, but he gave an approving nod to his general. "I trust your judgment, Bray, and you haven't steered me wrong yet. Plus, the victories have certainly helped with morale in the city. Do what you have to."

The two men stood from the table, everyone else following suit as the general extended his hand. "We'll brief you on the next battle's plans within three days, governor."

With a shake of hands, the meeting concluded. Everyone started filing out of the room while I made my way to Gunner and planted a kiss on his cheek. "Proud of you, love."

He hugged me tightly to his side, his smile beaming as he kissed my forehead. "Thanks, baby girl."

A commotion at the conference room doorway pulled our attention that way. One of the soldiers struggled against the stream of people leaving the room as he was trying to come inside.

"General! Is General Bray still in there?" he called.

"Yes, what is it?" Finn turned from a conversation he was having with some other soldiers.

People finally stepped aside so the man could come in. He was red-faced and panting like he'd ran across the entire city, and held up a manila folder stamped CLASSIFIED. "There's been another message from our contact in New Ireland."

"Andrea," I gasped.

Finn made his way to the messenger in three long strides, taking the folder from him. "Thank you, Private."

"It hasn't been translated yet, sir," the young soldier wheezed. "Would you like me to get Lieutenant Anurak?"

"Yes, please," the general said with as much patience as he could muster.

"Yes sir, right away!" Still, the messenger hesitated. "I didn't make a copy or anything yet, that's the original note. I…I thought you should see it first, sir." With that, he took off to find the translator.

Frowning, Finn opened the folder and his forehead only wrinkled more deeply at what he saw. Just as quickly, he snapped the folder shut and lifted his head. "Everyone out. The meeting's over, go on. This is a separate matter."

My husbands and I stayed as the room emptied, all of us immediately crowding around my father-in-law once we had privacy. "Is something wrong?" My heartbeat accelerated at his reaction to the note.

Finn met my eyes and tried to give a reassuring smile, but I could still see the worry tensing up his face. "We'll have to see what Anurak says when he gets here, but something is definitely unusual. This note is coming much sooner than our agreed-upon correspondence schedule with Andrea."

"Well, that doesn't have to be a bad thing, right? Maybe she just has more to tell us."

The general sighed and flipped open the cover. "I wish it could be as simple as that but I don't think so." He turned it around and slid the paper toward me. I couldn't read the characters of course, but quickly realized what he meant. The pounding in my chest quickened and seemed to rise up into my throat.

The first line at the top looked normal enough—glyphs written with a ballpoint pen sitting on top of the first line. After that was where it all went wrong. The symbols got bigger with each row, the pen strokes deep and shaky, like Andrea had been convulsing as she wrote. The last characters on the page were around two inches high, dragging all the way down to run off the bottom edge of the paper, which also had dark smears over the ink.

"Is that blood?" I pointed, but already knew. "Holy shit, that's her blood."

"We don't know if it's hers," Reaper said, although he didn't sound convinced himself.

A hand came to my shoulder, probably meant to calm me, but it made me jump. Shadow ran his palm across the top of my back, the motion only a little soothing as he inspected the paper over my shoulder.

"Whatever she's saying, it's repeating something," he observed. "It's the same two characters over and over."

Finn spun the paper back around to face him. "You're right." He didn't look comforted with that knowledge. "Down here where she draws them really big, she didn't even finish the whole character. It's like she dragged the pen off the page and just stopped."

"Fuck." I barely realized I had uttered the curse until Jandro came up to my other side, his hand rubbing my lower back while Shadow continued with my shoulders.

"No jumping to conclusions yet." Jandro pressed a kiss to my temple. "Let's find out what the translation is first."

I held on to him and Shadow while we waited. Anurak entered the room within the next few minutes, his face taking on the same frown as his general at first sight of the message. The lieutenant brought a pen and blank sheet of paper with him but didn't seem to need them. He set them slowly on the table as he looked at us all gravely.

"I'm very sorry," he said. "But I'm afraid our contact has been compromised."

"What?" I cried. "Why?"

"What does it say?" Finn demanded.

Anurak picked up the pen, holding it poised for a moment before writing on the blank sheet. "You remember the code is based on phonetic sounds, yes? This is the sound those two characters make."

He capped the pen and stepped away from the paper which read, *HA HA HA HA HA.*

THIRTEEN

MARIPOSA

"Comfortable?"

I was laying on my side with a pillow under my head on Shadow's tattoo table, which I was pretty sure had been a massage table at one point. I had my shirt pulled up to my waist and my underwear pulled halfway down my leg. My hip and thigh were bare, wearing only Shadow's touch as he ran a hand over my skin.

It had been a rough few days, monitoring Grudge's progress in the hospital, and then getting that haunting note from Andrea. When Shadow told me he'd finalized his surprise tattoo for me, I jumped at the chance to focus on something more pleasant than hospitals and enemies.

"Very." I curled my arm underneath the pillow, watching him set everything up. "Think I'll take a nap."

"You might," he said with a small smile. "This'll take a few hours."

"No hints?" I tried again just to prod him, knowing he wouldn't budge.

"Nope." He leaned in and kissed me quickly. "Unless you've changed your mind."

"Not a chance." Still, my eyes drifted to his sketchbook nearby, the cover closed. I knew whatever he was tattooing on me would be in there.

"You're sure?" He pulled on a pair of gloves, then spayed his alcohol solution onto a clean towel to wipe my skin with a firm, gentle hand. "Last chance to back out."

"I'm staying," I told him, the words carrying more than one meaning.

Shadow smiled as he uncapped a pen, holding my hip with one hand while he poised the tool above my skin with the other. "Then cover your eyes and take your nap, my love."

I stuck my tongue out before pulling the sleeping mask over my eyes and hugged my pillow. The next thing I felt was the light tickle of the pen moving over my skin as he started to draw on me. I had to bite my lip to not move—it was *too* ticklish in some spots.

Shadow's sketching and tattooing methods were polar opposites, I realized. He sketched quickly, making long sweeping lines and quick marks for necessary details. With the tattoo gun however, he was meticulous and slow. It was almost meditative, how much his focus narrowed during that stage of the process.

I tried to follow the strokes of the pen on my skin and match it to an image in my mind, but it was impossible to guess. Just when I thought I knew, he'd do something different in another area to make me second-guess. Whatever it was would be worth the surprise, but that didn't make me any less eager to know.

The pen lifted away after several minutes, Shadow's gloved touch lingering on me for a few moments longer.

"It looks good," he reported, excitement brightening his voice. "Just as I imagined. This is going to look amazing on you."

"Can't wait," I told him, smiling in the direction of his voice.

Another quick wipe of my skin and his machine buzzed to life to begin my outline. "Here we go," he said softly, moments before he touched the needle down and began the real work.

The sharp, scratching sensation faded to a gentle ache after several minutes, only the buzzing of his machine filling the air.

"Tell me a happy memory," I implored him at one point.

"I think this is about to become one." I couldn't see him, but heard the smile in his voice.

"Doesn't count," I teased. "What's something that happened to you before this that made you happy?"

"Well, there is the first time I tattooed you." The buzzing stopped briefly, and I heard his chair creak as he turned. "Did you know I purposely split up your sessions so I could see you more often?"

"You did?"

"Yes. You were the only woman I enjoyed talking to."

"Aww." I lifted my head from the pillow until his machine stopped again. "Kiss me?"

Shadow's mouth descended on mine in seconds. His beard felt especially, wonderfully rough against my mouth when I couldn't see it.

"Keep this up and it'll take even longer to finish," he chuckled against my mouth, kissing me once more before pulling away.

"Fine." I flopped back down to my side. "Tell me another good memory. One that doesn't have to do with me."

"That's a bit harder," he mused, gloved fingers holding my skin taut as his needles did their work. "Most of my good memories are with you."

"Challenge yourself." I probably sounded like an old professor from nursing school.

"Hm." Shadow continued my outline for several minutes before he spoke again. "I still have the first drawing I was actually proud of. I drew it in prison, after the...the cult."

"What was it of?" I asked, determined to keep his thought process in a positive direction.

"A dragon," he answered. "It was a tattoo I did for another inmate. I drew it pretty much from memory of a picture I saw in a book years earlier. I didn't even have a reference to go off of."

"Would you ever let me see it?"

"Hm." He sounded skeptical now. "I dunno. It's not very good by my standards now. But I was really impressed with myself at the time."

"I'm sure it's a fine drawing, love. What kind of

dragon was it?"

"Eastern-style, like a Chinese dragon," he said. "No wings, long curving body." Shadow paused in tattooing to drag a gloved finger over *my* curves. "Lots of scale details. It was big, too. The face was on the guy's chest, then it went over his shoulder and down his back."

"That sounds amazing."

"It was okay," he mumbled, the noise and prick of his gun returning. "He was a good client too. Young, maybe sixteen. I had to stick-and-poke him over several days, but he never complained and sat like a rock."

"Do you know where he ended up?" I asked, suddenly enthralled by this story.

"No. Jandro's the only person I stuck around with from then."

"You know what I'd love to do together?" I said after another several moments of quietness.

"I can think of a few things." There was that smile in his voice again.

"In addition to *that*," I grinned, "I'd love to just flip through all of your drawings and have you tell me about each one."

Shadow paused in his work, and for once the silence felt uncertain. "You'd *want* to do that?"

"Yes," I said earnestly. "Only if you're comfortable with it. I love how creative you are."

"Maybe." He still sounded unsure. "It's just that some of my drawings are really dark. Even some of the more recent ones. Doc told me I could use drawing as a type of therapy, as a way to process everything."

I stuck my hand out blindly, letting it hover in the air

until he grabbed it. "You don't have to show me anything you don't want to," I said. "Just because you've shared your past with me, doesn't mean you can't keep some things to yourself."

The next thing I felt was the warmth of his breath, and then his lips descending on mine, full of warmth and passion.

"I love you so much," he murmured. "Thank you for just…letting me be me."

"I love you too much to let you be anything else," I whispered back.

He groaned through the next kiss, and I felt the slight weight of his chest pressing down as he leaned over me. "I'll never finish this tattoo if you keep making me want you."

"I'm sorry." I grinned, not sorry at all.

Shadow laughed knowingly, lifting my shirt higher past my waist to plant kisses on my side. His beard and the light, teasing drag of his lips tickled me until I was squirming and laughing. He carried on with a few more kisses on my ribs before stopping abruptly with a light swat to my bare butt cheek. "That's your last chance to squirm. I need you to be still for me now."

It took me a few moments to gather myself, and he probably had no idea why. Shadow's dominance was sweeter, more playful than Reaper's, but no less demanding. His tickling kisses followed by the serious command lit me up like a match. A small part of me wanted to push his buttons a little more, to see how much he would really punish me, but he wasn't familiar with that kind of play yet. It would probably aggravate him more than anything.

And anyway, what I really wanted to do most was please him.

"*Fine*, I'll be good," I sighed dramatically.

Shadow let out a delighted hum, and I utterly melted at the sound. I should have known this tattoo would be the longest session of foreplay in my life.

My artist resumed his work and I stuck to my promise of being good for him. "I'll look through my drawings to see what I feel like sharing or not," he said after a few minutes.

"Completely fine with me," I assured him.

We carried on for a while in comfortable quietness, only the buzzing of his machine filling up the empty air. His hands on me were warm, comforting without being gratuitous. Even when working on me, Shadow was a complete professional. The only liberties he took were occasional kisses on my waist as he checked in on my pain and comfort levels.

After a while, maybe two hours by my guess, the buzzing stopped and Shadow's hands fell away. I heard a soft groan as he must have stretched, then the snaps and pops of his back cracking.

"Let's take a break, lover. I need to move around," he said with another light kiss on my waist.

I smiled, tapping my lips with a finger. "Kiss me here first and call me that again."

I heard his stool wheel closer over the floor, strands of hair tickling my face first as he leaned down and captured my lips. He'd taken the gloves off and his hands were bare now, knuckles stroking my cheek.

"My lover," he murmured sensually, lips grazing mine before descending on me again.

I rolled to my back, feeling blindly for a spot to grip on his shirt and pull him down. My thighs fell apart to make a space for him between them.

"Stop," he said with laughter in his voice. "After I'm done with you."

My core pulsed with the way he said that last sentence, but I let him go with a resigned sigh. "Can I get up and stretch too?"

"Of course. Just let me figure out how to keep this hidden."

We settled for tying a towel around my waist. Shadow helped me down from the table and secured the towel for me, then told me I could take off the sleeping mask. I whipped it off eagerly, blinking at the brightness of the room after being in the dark for over an hour.

My smile was indulgent the moment my eyes landed on Shadow. He was standing, tall and imposing as ever with his arms stretched above his head. His fingers rested gently on one of the beams in the ceiling, broad chest pressing forward as he stretched.

"I missed looking at this gorgeous man for the past few hours," I purred, coming closer to scratch down his chest and abdomen.

He broke his gaze from mine shyly, a smile still playing at his lips as he brought his hands down, touching them to my waist. "Want to eat something before the next session?"

"Sure." I tilted my face up for a kiss and he bowed over to indulge me.

As we poked around the kitchen, my lower left side throbbed and ached a little. It would be so easy to run to a different part of the house and take a peek under my towel, but I resisted. Shadow did narrow his eyes at me suspiciously when I excused myself to use the restroom, but I placated him with kisses and promises that I wouldn't look.

"Unless you want to come with me and watch?" I teased.

He huffed out a laugh and swatted my opposite hip. "No, do your business. I trust you."

It *was* tricky business hiking up the towel without completely unraveling it, or exposing the lower part of the tattoo, but I stuck to my word and didn't peek.

After some time to nibble and chat, we got back to it. Shadow re-sanitized the tattoo table, then I hopped on and pulled my sleeping mask over my eyes without any complaint. He untied the towel, exposing my lower half, and I shivered at the rush of air on my freshly inked skin.

"I think I've got about two hours of work left," Shadow mused. "I can get it all done at once if you don't distract me," he added with a playful tone.

"I won't," I laughed. "I'm dying to finally look at it."

"Just tell me if you need anything, lover." His kiss landed on my neck, hot and lingering with that deep, rumbling voice of his sending shivers down my spine.

"Now who's distracting who?" I huffed.

Shadow let out a throaty chuckle as he pulled on a

pair of fresh gloves, and then the buzzing started up again.

The next two hours went by slowly, which was both enjoyable and frustrating. I loved every moment Shadow's hands were on me—no matter the reason—but I was also dying to see my tattoo, his gift to me. His symbol of devotion and commitment as my husband.

At long last, the buzzing stopped and Shadow gently wiped my skin.

"It's done." His voice was neutral, a type of mask to hide however he was feeling. I knew he must have been nervous about my reaction.

"Can I look?" I was already reaching for the edge of the sleeping mask.

"Sit up slowly first," he said. "We don't want you having a spill like the first time."

"I thought we agreed there was no spill," I joked, but followed his guiding hands to sit upright.

"Stay like that for a second before you stand up."

"*Shadowww,*" I whined. "I want to see!"

"You will, I just want you to be careful. It's a big piece, and you've been lying down for a long time."

"You're just stalling," I teased, reaching a hand blindly for him. "Building up the anticipation, are you?"

His large hand wrapped around mine as he pressed a kiss to my palm. "I'm anxious for you to see it, but also a little worried you won't like it," he admitted.

"I'll love it no matter what it is. Because I love *you.*"

I felt his breath fan lightly across my hand as he sighed. "I love you so much."

I squeezed around his fingers and brought them to my lips. "Now can I please take this mask off?"

"Okay," he said after a beat of silence. "Go ahead."

I couldn't whip the thing off fast enough, then touched my feet down to the floor. My whole left side throbbed as I walked gingerly to the full-length mirror inside Shadow's closet door.

I was nothing short of stunned at what I saw, tears immediately springing to my eyes.

FOURTEEN

SHADOW

S he hates it.

I tried to stamp down the negative thought as Mari stared at herself in the mirror. But seconds ticked by and she wasn't saying anything. My heart hammered in my chest as I waited for a reaction from her. All the confidence and excitement I'd built up about this tattoo went out the window in an instant. I cursed myself for not letting her see it beforehand, that was a stupid fucking idea.

"I can cover it up." The words rushed out of me when the silence became too unbearable. "It needs to heal first, but I can—"

"Shadow." Mari turned to me slowly and my panic spiked at the sight of tears glittering in her eyes. "It's perfect. I can't…I'm sorry, I just don't know how to…" She laughed sheepishly, wiping her eyes as they started to overflow. "Thank you so much for this. I can't imagine a more perfect gift from you."

"You…like it?" She was smiling, so those were happy tears. I still couldn't always tell the difference.

"I'm completely in love." She looked at me, not the tattoo in the mirror, when she said that.

My heart was still going a mile a minute but for a different reason now. The panic had subsided and now it was bright, pure elation that filled my chest. I went to join her at the mirror, running a hand along the back of her shoulders as we looked at the tattoo together.

"I'm happy you like it."

It was the night-blooming Cereus flower, the center at her hip with the long white petals spreading out across her thigh, stretching toward her backside, and reaching up toward her waist. I added the green, thorny vines they grew on to fill in some background. The dark vines also provided contrast for the white petals, making them glow brightly against the dark, like that night we saw them together.

But my favorite part of the tattoo was the monarch butterfly sitting on a petal near the bottom center of the flower, casting a small gray shadow underneath it.

"Is this you and me?" Mari pointed at the butterfly.

"I thought it could represent us, yes," I said. "Not that I'm your shadow in the sense that I'm following you constantly, but more like we're always connected. A part of each other."

"I love that." Mari turned back to face the mirror, pivoting on the ball of her foot to look at the tattoo from different angles. "I love it so much. I love *you*. Fuck, I'm just in awe, Shadow. It's more perfect than I could have imagined."

"I'm glad you think so." My hand slapped to my chest, releasing a breath as I leaned against the tattooing table. "I'm fucking relieved, honestly. I thought you hated it for a second."

"I could never!" Mari's fingers began creeping down her hip to touch the design.

"Don't touch it yet," I warned her. "Give it a few hours. Let me bandage it for you." She headed back toward the table with a slight limp in her walk, and seeing her even in slight pain made my chest ache. She'd never complain but I knew her hip and thigh had to be sore from all the hours under the needle. Grabbing her waist, I lifted her off the floor and carried her the rest of the way, sitting her on the table's edge. "Let me be a medic to you, for once," I added with a grin.

"Excellent bedside manner, I told you," Mari beamed at me.

I taped a sheet of clean gauze over the tattoo, so her skin would be able to breathe while still remaining protected. The first few hours were the most susceptible to infection, as I was sure Mari already knew.

No sooner had I finished covering the artwork and began putting my supplies away than a small fist closed in my shirt and dragged me back to a hungry stare, lips parted and begging for a kiss.

I leaned down to indulge in a fast one, but Mari wasn't satisfied with that. Her teeth sank into my lip and held me in place, the light sting of pain rushing down to my cock.

"Mari," I groaned. Her good leg was already winding around my hip, her calf and foot gripping the back of my leg and pulling me forward. "You're hurt. Do you really want this right now?"

"I'm *not* hurt," she huffed with a pout. "And this tattoo has been an hours-long foreplay session, I want nothing else but you right now."

"A tattoo is an injury," I reminded her gently. "And yours is not a small one. You need to take it easy and heal from it."

"Okay, my leg is a little sore, but I don't care. I'm not *that* fragile." Mari's arms wound around my neck, pulling me down until my hands braced on either side of her. "You gave me this amazing gift. I've been blindfolded for hours while you touch me, kiss me, and tell me about your art. I just love you more every moment I spend with you, and I want you in *all* of my senses."

Lost for words, I lowered my forehead to rest on hers. My eyes closed and I just felt her there with me, breathed her in. How could this be real? After such a long, miserable existence, how was I able to find someone who loved me so genuinely and deeply? Who actively and enthusiastically *wanted* to have sex with me? Time and time again she reassured me, proved to me that every word she said was true.

She loved me, even lusted after me while I looked like this.

Keeping my hand high on her waist on her tattooed side, I grabbed her hip on her other side and pulled her flush to me, crashing my mouth down to hers at the same time.

"Hold on to me, lover." That was the only warning

she got before I anchored her to my body and lifted her off the table.

"Always," she purred, squeezing both legs around my waist before tangling her tongue with mine again.

I smiled through the kiss as I turned toward the bed. Supporting her back and hip, I rested my knees on the edge of the mattress and began to slowly lower her down until her back met the bed. Mari scooted up toward the headboard and I followed, crawling on my hands and knees over her. Our lips never disconnected for more than a quick breath, the two of us determined to stay locked together.

When Mari settled into the pillows and brought her arms around me again, I allowed more of my weight to rest on top of her. She let out a pleased moan through my mouth, securing her legs around my waist again. Every time we came together, I worried less about acci- dentally hurting her. Like she said herself, she wasn't some delicate, fragile thing. My woman had endured so much. There was a steely strength in her lithe, beautiful body underneath me.

Our kiss ended with panting breaths from both of us, the need for air keeping us separated for a few longer moments. I took the opportunity to rise up to kneel and peel my shirt off. In the split second I couldn't see, Mari's hands were already on me.

Her constant affection brought out a giddiness that made me want to grin. I'd seen how women fawned over other men—usually the likes of Gunner or Reaper, always trying to catch their eye and sneak a touch inside their cut. The other guys had enjoyed the attention with a kind of smug indifference, and I'd wondered if that was a result of always catching the eye of women. To them, maybe it got boring.

With Mari, I wanted to soak up and collect every touch she placed on me, and not just because she was the only one who did so. She didn't want anything from me, except to be with me as much as I wanted her.

When my shirt was gone, Mari had one hand on the waistband of my pants, the other still running up to my chest and back down my stomach. She was kissing my scars, as she liked to do. Each one a small touch of healing on a place where I'd been cut.

"Ahh," I groaned as her teeth closed around a small bit of flesh near my hip bone. She sucked a hard kiss there, tongue flicking as her mouth pulled until she released me with a pop of her lips. "That's a good one," I mused at the dark red mark forming at the spot. My skin was hot there, the pulsing of the bruise echoing down into my dick.

"Some of my best work," Mari agreed, smiling as her lips dragged below my navel. She unsnapped the button on my jeans and pulled me out, already half hard, as her kisses continued lower.

"Fuck..." My head dipped back toward the ceiling, eyes falling shut at the feel of her stroking me. Her mouth was near my base, then I felt her tongue chasing her fist as she stroked up my length. I looked down again just in time to watch her lips seal over my crown before the blissful, wet pressure of her mouth sent my head falling back again.

"So fucking good…" I felt blindly for some part of

her to touch, my hand finding purchase on her shoulder. She let out a small hum at my words and sucked me even deeper.

She likes it when you praise her, I realized.

"Your mouth…fuck, you're so beautiful…" As it turned out, talking and even forming thoughts was difficult when everything she did was this good. Mari seemed to understand the sentiment though. I looked down to see a smile reaching her eyes despite her mouth being fully stuffed.

My cock expanded with every drag of her lips over me, every hot slide of her tongue. Her free hand still wandered my body—dragging down my thighs as she shoved my pants down, running up my torso, or holding on to my waist as she sucked me harder down her throat.

Just when I was about to stop her, right before my pleasure really started building, she released me with a great gasping breath. I bent down to kiss her, sending her back to her elbows on the mattress. She was already naked from the waist down, dewy and flushed between her legs. My cock, now heavy and hard, dragged along her inner thigh as I resumed hovering over her.

We quickly made off with her top, and I had barely kicked my pants off when her thighs glued to my waist again, drawing me forward.

"Not yet," I murmured between her breasts before turning my head to draw a nipple into my mouth. Mari's frustrated groan made me chuckle, and I lifted my eyes to hers as I moved on to her other breast. "What, are you mad?"

"No, I just want *you*." She squeezed her legs around my waist for emphasis. "I told you, I already had my foreplay."

"Yes." I kissed below her breasts. "But it didn't make you come, so it doesn't really count, does it?"

"Shadowww…" she whined, her head falling back.

"Maaariiii," I taunted back at her, earning a bright laugh and her fingers scratching my scalp as I kissed lower.

Her frustrated grunts and groans soon turned to relaxed sighs and hums. I made sure not to jostle the gauze on her side, already eager for the day I could kiss her new tattoo. I kissed the small scar next to her right hip, one of my favorite places on her body. My mouth trailed lower and Mari's breaths quickened in anticipation. Just before reaching her clit, I pulled away, unwrapping my hand from her thigh to rest on my forearm.

Mari's head popped up from the pillows, shooting me a murderous glare. "Shadow I love you, but I'm seriously not in the mood for a bunch of teasing and denial right now."

"That's not what I'm doing," I assured her, running a hand up the inside of her thigh. "I just want to watch you."

I cupped my palm against her sex and got just the reaction I was hoping for. Mari's eyelids fluttered, her mouth falling open in a soft moan. I added pressure and small, circular movements with my whole hand, giving her the friction she wanted so badly. Her head fell back to the pillows as she started to lift and buck her hips against my palm.

"Yes, that," I whispered. Doc's pendulum had nothing on the hypnotic movements of her body as she chased pleasure. "I love watching you like that."

Mari's hooded eyes focused on me, the sexy, intimate eye contact making my cock jolt with need for her. "Keep talking like that. It's hot when you talk to me."

"Really?" I lifted my palm away from her, returning with two fingers to stroke and glide through her wetness.

"Yes," she gasped, thighs clamping around my wrist. "Tell me why you like watching me."

"Hm." I spread her legs apart and returned to playing with her, teasing her opening with a fingertip. "At first it was to make sure I was doing things right, but now I just love seeing you move, seeing how badly you want it."

"Want *you*," she added.

"Yes, me." I grinned, lowering another kiss to my favorite scar as I pressed a finger inside her. "But also in general. I love the sounds and movements you make when you're pleased."

She was making some beautiful ones now as I stroked her pussy, her hips tilting up for more sensation as her head tossed and she grabbed for the sheets next to her. I curled the digit inside her and dragged the pad of my finger along her slick walls, my eyes glued to everything happening above her waist.

"I love how flushed your skin gets," I continued, watching the pink of her cheeks deepen. "When your brows furrow and you bite your lips to keep from screaming."

She released her lip right then with a laugh,

returning my gaze. "I should have known, with how observant you are—ah!"

Her cry released with no lip-bite to hold it in as I added a second finger, spreading them apart inside to give her that feeling of fullness she craved.

"I love it when your legs clamp around me like you never want me to leave." The first knuckles of my hand rubbed her sex as I stroked deeper within her. "How you get so sensitive that you shiver no matter where I touch you. How your nipples get so tight and dark too."

My thumb swiped her clit and a beautiful shudder wracked her body then. Fuck me, she was a vision. I knew then, definitively, that I wouldn't mind one of the others joining us in the slightest. As long as I got to watch her being pleased, whether it was by me or someone else who had the privilege of loving her.

It was near impossible to tear my eyes away from her, but as I took small, biting kisses of her thighs, I knew what awaited me was just as sweet.

Her taste.

My mouth replaced my thumb as the weight on her clit, my fingers still driving deeply inside her with long, curling strokes. I flattened my tongue against the hard little bud to the sounds of her cries reaching a new height, her blunt nails raking across my scalp as her thighs held me in place. Despite my being in control of her pleasure, her sweet body had me trapped—not that I wanted to be anywhere else.

Mari's orgasm closed around my fingers as she whimpered and moaned, thrashing against me with ragged pants. As tempted as I was to watch, I didn't pull away from her until her thighs fell apart and her pleasure ebbed away to soft pulses.

"Come here." It was a soft, whispered demand as she reached for me, her eyes still hungry under her relaxed lids.

I couldn't bring myself to obey her fast enough, planting my hands next to her sides as I crawled up, bringing my face down for a kiss, and nudging my hips into the embrace of her thighs as I lowered the rest of the way to her.

Our bodies slid against each other in a few teasing, short thrusts before the head of my cock found her entrance. I pressed into her mid-kiss, pausing at her moan and just to *feel* her slick heat wrapped around me.

"I'm good, don't stop," she urged me, hands running up my back.

I brought my mouth to her neck as I pressed deeper, sucking lightly at her pulse but not enough to leave marks. She whimpered in protest as I pulled back, drawing nearly all the way out, then drove forward deeper than before. The motion had her arching off the bed with a ragged gasp, breasts smashed to my chest.

"This." I lifted away from her neck to watch her face, taking another long drag out of her before a deeper thrust inside. "I love watching you when I do *this*."

"Fuck!" Her face was in a beautiful grimace of pleasure as she clung to me with as much of her body as was possible.

Stripes of heat lanced up and down my back, her nails digging and grasping to hold on to me. It was a delicious kind of sharpness that radiated to every inch of my skin, and I wanted more.

"Fuck yes, *that*," I rasped, finding her lips with mine again. "Scratch me harder."

Mari smiled before I swallowed her mouth in another kiss, my tongue and cock mirroring each other as they surged deeper, always seeking more of her to taste and feel.

"Ohh fuck!" Her nails felt like they were scoring me, testing the limit of my skin as she dug in and dragged them from my ass to my shoulders. She didn't break the skin—I knew that feeling well enough. For some reason I could only feel pain with her, and it danced on the knife edge of my pleasure, heightening all the sensations as I moved through her silky heat.

"Too much?" Mari's hands flattened to rub and soothe where she just scratched me.

"No." I kissed her jaw, sliding my arms underneath to cradle her head and upper back. "Pain from you is so, so good."

She wouldn't ever truly hurt me, not like how I'd been before. That very knowledge was what made me crave these little samples of pain from her. I'd gone without the sensation for so long, her teeth and nails in my skin gave me just enough to feel and experience it like a normal person would. Exploring the line where it blurred with my pleasure was just an added bonus.

I rocked into her at a steady, even pace while Mari changed directions with her scratching. She ran her nails across my shoulder blades now, digging unabashedly into my decades of scar tissue while I moaned into another kiss. It felt like a fire was licking at my back—too close for cozy warmth but not quite burning me yet. It matched the heat of her pussy wrapped around me, searing, but so soft and pliant that I *needed* to sink in for more.

"You're mine." The possessiveness spurred me deeper into her body, a growl escaping me as my fist closed around a handful of her hair.

"Yours," she agreed, nails scraping along the back of my neck. "And you're mine."

"My wife," I groaned, drunk and delirious on every feeling and sensation racing through my body. Everything she showed me I was able to feel. "My lover."

"My husband," Mari answered in a panted whisper, her palms holding my face to look at me. "My love."

I tilted her hips higher, increasing the friction between us with every stroke of my cock. She clutched the backs of my biceps at that, soft moans turning into sharp cries and gasps. Pleasing her in bed had become my new addiction. Reading her body, listening to the sounds she made, and feeling the changes in the way her pussy gripped me—I wanted to drink it all down like there was an endless supply.

"Fuck! Shadow, yes!" She was getting louder, curling around me tighter with each snap of my hips. Her arms, legs, and even her lips trembled with wrought-up tension desperate for release. Seeing my woman on the precipice sent my own pleasure soaring, swelling and aching with every squeeze of her silky walls.

My face buried in her neck again, groaning against

her flushed skin as I drove into her, determined to see her to her finish.

Mari's orgasm triggered my own, the clenching of her sex around me stuttering my rhythm to the point of no return. I came in a rush of heat and sensitivity, every sensation heightened as she ran her nails up my back again. It felt like being struck by lightning, if that could ever be pleasurable. I shuddered and wrapped around her just as she did with me, the descent from my high slow and making me feel boneless.

I remained on top of Mari through the peak and the fall, my body still except for the great huffs of air I took. My pulse raced with dizzying speed. And still she felt so good, I didn't want to move. Her arms and legs remained hugged around me, like she didn't want me to leave either.

"I got you good back here," she mused after a few moments of quiet, palms caressing with a featherlight touch up and down my back.

"Am I bleeding?" I mumbled into the side of her neck. I didn't care if I was, except for giving her extra work in patching me up.

"No, it's just gonna be red for a while." Her fingers moved through my hair, running long, luxurious strokes over my scalp that made me want to purr like a cat.

"Good." I lifted my head to kiss her before rolling to my side. "I'll spend lots of time with my shirt off."

"Mm-hm." She grinned like she was pleased with the idea. "Never thought I'd hear you say that."

"Never thought I'd have long scratches on my back to show off." Mari rolled toward me and we fell into kissing some more—light, sweeping passes of our lips with how sated and sensitive we both still were. When we parted again, I touched the edge of her bandaged tattoo. "Did this ever bother you?"

"No." She scratched the rough bristles on my chin and smirked. "You're so good in bed, I forgot it was there."

A scoff escaped me as I rolled to my back. "Even I'm not *that* good." I smiled despite myself, running an arm around her waist to bring her down into the pillows with me. "You're just trying to give me an ego."

She wrinkled her nose and made more of her cute, frustrated growling noises until I scooped her onto my chest for more kisses. We settled into quietness after a few moments, her head resting over my heart while I traced her first tattoo, running my fingers over the inked lines on her back.

"You know what I realized?"

"Hm?" she mumbled sleepily against my skin.

"I think I might…really like seeing you with one of the others."

Her head lifted at that, eyes bright and curious. "You think so?"

"Yes." I traced her cheekbone, torn between staring at her endlessly or getting up to draw the beautiful planes of her face. "I love seeing you being pleased so much, I don't think it would matter who's doing it."

Mari returned her head to my chest, a giddy smile on her face as she settled on me. "Then we'll try it, whenever we get another fucking break in this war." Her head quickly lifted again, the smile wiped away. "And you know you don't have to—"

"Share you in bed if I don't like it, I know." I dropped an amused peck on her lips.

"And you know I never want to—"

"Ignore me or make me feel unwanted." I pulled her up higher to kiss her more deeply, banding my arms around her back while I reassured *her* for once. "Yes, I know that, my love." I tucked her head under my chin and held her to me tightly. "I know that better than I know anything else."

FIFTEEN

JANDRO

"I'm not fucking joking."

I bit back my smile as Mari paced in front of Reaper, Gunner, and Shadow, looking like the sexiest damn drill sergeant while the three of them stood stiffly at attention.

"You will not, under any circumstances, do anything stupid," she continued, pinning each of them with a hard stare. "Such as getting yourself captured by the enemy." Mari leaned aggressively into Gunner's face. "Getting stabbed, shot, or anything else that would put you at risk of a life-threatening injury. That goes for all of you!" She whipped around to face me and I schooled my features too late. I'd been staring at her ass and she caught me. "I mean it, Jandro."

"Yep, got it." I resumed my attentive stance but there was no hiding my smirk at her sexy-angry face. "That's why I'm hanging back on maintenance duty and not in the field killing some Blakeworth fucknuts."

Mari's features softened as she stepped closer toward

me. "You understand why I can't have all of you out on the battlefield, right? I just couldn't handle the possibility of losing all of you."

"'Course I do." I reached for her, my fingertips finding placement on the waist of her medic jumpsuit. "I'm happy to not be fighting, actually."

"Really?" Her eyebrows jumped at that.

"Believe it or not, I actually don't enjoy being shot multiple times or burned alive by explosives."

"You're not a great shot anyway," Gunner jabbed, resting his hands on the multiple guns holstered at his belt.

"Yeah, come tell me that when your Mini jams up 'cause you haven't cleaned it."

"Hey, I clean my shit!"

"You really should clean them more often," Shadow muttered under his breath.

"I'm sorry, what?" Gunner whirled on him, incredulous.

"I'm just saying, you have a lot of guns and it's been humid. They're definitely accumulating moisture."

"Alright, enough." Reaper raised a hand to stop the bickering. "We need to go. Sugar?" His voice softened. "We'll watch ourselves and we *will* come back. Promise."

She nodded at him, her body language fidgeting as if she was unsure about reaching out to touch him or not. "You better."

There was a tense moment of neither of them knowing what to do. Finally she rushed forward, squeezing him in a tight hug. Reaper wrapped an arm around her shoulders, the other around her back. His face lowered nearly to her shoulder, mouth angling toward her neck like he was going to kiss her there, but he stopped himself. Mari only squeezed him harder, the full length of her body pressing against his. For a simple hug, it was intense and sexually charged. Neither of them looked like they wanted to let go.

The other two and I looked on without comment, only patient curiosity. Mari and Reaper's relationship was a component of *us,* a greater whole, while still being independently *them* at the same time. The issues they had affected us all, but it still felt wrong to step in. Fixing what had gone wrong took time, and there was nothing wrong with that. None of us were going to tell her to hurry up and forgive him so we could all be a hunky-dory family again. Reaper had hurt her deeply—I knew that well enough from the nights of holding her crying after Shadow had been exiled.

By the same token, Reap was doing his best. He treated Shadow like a friend now, not a subordinate. He was thinking before he spoke more often, listening to others' input before jumping ahead to what he wanted to do. Of course he still wasn't perfect at it, but he was trying. The man knew how to admit he was wrong, and he didn't deserve to continue being punished for a wrong he acknowledged and regretted.

It might have been at a snail's pace, but Mari and Reaper seemed to be moving in a positive direction. And the best thing for the rest of us to do, was support them both.

The two of them finally released each other, and

Reaper came up to me as Mari said her goodbyes to Gun and Shadow.

"I want you, Larkan, and Slick out there after we're done," he murmured.

"Way ahead of you, Reap," I chuckled, slapping his shoulder. "You're crazy if you don't think we're scavenging some fancy Blakeworth machinery."

He grinned and thumped my chest. "Save the best shit for us and the Sons."

"Fuck yeah. Spoils of war, baby."

The three of them headed out to their waiting units. Mari came over to nestle into my side, and together we watched them go. She peered up at me once they were out of sight. "What were you two talking about?"

"Taking what's left of Blakeworth's goods after we beat their ass into submission." My arm rested on her shoulders as I dropped a kiss to her head. "I bet I can build you a whole new bike just from their parts."

"I like my dirt bike!"

"You're a president's wife, you gotta have at least two sets of wheels. More acceptably, three, but ideally, four."

"One for each husband?" she laughed.

"Something like that."

She hugged around me and lifted up on her tiptoes to kiss my cheek. "I should make sure the hospitals are all prepped and ready."

"Go on." I swatted her ass. "I'll swing by later to check on your generators."

With that, she headed off toward the two large white tents at the edge of the field. I chewed the inside of my cheek, watching her leave. We had nearly the whole hospital staff out here, and two field hospitals set up. A gnawing in my stomach cemented the reality that we'd likely be filling up hospital beds much faster than the first two battles.

We were on Blakeworth's doorstep, taking the battle to them now that we cleared the neutral zone of their spies. Gunner and T-Bone were able to piece together an aerial map of their capital city through Horus and Munin, T-Bone's raven. They marked the army's supply warehouses and government buildings, and the plan today was to take those out, essentially cutting Blakeworth off at the knees.

It was an aggressive move, and one in which we needed the element of surprise to pull off successfully. But there would likely be civilians caught in the crossfire.

After much back-and-forth and hesitation from Governor Vance, we finally decided this action was necessary. General Bray and Mari put together a unit of combat medics just to address civilians who'd get caught in the crossfire. Back in Four Corners, we posted a heavy artillery team facing east to watch for any activity from Tash but aside from that, it was all hands on deck.

I watched all the units move out until they were dark specks on the horizon. The shining towers of Blakeworth occasionally flashed as their glass panes caught the rising sun. I couldn't wait until we scaled those towers and put a Steel Demons flag at the top.

Some small part of me was wistful at missing out on the action. Battles used to be such a rush, on a different level than sex or riding or anything else. A year ago, I'd be out there right along Reaper's side, screaming like a madman while my gun lit up anyone who got in my path.

But battles took their toll on me. Even with the accelerated healing from Freyja, my back muscles still seized up. I'd been shot in both shoulders now, and the damn things couldn't move like they used to. I still got random pains in my lower leg, which Mari said was from nerve damage. Having gods around for healing didn't make me brand new, as I was beginning to figure out. They just sped up the process that was already going to happen, all the side effects and lingering pains included.

It wasn't just me who was battle-fatigued either. I could see it in the other guys. Even Gunner, who was fully in his element with that tactical mind of his.

We were tired. We wanted it to end.

And today was hopefully a big step toward that finish line.

I headed for the fleet of Jeeps and trucks we had standing by for a second wave if necessary. General Bray's mechanics were all good dudes who had taken well to me overseeing them, much like the foot soldiers who had taken to Gunner.

The vehicles were turned on and idling gently, ready to go at a moment's notice with a single radio call. Soldiers were relaxed but alert, hanging out with the doors and windows open, talking softly so everyone could hear if a call for back-up came in.

I wandered through the lines slowly, saying hello, but more importantly, listening for anything unusual with the vehicles. Everything should have been maintained and in top shape, but there was always a car or two that stubbornly didn't perform like it should.

"Jandro," one of the younger mechanics called, waving a wrench at me. "Can you come look at this?"

"Whatcha got, Holmes?" I came over, ears already pricked to the rattling under the truck's hood.

"Look underneath," the kid grumbled. "We just topped off the oil, but it's got a fucking leak."

I dropped to the ground, peering underneath the truck. "Yup, you're right. Go ahead and turn it off for me." He did so as I rose to standing. "We should take this one out of commission for now. Grab a flashlight and check out the engine for any leaks there. Did you just notice it?"

"Yeah, I think it's a pretty slow leak."

"So probably nothing that's a big break, a gasket or something is just not sealed somewhere." I patted the kid's shoulder, trying to wipe the frown off of his face. "It's not your fault man, cars are stubborn children sometimes."

"Just thought I did everything right," he muttered. He was young, probably not even twenty.

"I'm sure you did," I told him. "Sometimes you can do everything right and the damn thing still doesn't want to cooperate." I tilted my head, picking up a new grinding sound in the air from one of the other vehicles. "Like that, you hear it?"

The kid squinted as he concentrated on listening. "Uh, I think so."

"Something is messed up in there." I rubbed my chin as I turned around, trying to decipher which one of the vehicles it was coming from. "Someone didn't replace a belt, or a…"

I had turned toward the northeast and spotted a dark line on the horizon that wasn't there before, and was quickly growing bigger. I crossed my arms, watching the approaching unit with some confusion. Was there a second wave of back-ups that I had forgotten about? They weren't heading for us, but toward the field hospitals.

"Hey, who are they?" I asked the mechanic, jerking my chin toward the approaching vehicles.

He shrugged and shook his head. "I dunno."

I chewed my lip as I kept watching. Maybe Mari had called for more medics? She would have mentioned it though, and these Jeeps had guns mounted to the top, like makeshift battle tanks. A heavy sense of unease gripped me, and I shoved the mechanic toward the non-exposed side of the truck.

"Stay there. I'm gonna talk to your lieutenant," I told him, hurrying away to find his superior officer.

I hadn't jogged more than fifty feet before Lieutenant Davis met me in the center of the fleet of vehicles. "Who the fuck is that?" he demanded, pointing at the quickly approaching vehicles.

Fuck. Dread filled me up like a well of black ink.

"I was hoping you would know," I said.

"Shit." Davis grabbed for his radio. "General Bray, come in—"

He never got to finish the call. A projectile launched from a gun mounted on one of the Jeeps tore through the fabric of a hospital tent and engulfed it in flames.

SIXTEEN

MARIPOSA

"I mean, don't knock it 'til you try it." A hint of smugness bled into my voice as the young medics hung onto my every word.

"Doesn't it hurt?" a woman with curly black hair asked.

"Not if the guys prepare you well enough with lots of orgasms beforehand." I grinned, despite my face heating up. "And even then, they should go slowly, use plenty of lube, and most of all, listen and check in with you for any discomfort. It should never hurt if they're being attentive to your needs."

"Do your husbands ever…?" Another medic crossed her two index fingers and rubbed them against each other.

"No, they're all pretty focused on me." Somehow I was able to stay composed and resisted flipping my hair over my shoulder. "But if you're interested in that, I might know a sword-crossing trio." I grinned, thinking of the Sons and their occasional trysts with women.

"Oh, me, me me!" Several hands shot up and a tittering of laughter and good-natured teasing rose up from my staff. Warmth bloomed in my chest. It was so much like nursing school. When you had to work long, rotating shifts with the same people, you couldn't help but become a family. A family of people who were far too comfortable discussing various body parts.

"Alright, you perverts." I clapped my hands once. "Stay sharp. I'm going to check in on the other tent."

"Don't accidentally trip and fall on two dicks," someone called as I headed for the tent flap.

I walked out to the sounds of cackling, my smile wide as I headed for the neighboring tent. We needed this, all the laughter and crude conversation. We were about to get overrun by carnage, chaos, and death. Might as well enjoy these moments of peace while we had them.

Most of the injured from battle would be directed toward the first hospital tent. The second tent was reserved for major operations, such as amputations or removing large pieces of shrapnel from victims. Dr. Books and Rhonda were chatting quietly over tea in the second tent when I stepped inside.

"They're ready over there," I said, angling my head toward the direction I came from.

"You sure?" Rhonda teased. "They sound like a pack of hyenas."

"Just conducting the usual interviews about my sex life." I shrugged, my grin returning.

Dr. Brooks hid his blush and soft laugh behind a sip of tea, while Rhonda remained stone-faced, peering at me shrewdly. "Is everything okay at home, Mari?"

I pulled in a breath, knowing the longer I took to answer, the more obvious the answer would be no. "As okay as it can be." I forced a smile. "Given the fact that, you know, we're in the middle of a war and my whole family is fighting in it."

"Forget the war for a second." Rhonda set down her tea cup and Dr. Brooks took the opportunity to check on some machinery at the opposite end of the tent. "War is hard, you and I both know that." Rhonda's steely eyes bore into me. "I'd venture a guess that neither of us ever took out the pain of our jobs on our loved ones."

"Please, Rhonda." I held up a palm to stop her. "We're both experienced enough to know that trauma expresses itself differently in everyone. My men aren't perfect but they love me. Have they hurt me? Yes. Have I hurt them? Also yes. Maybe not in the same ways, but no one has made it through the last decade unscathed."

Rhonda didn't speak, only kept looking at me with that dissecting gaze.

"There's no one I'd rather see at the end of the day than those four men out there." I pointed outside the tent. *Yes, even Reaper,* I realized. "So when you ask if everything's okay, yes. We're doing the best we can, but we're not in a vacuum, Rhonda. We can't just subtract the war from the equation, because it has taken its toll on all of us."

The head nurse opened her mouth like she was about to speak, but a thundering crash rocked the tent like an earthquake. I was nearly knocked to my feet, and

Rhonda slid off the table she was sitting on and hit the floor.

"What's happening?" she demanded.

Searing heat coated my skin like a sudden fever. Bright, flickering light lit up the canvas walls of our tent. The most obvious sign came a moment later—the smell of smoke.

"The other tent's on fire!" Dr. Brooks sprang into action, grabbing gallons of the distilled water we used to wash equipment, and ran for the tent flaps.

"Oh my God, everyone's over there!" I hurried to pull Rhonda to her feet, but she moved slower with her bad leg and pushed me away.

"Go help the doctor!" she ordered me.

"I'm not leaving you alone!" I screamed back.

"I'll be alright, kiddo, those young medics need you. Save them!" She grabbed her cane and actually whacked me in the leg with it. "Go!"

I kept my eyes on her as I headed for the exit, staring at the tough-as-nails nurse until the last moment when I stepped outside. And holy fuck.

The battle was right fucking here.

Soldiers ran and shouted orders. Gunfire erupted, already making me duck and my ears ring. And right next door, our hospital was engulfed in flames.

I ran to help Dr. Brooks douse the flames with water, but it was hopeless. We might as well have been using squirt guns on a forest fire.

"Did anyone get out?" he yelled, swinging his arms back and forth to get more water out of the container. We didn't have hoses, so I copied his movements.

"I…" The horror hit me like a shot to the chest, cracking me wide open.

Fuck.

No.

I had *just* been in there, not even five minutes earlier. The medics' faces floated through my mind—their wide eyes, their smirks and giggles at the sordid details of my sex life. We were all just having a moment of lighthearted fun before a long day of work began. They were ready. They trained under me to save lives.

And, oh God no, they were *so* young.

"…I was the only one that left the tent."

The empty water container fell from my hand and my feet pressed forward, the flames already feeling close enough to singe my hair. A strong hand immediately clasped around my arm and pulled me back.

"No, Mari!" Dr. Brooks' voice sounded so far away. "You are *not* going in there!"

"I left them!" A sob rattled through my chest. "I walked away, I left them in there!"

"It's not your fault, sweetheart. I don't know how this happened."

The doctor's arms banded around me, pulling me back once he realized I fully intended to run into that tent, which had now collapsed into a wide circle of flames. The blaze didn't reach very high, but the fire was spread out. I could see some of the metal frames of the hospital beds and shelving we used. Flames just engulfed everything, covering shapes of every size. I couldn't even tell what was equipment or a person, and that made me scream a heart full of rage and pain at the carnage right in front of me.

"Mari? Mari!"

Someone was shouting my name, growing louder by the second. Dr. Brooks loosened his hold on me just a fraction and I tried to seize the chance to run into the fire, but he held on tighter when he sensed me pulling away.

"Mari! Oh my God, thank fucking everything."

Someone else was holding me now. Jandro crushed me to his broad chest, touching my cheek with a shaking hand. His eyes were tear-filled and full of relief, lips trembling as he said my name over and over.

"You weren't in that tent," he whispered. "Thank all the fucking gods, you weren't in that tent."

"Jandro, they were all inside!" I cried, trying to push on his chest to make him let me go. "I left them there! I have to go see if anyone—"

"Mari, babe." His voice hardened, holding my cheek firmly to make me look at him. "There's nothing we can do. We have to run."

"Run?" I blinked at him. "No, we have soldiers here. We have to fight. Someone attacked the *hospital*."

"It's Tash's army," he said quickly. "They over-whelmed the backup unit, a quarter of them are already gone. We have to run now."

"What?" I didn't understand, his words weren't computing. Before I could process what he said, he was pulling me away from the fire and breaking into a run. Dr. Brooks ran alongside us and I grabbed his arm. "You have to get Rhonda!"

"Going there now. The two of you keep moving!" He disappeared into the second tent that was still standing and a new spike of panic hit me. Would I see him or Rhonda again?

Jandro wouldn't let me stop or slow down to look around. Chaos surrounded us and I was still just trying to make sense of everything.

"Jandro, please wait!"

"Mari!" He barked my name out more harshly than I ever heard him say before. "If we stop, we're dead!"

"What about the other guys?" I hurried to keep up with his pace. "Has anyone called them?"

"I tried, didn't get an answer," he said. "They're busy with their own battle, or Tash might be interfering with our radio signals."

A barrage of rapid gunfire kicked up dirt right in front of our feet, making Jandro and I skid to a stop and throw our arms up to shield our faces. Before he pulled me to run in a different direction, I saw the armored Jeep with a massive assault rifle mounted to the roof coming straight for us.

"Fucking surrounded," Jandro hissed between his teeth, his hand an iron grip around my own.

"Are you hurt?" I asked him.

"No."

He pulled me around one of our own equipment vans and there, we stopped. Our backs pressed against the vehicle for cover, the two of us breathing with hard and labored gasps.

"Jandro——"

"Shh."

He turned to peer through the passenger window of the van, then carefully opened the door, making as little sound as possible. After rummaging around the seat for a few moments, he popped open the glove box to reveal a small handgun and a magazine of ammo.

Jandro looked at me and whispered, "You got your gun?"

I nodded shakily, my hand finding purchase on the weapon on my hip.

He took the gun from the glove box and cursed under his breath. There was no mag inside. The cartridge lying next to the gun contained the only bullets.

"You fully loaded?" Jandro asked me.

I nodded again. "How many shots do you have?"

"Fifteen." He dared to huff out a laugh. "And Gunner was right. I am probably the worst shot out of all of us."

"Jandro…" His name came out as a weak whimper on my lips. I didn't even know what I was trying to say.

He cupped my cheek and placed a tender kiss on my forehead. "I love you so much."

"Is this…" My eyes blurred with tears. I stared at the patches on his cut, inches from my face. The thread, the stitching. His club symbol was a skull with two wrenches crossed behind it. I'd never looked at it so closely before.

Jandro tilted my face up to his, wiping my tears with his thumbs before kissing me too softly, too sweetly on my lips, his mouth so soft and lingering, which only made me cry harder.

"If they get me first," he whispered. "Run south, back to Four Corners."

"No," I said weakly, clutching at him. "I...I can't lead them back to the city. All those people."

"If the others come back, they *have* to find you alive, Mari."

Glass exploded, raining shards down on us as we ducked low. The windows and windshield of the van were gone.

"They'll let me live if I tell them I'm a medic." I was just babbling now, my mind desperate to find another way out of this situation, one that didn't lead to the slaughter of thousands. One that didn't mean I was about to lose Jandro. Lose *everything.* "I'll...I'll help them at first. Buy us some time."

Jandro only shook his head, the warmth and love in his eyes hardening. "Do *not* let them capture you under any circumstances."

"But—"

More rapid-fire cut off my argument, bullet holes appearing in the side of the van just above our heads. Jandro shoved me next to the front tire just in time, and he rolled next to the rear tire just as a series of shots tore through the lower half of the van where we'd just been crouching.

Jandro leaned with his back against the tire, holding his gun to his chest as he peered around the back of the van. "They're right there." The sound of defeat in his voice was heartbreaking. He looked back at me. "Promise me, *mi amor*, you won't let yourself get captured."

"I…"

This couldn't be the last conversation I was having with my husband. Not this. We still had so much to talk about. So much to do together.

"Mari!" Jandro hissed through his teeth to keep his voice down. "Promise me *now*."

"I promise." My voice had no strength, it was barely a whisper. "I love you so much, *guapito*."

He forced a grin, though it looked more like a grimace. "You're the best wife a man could ask for." With a deep breath that seemed to calm him, he looked up briefly, then back at me. "Ready?"

I gave a shaky nod, still numbed by the disbelief that this was actually happening. He gave me no instructions because we were about to die.

Jandro returned my nod and let the back of his head fall against the van for a moment. "On three," he said, voice at normal volume. "One…two…*three!*"

I rose to my feet, pointing my gun through the shot-out windows of the van. Five Jeeps were lined up on the other side, each with a driver, two passengers, and a gunner manning the assault rifle on top. Only they weren't driving, so everyone in the Jeeps had weapons drawn and pointed at us.

There was no way we could win.

I started firing, hoping to take at least one of them out before I went down. They returned fire, and I ducked on instinct. Looking over at Jandro, he had done the same, waiting for a pause so he could resume shooting.

When we moved to shoot again, the gunner was

taking aim from the Jeep's roof. When he fired, I thought my eardrums would burst. Pain split through the sides of my head, and then I was falling backwards. The van…it looked like it was about to fall on top of me.

I brought my arms up instinctively, despite knowing I'd never survive being crushed under a massive vehicle. Something grabbed around my waist and flung me roughly in a different direction. *Oh fuck, no! I can't get captured!*

I thrashed, kicked, and screamed. I couldn't hear anything besides the painful ringing in my head, couldn't make sense of up, down, or any direction. *Jandro! Where's Jandro?* I tried screaming at the top of my lungs but still couldn't hear myself.

Someone was touching me, dragging me somewhere, and I fought with all of my remaining strength, which was quickly draining away. Then something appeared in front of my face, a hand. Fingers were snapping in front of my eyes, the sound muffled and far away.

And then, a man's face. He looked familiar and I squinted in my effort to recognize him. Silver hair and kind blue eyes.

"Hey there, angel." His lips moved slowly enough for me to understand. "Sorry we're late, but Jerriton's here. Told ya we'd stand with Four Corners."

SEVENTEEN

JANDRO

Once that projectile fired off from the top of the Jeep, I knew we were done for. This was it, fucked over by an ambush we never saw coming. An attack on the hospital, of all things.

The van rocked onto its two passenger-side tires from the close impact of the missile. Mari had been shooting through the windows and the force knocked her back. Before I could dive for her, someone grabbed my cut and yanked me back as the van fell onto its side.

"MARI!" Someone had grabbed her, a guy was hauling her away from the overturned van with an arm around her waist. He was dressed in the all-black of the troops who just ambushed us. "Put her down!" I yelled, raising my gun toward them.

The guy ignored me, but something else was off. He seemed to be handling her…carefully. He sat her gently on the ground, and his partner crouched in front of Mari's dazed face, snapping his fingers in front of her eyes.

I tore out of the grip holding me and whipped around, my gun at the throat of a kid in his twenties. "Who the fuck are you?"

"Jerriton," he said quickly, raising his arms to his sides. "The People's Army of Jerriton, we're on your side."

"People's Army?" I pulled my gun away a fraction of an inch. "You the rebels that broke out of the prison?"

"Yes, sir." His eyes were wide as his head bobbed up and down in a nod. "We escorted Mariposa and Shadow back to Four Corners."

"Well shit." I lowered my gun and somehow in my shock, remembered to take in my surroundings.

There was no need for cover, as I soon realized. Jerriton was everywhere, shooting at the black-clad troops wearing similar, but slightly different uniforms. Everyone that had been shooting at Mari and me was either dead or had been detained.

"Okay, what the fuck is happening?" I demanded, turning around in a circle. At quick glances, it looked like our attackers had turned against themselves. "Did you shoot down our hospital?"

"No, I swear!" The kid shook his head, his wide eyes still on my gun. "We were on our way to help and saw *them* marching toward you. None of them even glanced at us. They were like robots, it was fuckin' weird. It was dark and we just kind of followed them in. Uniforms must've looked similar enough that it didn't raise alarms for them."

None of that shit was making sense, but I had more

pressing matters to deal with. "Hey!" I hollered, walking up to the two guys surrounding Mari. "Get the fuck out of my wife's face!" I grabbed the shoulder of the guy crouched in front of her, shoving him to the side.

"Easy, man." He was an older guy, roughly Reaper's dad's age, with hair and a beard that were mostly gray. His blue eyes narrowed at me. "I've had some medical training, I'm just checking her for a concussion."

"Jandro, this is Samson." Mari was lucid enough to sound amused. "He led the Jerriton resistance that got me and Shadow home. Sam, Jandro is one of my husbands."

"Like that wasn't clear." Samson chuckled as he rubbed his shoulder, and a twinge of guilt sat in my chest.

"Sorry, man," I muttered. "Here, let me." I held my arm out to help him up.

"It's all good. Thanks." Samson grabbed my forearm and allowed me to pull him to standing. "She's fine, by the way," he added a bit smugly.

"Fuck, both of us are." I ran my hand over my head, still stunned at this drastic turn of events when we were down to our last bullets. "I don't…I don't know how many of us are left."

"Dr. Brooks and Rhonda! We have to find them." Mari held her hands out and I grabbed them to pull her to her feet and into my chest, wrapping her up tightly.

"Lady with a cane and tall, black guy with glasses?" piped up the kid I'd been talking to earlier. "Red crosses on their jumpsuits?"

"Yes!" Mari tore out of my embrace to look at him. "You've seen them?"

"Yes, ma'am. They're fine," he said with a dip of his head. "They found cover behind a pile of debris, and we took out the ones shooting at them."

"Oh, thank fuck." She slumped against me, only to lift her head again. "The guys! Did you try radioing them again?"

"I will in a sec." My hand came to rest on the back of her head, bringing it to nestle in the center of my chest again. "Just let me hold you like this for a minute."

I'd made peace with dying today. I had expected it, even welcomed it. But something—the universe or the gods—decided that today was not my day. I still had more time with my wife, my family, and I wouldn't take a single moment of that for granted.

Mari's arms came around my waist and she held on to me just as tightly.

————

"OUR DEEPEST APOLOGIES for not coming to your aid sooner." Samson stood at the end of the conference table two hours later, cleaned up in a polo shirt and slacks for this meeting with the entire Four Corners leadership. Even some of Governor Vance's cabinet members who weren't directly involved in the war effort wanted to meet the People's Army of Jerriton. "We wanted to ensure things were stable enough back home before involving ourselves in other territories' disputes."

"Stable enough, meaning…?" General Bray implored him.

When Samson hesitated in answering, Governor Vance piped up. "Speak freely, sir. You've just saved my territory and will not be tried for any crimes here."

"You can trust the governor and the general," Shadow added. "They've been good to us."

T-Bone muttered something under his breath, earning some side-eyes, but Shadow's encouragement seemed to be what Samson needed to hear.

"We overthrew the governor that Tash left in charge," he said with an air of pride, lifting his chin. "And took back our territory, our home."

"Fuck yeah," Gunner muttered, his face splitting into a grin as his hand curled into a victorious fist. Louder he said, "Congratulations. It's the least of what you deserve."

"You're renaming the place, I take it?" Reaper asked, a smile also growing on his face.

"Thank you, and yes." Samson gave a lighthearted shrug and grinned sheepishly. "Probably Colorado, like how it was before."

"Once we're able, Four Corners will support you in any way you need," Vance said.

"Again, thank you." Samson lowered his gaze to the table. "After this war is over, we plan to hold elections."

"Just like the good old days." Even Reaper's dad was beaming at him from across the table. "You're running, I hope."

Samson shrugged humbly again. "I'm not sure yet. We'll see."

Vance's assistant Josh cleared his throat to grab the room's attention. "This is very exciting but if you don't mind gentlemen, we do need official reports of today's events."

"Right, of course." Finn turned to his son next to him at the table. "Why don't you start, and then we'll get into what happened with the hospital."

It turned out Reaper, Gunner, and Shadow's units had mopped the floor with Blakeworth. They demolished important government buildings and supply warehouses, just as planned. Sadly, as we also predicted, death and injury among civilians was also high. Their medic team was able to take over a well-stocked hospital reserved for the elite class, and stayed there to treat the injured without having to transport them back to our field hospitals.

After their battle was over, everyone stayed to look for more injured in the rubble. They filled the Blakeworth hospital, and still carried truckloads of civilians back to us, unknowing of the situation we were in. They never received a single one of our distress calls until after Jerriton saved our asses, which strongly suggested that our attackers interfered with our signals. Once Reaper concluded his report, all eyes swiveled to those who rode in and saved us, the real stars of the show.

"Samson, the floor is yours." Governor Vance folded his hands patiently, but I could see how he too was eager to hear this story.

"Thank you, sir. As I said, we wanted to stabilize our territory before offering aid. But recruiting a sizable army was a high priority as well." He looked to the side, toward Mari with a small smile. "We never forgot how Mari and Shadow freed us, allowing us to take our home back. I promised them that Jerriton had their back and wanted to make good on that promise. We headed out as soon as we had the numbers and the artillery."

"She told us to expect you." Finn smiled at his daughter-in-law. "To say we're grateful is the understatement of the century."

Josh cut in with another clearing of his throat. "And you said you encountered another army on your way toward us?"

"That's correct." Samson nodded. "We didn't have uniforms, the closest we could get was wearing all black. Well, this other army had all-black uniforms."

"So you figured they thought you were part of them but a separate unit?" Josh asked.

"We thought so at first, but actually no, they…they didn't seem to register as us being there at all." Samson looked visibly nervous for the first time, combing one hand back through his hair. "It was like all the soldiers had a one-track mind. There was no variance to their marching, not a single arm or foot out of place for miles. No one talked, smoked, broke formation, any of the normal shit soldiers do when they're going somewhere and there isn't a commander watching them. It was very bizarre to see."

"Would you say they acted robotic?" Reaper asked. "Like someone could control them with a flip of a switch?"

"Yes," Samson agreed. "It was exactly like that. Like a string could be cut and they'd all collapse."

"Did you interact with them at all?" Josh peered over his glasses, writing hand poised over his memo pad.

"No, we didn't want to risk a confrontation. We let them march ahead of us for several hundred yards, then followed. They were heading in the same direction, so we at first thought they might have been your own people." Samson's expression soured, mouth turning down as he stared at the tabletop. "We should have stayed closer. Otherwise we might have been able to stop them."

"You couldn't have known," I said, speaking up for the first time. "I saw them coming and thought they were another back-up unit too, at first."

"It was poor planning on my part," Gunner said, swallowing thickly. "I was so focused on keeping defenses up in the city, I didn't think to have extra guns around the hospital."

"You're not to blame either," Mari said to him. "The whole time I've been a traveling medic, no army has directly attacked a field hospital, until now. It's just not done. It's…" She took a shaking breath and I reached under the table to squeeze her hand. "It's an atrocity," she finally said, a dark heaviness in her voice.

"Mari, I know you've had an extremely hard day but if you don't mind," Josh broached gently. I wanted to smack him. He couldn't handle half the shit she'd dealt with, so fuck him talking to her like she was some delicate thing. "Can you tell us who was lost in the hospital? And your current patient count with the new intakes?"

Mari looked like she wanted to smack him too, but she took a steadying breath and placed her hands on the table. "We lost eight medics today," she began, her tone steady while still charged with emotion. Everyone bowed their heads and listened intently as she said their names. Josh quickly wrote them down, his pen the only sound in the room aside from Mari's voice. The first moments of silence and respect for those we lost today.

"We've lost twenty-nine soldiers from the backup units," Mari continued. "I'm sorry, I'm afraid I didn't know all of their names."

General Bray looked up. "May I?" At Mari's nod, he picked up a roster sheet and recited the names of the fallen soldiers, some of which I'd just been talking to before the attack on the hospital. He said the name of the young mechanic I was talking to about the oil leak in the truck, and my head bowed lower. This time, Mari reached out and squeezed my hand.

"Thank you, General," she said when he finished. "On a happier note, we have twenty-four survivors from that unit. Nine of them have critical injuries. The injured civilians from Blakeworth add another seventeen. Of those who attacked us and have been detained—"

"Should be executed," someone muttered under their breath.

Every one of Mari's husbands shot murderous looks at the random sergeant who spoke out of turn, but it was General Bray who slapped the table with his palm and jumped to his feet.

"Get out, Sergeant Burns," he barked, pointing at the door.

Burns shrank down in his chair, eyes wide at his boss. "Sir?"

"You heard me. Out. We're compiling reports, not sharing opinions. I'm not in the mood for anyone's smart remarks, so you can fucking leave."

The soldier scrambled out of his seat toward the door, muttering apologies as he made himself scarce.

"You interrupt anyone at the next meeting, I'll have you demoted," Bray growled. "I'm sorry, Mari. Please, continue."

She bit back a smile, keeping composed to deliver the rest of the report. "Of the attacking unit, we're treating twenty-two with serious injuries as well. But the most compelling thing about those soldiers is that they all show signs of major physical and psychological trauma, taking place long before the battle began."

General Bray paled as he exchanged a long, worried glance with Reaper. "How do you know this?"

"A few of them have spoken to us with no memory of the battle or how they got there," Mari said. "Nearly all of them have old injuries, burns mainly, that appear to be inflicted by torture." She took a deep breath, eyes casting over me and her other men before speaking again. "Some of them have had to be sedated because all they do is scream."

"Fuck," Reaper muttered, looking toward the ceiling.

"They all have damage to the ear canals as well," Mari said.

Finn scrubbed a hand tiredly down his face. "Do you have any theories as to what this could mean?"

"I can pretty confidently say these soldiers are being tortured or possibly even brainwashed into compliance," Mari answered. "Although it's to varying degrees. Some of them are lucid and talking to us, while others are nearly catatonic."

"Do you believe they're unaware, or possibly not in control of their actions, when they attack us?"

"That is a possibility," she said sadly. "We need to find out more to be sure, but it's clear they're not fighting of their own free will."

Fuck, I thought. *And we sent Andrea right to the center of it.*

"Is there anything else?" Bray asked, sounding more weary than I'd ever heard him before.

"There is one thing." Mari glanced at the table for a moment, looking hesitant as she chewed her lip. "The loss of eight medics coupled with a much bigger patient load is…stretching us very thin."

Now she was the one who looked weary, and I wanted nothing more than to remove her from this room and take her home to rest.

"We'll be training new medics as quickly as we can, but that still doesn't help us with our patient load right now," Mari continued. "So Dr. Brooks gave me permission to seek hospital volunteers. They won't do anything complicated, just help us with basic tasks for the patients. If anyone—"

"Me." I leaned toward her, dropping a fast kiss on her shoulder. "I'll help. Anything you need."

"I'll help too," Reaper piped up from across the table. "Just tell me what to do and where to go."

"I volunteer as well, ma'am," one of the soldiers piped up.

"What a great idea to give back to our people." Governor Vance slapped Josh's shoulder. "Count both of us in."

All around the conference table, people echoed their willingness to volunteer. Even Samson and his people from Jerriton said they would be willing. Mari smiled humbly down at the table, her shoulders just a little more relaxed than they had been.

"Thank you, all of you. I guess we can make a sign-up sheet and a volunteer schedule."

"I can definitely help you with that." Josh turned to a fresh page in his memo pad. "Everyone who's volunteering, come see me."

The meeting concluded shortly after that. A line formed in front of Josh, and Mari had to return to the hospital.

"When are you coming home?" I asked, grabbing her hip like I never wanted to let her go. I thought we would die together today, and now I didn't want her to leave my sight.

"I don't know, honestly." She looked up at me apologetically. "Maybe I'll have a break for a couple hours in the morning."

"You want me to bring you food? Coffee?" I laced my hands at the small of her back. "I can go with you, just start volunteering right now."

"We're still trying to get all the patients situated. No one's got the spare batteries to train volunteers right now." She stuck her hands inside my cut, hugging around my waist. "Food and coffee would be amazing, though."

"You got it." I kissed her forehead, running my hands up her back. "I'll sign up with Josh, then see what we got at home."

"Thank you." She tilted those beautiful lips up, kissing me a few times before we reluctantly untangled our limbs so she could say goodbye to the other guys.

No sooner had she left the room than one of Samson's officers approached me, a woman maybe a decade older than me that looked tough as nails, like she'd been in the military her whole life. "Excuse me, I didn't want to interrupt you with your wife but, you're Jandro?" Her eyes fell to the patch on my cut.

"Yeah, and you are?" I held my hand out to her in greeting.

"Nora." She stared at my hand, not taking it. "Are you Angelica's brother?"

My hand fell limply to my side, my once-calm heart rate now hammering in my chest as I stared at this woman. "You know Angie?"

Nora nodded. "I have a letter to you from her." She was still wearing a bulletproof vest and quickly worked to remove it as she talked. "I met your sister in Oregon —well, Cascadia now. She showed me pictures of you two when you were kids, and I used to babysit her daughter."

"Her daughter?" I repeated numbly. "My…niece?"

"Yes, Sofia. My lord, she's gotta be almost four now." Nora finished removing her vest and pulled an envelope from a pocket inside her sweater. "She sent this to your old address in Arizona over a year ago, but it got returned." She held the letter out to me and it was all I could do to not snatch it from her hand.

"How did you end up with this?" My hands shook as I struggled to unfold the paper. "How is she? She's okay?"

"She was fine last I saw her," Nora assured me, then added with a small grin, "Pregnant with her second baby."

"Another baby..."

I finally managed to unfold the letter, the words on the paper blurring, but the photo enclosed was crystal-clear. There was my sister, looking exactly as I remembered her the night she left. Angie sat on the ground behind a dark-haired toddler, hugging the little girl and smiling. Fuck me, I couldn't remember the last time I saw her smile like that.

And behind Angie, a man hugged around both her and the toddler, his eyes closed as he kissed the back of my sister's head. I wondered if that was Drew, who she ran off to be with, or some other guy she met there.

"Colorado was where I grew up," Nora explained to me. "When I heard about the oppression going on, I decided to move back to check on my extended family. Angie gave me the letter on a whim, saying you were probably riding all over on your motorcycle and to give it to you if I ever saw you."

"Fuck," I laughed in disbelief, still staring at the photo. "What are the odds, huh?"

"I was staring at you like a creep during the whole meeting, wondering why you looked so familiar," Nora chuckled. "It finally hit me, and thank God I've carried the letter on me everywhere since I left, just in case."

"I'm grateful," I said, looking up at her. "Thank you so much for this."

"I'm just glad I could pull through for a friend." Nora smirked. "And meet the little brother she told me so many stories about."

"Aw hell," I groaned. "I'm afraid to find out what you've heard."

"You should be," she goaded me with a laugh.

I carefully folded up the letter to read later, when I had a moment alone. "When did you last see her?"

"Oh, it's been about eight months or so." Nora tilted her head with a smile. "She's definitely had the baby by now."

"This is her same address?" I tapped the faded ink on the envelope.

"Yes, she's lived there for the past four years."

"I'll write to her myself," I decided out loud. "I know it's a fifty-fifty chance she'll even get it, but I want her to hear from me directly."

"If we get lucky and win this war," Nora shrugged hopefully, "we might even get working phone lines again and you can give her a call."

"That would be nice." I returned her smile. "Something to look forward to. Hey!" I held an arm out to indicate the rest of the Jerriton army in the room. "Do you all have somewhere to stay?"

"The governor's staff has set us up with accommodations, thank you."

"Good." I made sure to catch Reaper's eye as I

tucked the letter away safely. "Well, you're welcome at our home any time. You've been there for my sister, so you're family as far as I'm concerned."

"Thank you. My wife wasn't present for the meeting, but we both love Angie, and she'd love to meet you too."

"My wife had to leave, but she'd love to have you both over." I smiled a bit sheepishly. "When she's not overworked and exhausted, I'm sure."

Nora laughed, amusement deepening the lines around her eyes. "You've certainly grown up from the troublemaker your sister told me about."

"Had to," I said with a small shake of my head. It was the simplest answer for everything that transpired in the last few years. "Thank you again. It was great to meet you, but if you'll excuse me," I touched a hand to Nora's shoulder. "I have to run home and make some food and coffee."

EIGHTEEN

MARIPOSA

"You're sure you don't mind?"

I smiled at Finn, trying to ease the concerned frown etched into my father-in-law's face. "Not at all. The more information we have on official record, the better."

"You're working harder than any of us," he said. "And training the volunteers, on top of your regular job."

"It's not much to train them," I said, scanning the wall of clipboards for the patient we were about to see.

"Still, it's more than what you should be doing."

"That's being a battle medic in a nutshell." I found the one I was looking for and snatched it off the hook, quickly flipping through the paperwork to get a refresher on the patient's intake report.

He was from General Tash's army, and one of the more lucid soldiers, talking to us readily despite not remembering much. Every day he grew stronger and seemed to remember a bit more. When Finn asked to speak to some of those from the opposing army, this patient seemed like the best candidate. He was still skittish and prone to headaches, but his CT scans showed improvement and all his vitals were strong.

I looked up at Finn, sharp and handsome in his military uniform as he waited for me to finish reading the patient's chart. "Ready?"

He held an arm out to the side and smiled at me warmly. "After you."

I led the way through the hospital corridor, walking fast enough that the general had to quicken his march to stay at my side. My medic-march, as we in the hospital called it, was on autopilot at this point. I was so exhausted, I could barely perceive my walking speed anymore. I'd hardly spent any time at home in the last few days, only crashing there for a shower, quick meals, and a few hours of sleep. The volunteers were beginning their shifts soon, which would ease the burden on us slightly. I figured I might be able to manage one full day off soon.

My feet stopped robotically just outside of the patient's room and I took a moment to re-center myself. I had to be a person now, not a machine, and that took a different kind of energy.

Rapping my knuckles softly at the door, I turned the knob and cracked it open a few seconds later, sticking my head in with a smile. "Hi, John. How are you feeling?"

We called all of the male patients from Tash's army John, as in John Doe. None of them remembered their own names.

This John was fair-skinned and freckled, with strawberry blond hair and blue eyes. He'd suffered second-degree burns and severe lacerations from shrapnel during the battle. Both of his arms and his torso were wrapped in thick white bandages.

"Oh, hi. Um, good..." He squinted for a few moments as if concentrating. "Mari, right?"

"Yes, you got it!" I opened the door wider, allowing him to get a view of Finn right behind me. "Is it okay if the general sits in with us today?"

John's eyes widened as he shrank back in his bed, bringing the hospital blanket under his chin as he rapidly whispered something under his breath.

"You don't have to be afraid, son." Finn leaned in closer. "You're not in trouble, no one's gonna arrest you. I just want to listen and help figure out what happened."

"I don't know…" John broke eye contact as he shook his head. "Four Corners army, they want me to kill…"

I turned toward my father-in-law so only he could hear me. "It might help if you took your jacket off?"

"Oh, certainly." He started unbuttoning his uniform immediately. "I probably should have thought of that."

"It's okay. We're still learning everyone's triggers."

In the time it took for him to take off his jacket, a small black form had jumped onto John's bed and began kneading the blanket, purring up a storm.

"Freyja," I said in surprise. "I was wondering where you've been."

The black cat's presence immediately seemed to calm John, who held a hand out to her. "She visits me every day," he said softly.

We watched from the doorway as the cat nuzzled into his hand, walking higher up the bed until she settled into his lap.

"John?" I decided to try again. "General Bray has taken his jacket off. He just wants to listen. Is it okay if he stays for a few minutes?"

John's hands scratched through Freyja's fur. The cat seemed to soak up all his fear through his pets and give him back some bravery, at least temporarily.

"Yes, I think that would be okay," he voiced softly.

"Thank you. We'll be fast and then we'll let you rest."

Finn and I made our way into the room, he was now in his white T-shirt with the top of his uniform draped over his arm. My father-in-law took a chair at the back of the room while I pulled up to John's bedside.

"So you didn't call for morphine this morning," I noted, my pen hovering over his chart in my lap. "How was your pain level when you woke up today?"

"My headache was completely gone." There was a brightness in his voice, excitement making him light up. "I think…I think I remember more too."

"Really? That's great!" I made a quick note of it and set my pen down. "Would you like to share what you remember now or…" I let the question trail off, giving him ample permission to refuse if he didn't want the general to know.

John's eyes flicked toward Finn for a moment, then back to me. "I think, I'm pretty sure my name is Robert." He nodded to himself, as if speaking aloud made him more confident in that answer. "Yes, Robert.

Some people call me Rob, I think. Yeah, I'm pretty sure."

"Excellent, this is all good news." I crossed out *John Doe #17* at the top of his chart and wrote in *Robert*. "Do you happen to remember your last name?"

He thought for a moment. "Anderson? I think it's Anderson."

"Robert Anderson," I repeated back to him. "Does that feel like it's you?"

"Yes, it does!" He beamed, looking the happiest I'd seen him since we took him in. "My name is Robert Anderson."

"Well, it's wonderful to meet you, Robert. You're making great progress." I made a few more notes on his chart. "Is there anything else you remember?"

The excitement drained from him slowly, his smile fading as his eyes took on a distant, vacant look. "I remember feeling…trapped in my head."

I glanced at Finn, who started leaning forward in his chair. "What do you mean?" I asked Robert.

"Like I wasn't in control of my body. Like…" He brought a hand up to rub at his temple. "Like someone had broken into my brain and they controlled me from the inside. I could still think and stuff but…something else was there." Robert swallowed thickly, his hand returning to petting Freyja to ease some discomfort. "I remember it just…hurting *so* bad."

"Did you hear laughing?" Finn inquired.

Robert nodded. "We all did."

"Who's we?" I asked him. "The other soldiers you were with?"

223

Robert shook his head. "We were never soldiers. Not willingly, anyway. But yeah, we were all crowded together, and…" He grabbed his head with his palms. "There were so many faces, so many of us in pain. I can't even remember them all."

Finn and I exchanged a look. My father-in-law was now on the edge of his seat. "Do you remember the battle three days ago?"

"Three days?" Robert muttered to himself, his brow furrowing. "The time sounds weird. It feels like longer than that but I remember flashes, like it was a dream. It doesn't feel real." Robert rubbed his forehead. "I'm sorry, I'm starting to get a headache again."

"I'll get you some Tylenol." I rose from my chair to reach over and touch his shoulder. "Thank you so much, Robert. You've been incredibly helpful."

"You're very brave, young man." Finn made his way to the door. "And you're safe now. Thank you for letting me listen."

We left Robert's room, closing the door quietly as he sank into his bed, Freyja making herself comfortable on a new spot on his blanket. Finn and I just stared at each other for a moment of stunned silence in the hallway.

"Well, what the fuck do you make of that?" he breathed out in disbelief, sliding his arms through his jacket to put it back on.

"Wanna talk it out?" I jerked my head toward an empty break room.

"Yes, please."

We headed that way to find none other than Freyja sitting on the counter next to the outdated microwave.

"What the?" Finn looked down the hallway, then turned back to the cat blinking slowly in front of him. "How did she…?"

"Gods," I said with a shrug. "You get used to them popping up everywhere."

"Huh." He chuckled softly as he resumed buttoning up his jacket. "Well, alright then." Once he was dressed as the general again, he looked at me with a serious expression. "So what do you make of our friend Robert?"

"He's in probably the best shape out of everyone from that unit," I said, leaning against the counter next to Freyja. "Most of them are non-verbal, non-responsive to stimuli at all. It's like they're not even there." I scratched the cat's cheek. "The ones who do talk, it's just babbling. They're confused and don't know who or where they are."

"So there's varying degrees of this…this trauma they've endured?"

"I think we're seeing different stages of the same process," I answered. "With Robert, maybe he was a newer addition. If he wasn't conditioned for very long, it makes sense as to why he's recovered so quickly."

Finn nodded, following my train of thought. "And the ones who haven't recovered?"

"They've probably been conditioned for much longer." I let my hand drop from Freyja's head. "They may be even too far gone to save."

"And so the ones who are speaking but confused, are somewhere in the middle," my father-in-law concluded.

"Yes, exactly. Some of them have improved slightly, but it's slow-going."

We both found ourselves looking at Freyja, blinking slowly and sitting calmly on the counter next to me. The cat seemed to grow bored of the staring contest and proceeded to lick her paw.

"Do you think she has anything to do with Robert's recovery?" Finn asked in a low voice, barely above a whisper.

"I'm almost certain of it." I smiled, petting down the cat's back. "She's basically lived here at the hospital, wandering in and out of patients' rooms."

"Amazing," the general breathed, reaching out to stroke Freyja gently.

I cannot do more for the empty vessels. Freyja's warm voice was heavy with sadness, filling the room and my head with a gentle pulse of energy. *There is no humanity left for me to nurture.*

"Did you hear that?" I asked Finn.

"No, but I felt…something." He rubbed his own arms. "Like static in the air, but not as harsh."

I repeated what Freyja said and he nodded slowly. "So they are too far gone then."

"Sadly, yes."

"What I want to know is," he rubbed his jaw, "why send a mix of them to attack us? Why not a whole unit devoid of their humanity? Rory and Shadow seemed to deal with a mix at the first battle too. Some screaming and struggling, others just…empty."

"Maybe the victims respond to it differently," I suggested after a few moments of thinking. "Some might be more susceptible to the torture, while others are more resistant."

"What would determine that, in your opinion?"

"I really don't know," I said with an apologetic sigh. Doc and Dr. Ellis would probably have some compelling theories, but digging this deeply into psychology was beyond my realm of expertise. "Torture of any kind seeks to exploit weaknesses. They can't do extensive physical torture because they need the soldiers in good enough shape to fight and march long distances."

A thought hit me suddenly. "What if they're still experimenting?"

Finn narrowed his eyes. "What do you mean?"

"Whoever's torturing them is…they're refining their technique," I said. "We have more catatonic patients from this ambush than in the first battle. That means whoever's doing this is becoming more efficient at torturing them. After we won the first battle, they realized they needed better soldiers, which for them means less humanity. Less free will."

"So they're testing their levels of control. That could explain why they attacked the hospital this time instead of meeting us in an actual battle," Finn mused. "Or this was a unit of rejects that they just wanted to dispose of quickly."

"We were still completely outmatched though." I petted Freyja again, trying to shove away the events of that day. The burning hospital tent was not a memory that would leave me easily. "If Jerriton hadn't showed up when they did, that would have been the end for us."

"But it wasn't." My father-in-law reached out to give

a gentle squeeze to my shoulder. "We're all still here to fight another day."

"Yeah," I agreed with a sigh, the exhaustion settling into my limbs again. "Still kickin'."

Finn released me, his face taking on a conflicted expression before speaking again. "You know I love you no matter what, right sweetheart?"

I blinked for a moment, taken aback. "Finn, I—"

"No matter what happens between you and my son, I mean," he clarified. "You'll always be a daughter to me."

I looked down at my shoes, a mixture of embarrassment and relief surging through me. My pride was a little wounded, to be sure. I didn't want anyone outside of me and my husbands knowing how Reaper and I were struggling to reconnect. But Finn had become a father figure to me too, and with the absence of my own parents, his presence was a comfort I hadn't realized I needed.

"You know all about that, huh?" I said a bit sheepishly.

"No, very little actually. He's been just as tight-lipped as you." Finn smiled reassuringly. "And I won't pry. Lis and I just miss you, that's all. If you ever have a free moment to come by, by yourself or with one of the others even, we'd love to have you."

"Thank you, I appreciate it." I wasn't sure how much I believed him. Parents always favored their own children over their children's partners, didn't they? In all honesty, I was too exhausted to give it much thought.

More patients needed to be seen. "Was there anyone else you wanted to see while we're here?"

"No, thank you for allowing me to listen." Finn clasped his hands behind his back, readily accepting my change of subject. "I should report back to the governor and my lieutenants."

"I'll walk you out."

Freyja jumped down from the counter as we left the room, tail high in the air as she trotted down another hallway.

"A god's work never ends," Finn chuckled, watching her leave.

I held on to his elbow as we walked together toward the front entrance. "Does any of this change how you're going to prepare for upcoming battles? What you heard from Robert today?"

"I don't know," he said with a weary sigh. "Ideally, we would. I hate the thought of killing people who aren't aware and have no control of what they're doing." He gently removed my hand from his elbow and turned to face me when we reached the door. "But I don't know of any alternatives," he added sadly. "If only we could target the source of what's doing this to them."

"I understand," I said. "Above all, we have to protect our own people from outside threats."

"Correct." The general smiled warmly at me. "It's good to see you at the war meetings. I hope you keep coming to them."

"If I have time," I laughed humorlessly. "Which I never have enough of. But it's been good to see you too."

Finn leaned forward and kissed my forehead. "I'll see you later. Take it easy, sweetheart."

"You too, General Bray."

I watched him walk down to his waiting SUV, then went back inside for another long hospital shift.

NINETEEN

MARIPOSA

"You know if I close my eyes and just forget everything that's been happening, I can almost pretend like we're not in the middle of a war right now."

I was stretched out length-wise on the couch with my feet in Shadow's lap and my head in Jandro's. At one end, my skull and neck were being rubbed, my headache being soothed away into the blissful pressure of Jandro's firm fingers. He tried braiding my hair at one point, but quickly gave up on that endeavor to massage me instead.

At the other end, Shadow thoroughly experimented with all manner of touch on my feet, just as he did with the rest of my body. My initial instructions were all he needed. He picked up the rest from the sounds I made and how I utterly melted at his touch.

"Is this helping you pretend?" Shadow asked with a small smile, running his thumbs up the length of my arch.

"Mm-hmm…" My eyelids were falling shut from

relaxation. "Both of you are helping my imagination along very much."

The guilt still wasn't going away—that remained my biggest tether to reality. Guilt over the medics we lost. None of us were able to mourn them, we had too much work to do, patients that needed us, but most of whom we didn't know how to treat. And then there was Andrea.

Andrea. Tessa still didn't know about the latest message we received. What could I tell her?

I still wanted to hope that Andrea hadn't been compromised—that she wasn't under control like all those robotic soldiers from Tash's army. But what else could the note mean?

Either way, I was still determined to get her out. We suffered some losses, but we were still winning this war. Whenever Tash surrendered to us fully, we'd take over their base and find her. After she risked everything for our cause, bringing her home was the least we could do for her.

Jandro's warm fingertips came to my forehead, smoothing out the tension that built up there while I thought of Andrea.

"Keep on pretending, *Mariposita*, just for a little while. We'll be back to reality tomorrow."

I nodded, releasing a deep sigh from my chest. The hospital was full of our own people, Jerriton citizens, Blakeworth and Tash troops. We had to keep the one field hospital up just to contain the overflow of injured. The rush of volunteers eager to help did give us a tiny bit of breathing room. It was the only way I was able to take this evening off.

Even with the extra help, I expected to be on my feet for no less than sixteen hours tomorrow. So I'd do my best to enjoy this evening and release the guilt over pretending that all this fighting and suffering didn't exist.

My two men seemed to have similar ideas. Shadow's touch crept higher up my legs, fingertips pressing a delightful circular massage inside my knees. Jandro's hands moved lower, running below my collarbones to the top of my chest.

"Are you boys getting fresh with me?" My eyes were still closed, teeth sinking into my lip as I tried not to smile too hard.

"What, us?" Jandro's fingers glided down over my arms. "Wouldn't dream of such a thing."

"Mm-hm…" I spaced my legs apart in Shadow's lap to make more room for his hands. He saw where my mind was going, bringing his massage higher up my thigh. I started to squirm, sensitivity prickling along my skin from both of their touches.

The thought of having both of them had been heavy on my mind since Shadow told me he'd be interested in sharing. Now, excited flutters filled my stomach at making that a reality. I wanted to jump up, start kissing them both, and touch them at the same time. But we'd barely started and Shadow could still change his mind.

So I stretched out long between them, pointing my toes and arching my back, letting them set the pace. Jandro would be mindful of Shadow's feelings too. As I reached my arms over my head, Jandro clasped my wrists together with one hand, leaning down over me with a playful smile.

"What does our girl want?" he asked in a low voice, lips hovering over mine.

"Both of you," I whispered back, keeping my eyes locked on his while I rubbed my foot against the front of Shadow's pants, who grunted out a soft moan at the contact, his hand between my thighs squeezing slightly.

"You down for that, big man?" Jandro looked toward his friend, whose eyes kept running up and down the length of my legs.

"Yes." Shadow breathed the word out softly, but there wasn't a hint of hesitation. More like he was trying to contain his excitement.

I rolled up from Jandro's lap, looking behind me to kiss him. This would be a gentle enough start—Shadow had seen me kiss him and the others plenty of times.

Jandro turned on the couch to support my back with his chest, arms coming around my waist to kiss me over my shoulder. I let his body hold me up, leaning my weight against him as I sank into his kiss. The warm flutters extended down to my toes, where I could feel Shadow growing hard beneath his jeans as he watched us.

Shadow's hand continued his firm, kneading massage of my inner thighs, while Jandro's touch spanned my stomach and waist. Already I was languid, just wanting to fall limp and let their four hands explore me.

Jandro broke away from my mouth, dragging his lips

to the nape of my neck and my upper back as he started lifting my shirt from behind.

"Come here." Facing forward again, I reached for Shadow and he scooted closer to me while Jandro got me topless. "Hi, love." I smiled, pleased to have him within kissing distance.

"Hi." Shadow returned my smile, his hands now resting on my hips as our kiss connected. My hands went around his neck, then smoothing down his solid chest to dip under the hem of his shirt. He pulled away to remove it, and I audibly sighed at the beautiful sight of him. All the while, Jandro placed kisses down my spine, amplifying the flutters running through me.

It was a nervous-excitedness with the two of them, probably because it was the first time. Despite having had plenty of threesomes by now, this one was different.

"What would you like right now?" I asked Shadow, leaning forward into him. I kissed the scar on his cheek before moving down to his neck, relishing in the soft sighs and moans he made. *You will never be neglected again.* I repeated the promise mentally with each taste of his warm skin.

"Mm, I want…" he murmured, hands running from my hips up my sides.

"Yes?" I urged him, taking a nibble between his neck and shoulder.

"I want to watch Jandro please you," he confessed.

"That can be arranged," Jandro said behind me, stroking lightly down my lower back. "Come here, *Mariposita.*"

I pulled my legs out of Shadow's lap and swung

them around toward Jandro, coming to my hands and knees between my two men. Jandro's kisses continued working their magic on my spine as he pulled my shorts and underwear over my ass and down to my knees.

"Damn, I love this tattoo." Jandro caressed over my hip, admiring the Night-Blooming Cereus, which was almost completely healed. "Some of your best work, man."

"I agree." I grinned, dragging a biting kiss over Shadow's shoulder.

"I have the best canvas to work on," Shadow answered humbly.

When Jandro swiped his first touch between my legs, I gasped and Shadow let out a rumbling moan that sounded like a purr. I leaned my forehead on his shoulder, nipping at his collarbone and the top of his chest.

Jandro's touches were light and teasing, only his fingertips dragging in circles around my sensitive flesh. My hips rolled, chasing his hand for more friction, and I got swats to my ass for my impatience. I whimpered against Shadow's shoulder, looking up to see him focused on what Jandro was doing behind me.

"Kiss me," I pleaded, running my mouth up his neck.

"You kiss *me*," Shadow retorted with a smirk. "I'm watching."

I wanted to pout and whine. He *loved* to kiss and make out, and now he was refusing me? But I was also a puddled, proud mess inside. He was taking pleasure for himself, now confident enough to tell me what he wanted. It was insanely hot and made me so eager to give him all he asked for, and more.

I kissed his throat, tongue licking the hollow between his collarbones, and moved lower, sending my hips higher.

"You're making her wet, man." Jandro grabbed one side of my ass, holding me with a strong grip as he finally rubbed more firmly between my legs. He still ignored my clit, but stroked through my sensitive flesh, coaxing even more wetness out of me.

"Am I now?" Shadow's chest vibrated against my lips when he asked the question, hands caressing my face as he pulled my hair out of the way. He cupped my cheek and tilted my face up to look at him. "You like kissing me that much?"

I licked my lips, tongue darting out to lick his thumb. "I like it when you tell me what to do to you."

His lips parted, eyebrows raising like he didn't expect that answer. "You…do?"

I grinned at him, enjoying his reaction immensely. "Very much." *Take some power back, love. You deserve it.*

Shadow drew my face up to his, kissing me with a warm tenderness, like he was silently thanking me for this trust, for this freedom to explore more of a power dynamic between us. To exercise a type of control he never had before in his life.

Our kiss parted with a dizzying breath, my face lifting up with a gasp at the feel of Jandro's tongue gliding along my slit, his lips sucking and kissing between my legs. Shadow cupped my face again, bringing my gaze back to him. "Make me hard for you, lover."

I couldn't obey fast enough, my hands scrambling over his jeans as I kissed down his chest, leaving nips and bites on his body because I knew he liked them. He ended up helping me with his pants—Jandro was just too good at playing with me back there and made it impossible to concentrate.

Shadow was already at half-mast, his cock slapping his stomach softly as he shoved his jeans down. I grabbed his thick base and slid my lips over his crown, already eager for something to fill me somewhere, whether that be my mouth or my pussy.

"Ugh, fuck…" Shadow drew my hair out of my face, running an affectionate touch down my back. "That's so good."

Jandro's mouth pulled away from me, his fingers driving through where his tongue had just been and filling me from the other end. "She's the best at sucking dick, man. Literally nothing else compares."

I only had a moment to bask in the praise, drawing more of Shadow into my mouth and moaning at Jandro's fingers fucking me, when I heard a loud slap above my head.

Releasing Shadow's cock, I looked back and forth between two of them incredulously before they could save face. "Did you guys just high-five?!"

Jandro burst out laughing, lowering his forehead to my back and planting a series of kisses there. "I'm sorry, I just…I've always wanted to do that."

"He kept raising his hand when you weren't looking." Shadow was chuckling softly. "I did it so he'd finally stop."

"You guys are the worst," I groaned, bringing my forehead to Shadow's thigh. Despite me, a few snickers escaped, and then moans as Jandro's hand returned to its duty of pleasing me. His thumb rolled over my clit, fingers curling as they dragged against my walls.

"I dunno, *Mariposita,*" my cocky man mused. "Seems like we're doing pretty good."

Shadow gripped my chin in his fingers, the touch light, but firm. "I didn't tell you to stop sucking me." Oh fuck me. He was enjoying this just as much as I was, if not more.

With my next breath, my mouth was on him again, tongue and lips gliding over rigid muscle and velvety skin. He muttered curses and praised me, hands running over me with so much tenderness and care that I wanted to melt in his lap.

Ever the jokester, Jandro seemed intent on distracting me and fucking up my blowjob to the best of his ability. He kept varying the speed and depth with his fingers—fucking me intensely with his hand until I had to release Shadow's cock to cry out, only to slow the pace way down just as my release started building. That was his style, dangling an orgasm in front of my face only to yank it away when I got close.

He did that several times, even switching up between his hands and his mouth to bring me to the edge, only to leave me hanging. My knees gave out, and I laid on my stomach stretched out between the two of them.

"Jandro, please," I whined, my head resting on

Shadow's thigh to give my jaw a break. I kept stroking my gorgeous, scarred man who was now fully hard and pulsing in my hand, looking up at him with pleading eyes since Jandro wouldn't listen.

Shadow stroked my cheek, the sweet touch wrapping around to caress the back of my neck. "Let her come, Jandro. She's been good."

I heard a sigh of mock disappointment from behind me, along with the rustling of clothes as Jandro got undressed. "Guess I'm outvoted."

With renewed energy I rose up to my hands and knees, Shadow and I leaning toward each other for a kiss. A loud smack on my ass was the only warning I got before Jandro's wide cock pressed through my flesh, striking deep into my core with everything I'd been needing. He barely pulled back to drive forward again when the release hit me like a crashing wave. Shadow held me up by my shoulders while I convulsed, shuddered, and barely breathed.

Even as it ebbed away and the aftershocks zipped through me, my arms gave out and I found my head cradled in Shadow's lap once again. I realized it was quickly becoming one of my favorite places to rest.

"You always get mad at me for that." Jandro grinned from behind me, gliding in and out of my body with long, slow strokes while I recovered. "But isn't the release worth all the build-up, *Mariposita?*"

"Fuck you, a little bit," I mumbled, pushing up to my hands again. Leaning back, I left Shadow alone for a moment while I wrapped my arms around the back of Jandro's neck, arching to kiss him over my shoulder. "It is *so* fucking worth it," I whispered, dragging kisses from his cheek to his ear. "I just can't help being a brat."

"Don't I know it." Jandro hugged around me, bringing my back flush with his chest as he sucked along my neck and shoulder. "I just want to make you see other realities when you come, that's all."

I laughed lightly as I covered his hands with mine, enjoying this private moment between us, however brief it was. "You like bringing the brat out of me too."

"Also true." He nipped along the back of my neck, squeezing me in a hug that was both endearingly sweet and a testament to his strength. Jandro could snap an enemy's neck with these arms, but he'd rather take bullets and jump in front of bombs to protect me.

"I love you," I whispered against the side of his face, wishing I could become smaller only so he could hold me tighter.

"*Te amo,*" he answered, loosening his arms around me with a final kiss.

I returned to hands and knees, my eyes meeting Shadow's as Jandro's hands shifted to my hips. "You okay, love?" I searched Shadow's face, his mismatched eyes, for any sign of discomfort. Jandro and I were wrapped up in each other for less than a minute, but I made the same promise to him and every one of my other men—I'd never neglect them for someone else.

Shadow returned his hand to my cheek, leaning in to kiss me in answer. My worry relaxed away as our lips pressed and our tongues tangled. Jandro started fucking me in earnest then, making me moan through kissing Shadow as his cock filled and emptied me.

"Is Jandro pleasing you?" Shadow smirked, his lips hovering over mine as his best friend drove into me harder.

It took me a moment to form a simple answer. Jandro's thickness pressing through me stole my breath away, and each drag of him pulling back felt like it hit every nerve ending in my body.

"Yes, ah! Fuck…yes," I panted in reply.

Shadow's eyes flickered from my face to watch the action behind me, his touch dragging down my chest until he kneaded a breast in his hand. Sparks of sensitivity made me cry out louder when he rolled a nipple between his fingers.

"Then I'm so much better than okay," he growled, eyes roving my entire body as I shook and swayed from the impact of Jandro's thrusts.

"You are?" I reached for Shadow's cock again, and he inhaled sharply at the contact. My pleasure swelled at his reaction. The poor thing hadn't gotten any attention for a whole minute and I needed to rectify that. "You're really enjoying this?"

He touched his forehead to mine, hands caressing me and heightening my pleasure over every inch of my skin. "Not just enjoying it. I see how right Reaper was about sharing a woman we love."

"How do you mean?" I breathed. Jandro slowed his thrusts behind me as if he too were waiting to hear an answer.

"This is…not just sex," Shadow muttered. "This is all about giving you more of what you deserve. All the pleasure you can handle." He pressed a warm, dizzying kiss to my mouth, then broke away to stare at me reverently. "I love you more than I can ever express. I want you pleased and cared for more than I could ever physically do by myself." His eyes flicked up to Jandro. "So I'm glad you have the others. You've always deserved more than one man."

"Oh, Shadow…" My throat tightened, a sob threatening to choke out as I planted kisses everywhere on his face that I could reach. "I love you so much."

"Shadow-man gets it." Jandro's palms smoothed down my back. "On our own we all fall short but together, we can be exactly what you need."

"Yes, that's it," Shadow agreed.

One of Jandro's hands came away from my skin. "Come on bro, up top."

"No!" I tried to glare as I looked back at him but couldn't hold in the laughter. "No more high-fives."

"Just one more, then I'm finished being a dumbass, I swear," Jandro pleaded.

I groaned but didn't keep arguing. Shadow rolled his eyes and relented, slapping Jandro's palm with far less gusto than the first time.

"Pretty weak, but I'll take it. All your strength's in your dick right now."

"So's yours," Shadow moaned as I gripped his length again, wetting him with my tongue before sucking him into my mouth.

All the talking finally ceased. Only slapping skin, moans, breaths, and whispered curses filled the air as the three of us found our rhythm. Jandro tried to pace himself as he fucked me from behind, but I could feel how closely he edged toward release. His breaths grew louder and ragged, his already-thick cock swelling against my walls.

I lapped at Shadow's cock like he was made of ice cream, moaning at how he pulsed under my tongue and how Jandro filled me with each drive of his hips. With a heavy moan, Shadow pulled me up for a breathless kiss, his hand stopping mine when I continued to stroke up and down his length.

"You don't want me to touch you anymore?" I teased, smiling against his lips.

"I want to last long enough to fuck your sweet cunt."

The words were filthy, but his tone was the same warm, tender voice he always used with me. The combination of the two was like an orgasm for my brain, sparking as it processed the mental pleasure this man gave me, before filtering it through the rest of my body. His dirty talk tingled down my spine, accelerated my heart, and made my core squeeze around my other husband.

"Fuck, babe," Jandro grunted, still rocking me forward with each thrust of his cock. "Thanks for the warning."

"Sorry I, ah…fuck!"

Words left me as he reached around for my clit. He tipped me over the edge, pausing his thrusts while fully seated inside me. Both men petted and praised me as I shook and whimpered through another release, my skin now coated in a sheen of sweat. Jandro withdrew from me and kissed my back as I floated down from bliss.

"Never say sorry for feeling good," he rasped before

sitting back on the opposite end of the couch, chest heaving with loud breaths, his cock erect and stiff. "Even when I do gotta take a breather," he added with a sheepish smile.

He looked so damn delicious, I wanted to run my tongue all over him. And I would, once he had a moment to cool down.

I sat up to kneeling, bracing my hands on Shadow's shoulders for balance as I threw a leg over his lap.

"Ready for me already?" He gazed up at me, hands already trailing up the backs of my thighs.

"Told you I recover quickly." I was still a little breathless but started lowering down eagerly. As wonderful as tasting him was, I was more than ready to feel him inside me.

Taking him was easier after having Jandro and a couple of orgasms already. Shadow's cock spread me open with ease, the pressure of him so filling and delicious as I sank down.

"Fuck…" His eyelids fell shut as his head tipped back, palms smoothing over my ass and running over my waist.

"No. Look at me, handsome." I placed a finger on his lips and his eyes fluttered open again. "You like to watch? Then watch me ride you."

"You fucking undo me," he groaned as I began a slow rise and lower, savoring every inch of him gliding through me.

"You're…fuck, God…" My legs were already shaking at the effort of riding him, most of my strength already zapped from earlier. Shadow was right there for me, guiding me with a hand on my waist and rolling his hips underneath me.

"You're so beautiful when you're spent and well-fucked," he whispered, the tenderness in his voice taking on a rough growl. "So good and perfect for us."

"You're so perfect for me," I panted. Our skin glided hot and wet against each other at a quickening pace, both of us swept up in this urgent need for each other. "You're mine. Mine."

"Yours." Shadow's fist closed in my hair, bringing my mouth to his for a hard kiss. "Only yours."

I leaned my forehead on his, resting my upper body against him while we crashed and rode each other down below. Turning my gaze to the side, I saw Jandro stroking himself as he watched us, his cock flexing against his hand.

"Keep going," he urged with a grin. "Don't stop on my account."

"Shut up and come here," I demanded.

Jandro scooted closer, moving up to sit on the back of the couch so I could reach him easily while riding Shadow. Bracing one arm on Shadow's shoulder, I could touch and taste Jandro with the other as I pleased.

"Oh, Jesus…" Jandro hissed, gripping the couch on either side of him as I pulled his thick head between my lips, letting the rise and fall of my body on Shadow's cock determine when my mouth slid up and down on his. "So much for that fucking breather. I'm not gonna last through your mouth doing *that*."

"I'm getting close too," Shadow moaned through gritted teeth. His grip tightened on my waist, lifting me high off his cock so I could reach more of Jandro. When he slammed me back down, he struck a new place deep inside me that had me seeing stars, and moaning for more.

"Gonna come for us one more time, *Mariposita?*" Jandro ran a touch down the front of my body, grabbing my breasts and making me whimper louder with his pulls on my aching nipples.

"She's right there," Shadow growled out. "Fuck, she's squeezing me so tight." He wrapped around me, holding me in place as his powerful hips snapped up and crashed his body against my clit.

My whole body shook from the impact and I was screaming as loud as I could with my mouth stuffed full. The orgasm hit me harder than Shadow's thrusts, convulsions sweeping through me as though I'd been electrocuted. And then warmth filling my mouth, pulsing into my core. The release of my men dragged out my own pleasure, their bodies rigid and their expressions furrowed in sexy grimaces as their moans and gasps for air filled the room.

Shadow's hands fell limply to his sides. The two of us rose and fell with his breaths, our pulses thrumming together. With me slumped across his chest and shoulder, I laid my head on Jandro's thigh, who looked to be in danger of sliding off the back of the couch.

"Don't fall," I whispered drowsily.

"Hm?" Jandro bowed forward, leaning over me to place more kisses on my back, then rested his forehead between my shoulder blades. "Damn," he panted.

"Yeah," Shadow agreed on a deep exhale, returning

one hand to caress up my leg. He kissed my shoulder that was nudged against the side of his chest.

I reached for his face, stroking his bearded cheek while rubbing Jandro's neck with the other hand. "I don't wanna move," I confessed, utterly blissed out in this place with my two men.

"Me neither," said both of them in unison.

"Shadow-man, want to carry her to the shower?" Jandro suggested. "She might be sore."

Shadow grunted out an affirmative and brought his hands to my ass to secure me. He started scooting off the couch, but I held on to Jandro before we stood up.

"You're coming too, right?"

Jandro slid down onto the couch and jumped up, cock still wet from my mouth and bouncing on his thighs. "Shadow, you gonna scrub my back?"

"No."

I giggled as Shadow rose from the couch with one swift press of his strong legs. He held me easily, but I still wrapped my arms and legs around him, pressing a kiss to his mouth. "Will you scrub mine?"

He grinned. "Yes, of course."

Jandro sighed in pretend disappointment, gathering up our discarded clothing. "Don't sulk," I chided him. "I'll wash your back, *guapito.*"

"Fine. I'll deal with washing your front, I guess." Then he smacked my ass with his free hand and ran ahead of us to turn on the shower.

TWENTY

REAPER

I didn't love my volunteer shifts at the field hospital at first, but my time spent there grew on me after a few days. Since I had barely any medical knowledge, my duties mainly consisted of bringing the patients food, water, blankets, or whatever else they needed.

Sometimes they just wanted someone to read to or sit with them. For some reason, I found this the most difficult to do, despite it being the easiest task. But it wasn't about me, as I was quickly learning. None of my volunteer hours were about me, or how it would make me look to Mari. Admittedly, being in closer proximity to her and having her see me do this kind of work played a part in signing myself up. I had the small, lingering hope that it would help bring us back together.

Rhonda ended up putting us on opposite shifts, so Mari and I were never at the hospital at the same time anyway. I had a feeling that the crabby old nurse did that on purpose. She wasn't a big fan of mine. Not that it mattered, anyway. I got a firsthand look at what Mari dealt with every day, and after my first few shifts, I was beginning to see why she was so dedicated to it.

Day after day, after changing endless sheets on the makeshift beds, running back and forth to fetch all manner of things, or just sitting and holding someone's hand as they told me their life story, I started to think there was hope for a selfish prick like me after all.

Jandro and I worked together sometimes, although he was usually put on maintenance duty to fix machinery or the hospital vehicles. I saw Freyja every so often too. The black cat seemed to have become a fixture at both hospitals, wandering around beds and accepting scratches wherever she went. No doubt she was spreading some of that healing magic too. She put the patients at ease, which made the medics' jobs easier.

Hades on the other hand, stayed far away from the hospitals. If he followed me, he usually hung back near my bike until my shift was over. Maybe there was something unsettling about a god of death hovering around a place trying to prolong people's lives.

A slew of new patients had just arrived when I showed up today, a mixture of our own injured, Blakeworth citizens, and Tash's soldiers. Governor Vance was still optimistic about giving Blakeworth citizens refuge in Four Corners, *if* they had been conscripted to fight and didn't have loyalties to the cause. They would be treated for injuries first, and then questioned by my dad's lieutenants when they were well enough.

The soldiers from Tash's army were wild cards, though. We were beginning to question if they were soldiers at all, or people just unlucky and vulnerable enough to fall under the mind control they were subjected to. At least more of them were talking now, although a great majority of them still didn't remember their names or how they ended up here.

I stepped into the hospital tent and nodded at Jandro on the other side. Today they had him replacing filters in the air purifiers. Grabbing a pitcher of water, some towels, and snacks, I started making my usual rounds.

Most of the Tash patients were dead silent, but the ones that weren't catatonic had eyes watching me like hawks. I wondered if any of them recognized me from previous battles. The medics warned me the patients were skittish, especially around loud noises, so I did my best to speak to them in a low voice and not make any sudden movements.

One guy however, stood out as being particularly chatty and couldn't seem to sit still. Even Freyja, sitting at the end of his bed, had her ears pointed back in irritation.

The guy's head was wrapped up in bandages, covering one of his eyes. I could hear him talking rapidly to himself from across the tent. As I got closer to his bedside, I realized he was speaking Spanish.

"Hey man. Do you want some water?" I rolled my small cart up next to him and held up the pitcher. "*Agua?*"

He'd been lying on his back, but sat up abruptly the moment he heard me. The movement sent Freyja jumping down and walking off to tend to someone else. The guy tried turning to me, but his weakened state, and probably the drugs, nearly had him careening forward.

"Whoa, whoa, easy!" I grabbed his shoulders to hold him up, then placed a hand on his neck to keep his head still. "You shouldn't move so fast with a head injury. I'll get you whatever you need."

"*Señor, por favor*," he whimpered before talking in a rapid string of Spanish too fast for me to understand.

"It's okay, buddy. Let me lie you back down. You gotta watch your head." I pointed to my temple. "*Tu cabeza*."

He clutched my shirt and started pushing back against me, which was alarming. No patient had ever fought me before. I didn't want to use force on this guy and potentially injure him further.

"Hey man, you gotta lie down," I told him more firmly. "You're hurt. You need to rest."

"*Por favor, mi esposa*!" he pleaded. That was all I caught before he started speaking rapidly again.

"Okay, okay." I heard the word *esposa* a few more times before his strength gave out and he allowed me to lay his head back on his pillow. "Take a drink, man. It's gonna be alright."

The man accepted the water I held to his lips, swallowing several gulps and gasping before speaking, no, begging, rapidly again. He held on to my forearm and I saw a tear trail out of his one visible eye.

"Okay, listen. I'm gonna get someone who can talk to you." I patted his shoulder, then looked behind me to make sure Jandro was still in the tent. "We'll figure out what's going on with your wife, okay? *Un momento.*"

Seemingly placated, he finally released me. I moved the supply cart out of the way and headed for the back of the tent, feeling his stare on me the whole way. Jandro was elbow-deep in an air purifier when I came up next to him.

"Hey 'Dro, I need a favor real quick."

"'Course you do," he chuckled. "Why else would you come up to me in the middle of your Mother Teresa shift?"

I ignored his jab. "There's a guy here who keeps asking about his wife but it's all in Spanish. Can you talk to him?"

"Ooh, I'm an interpreter now," Jandro said with fake excitement as he pulled a small motor out of the air purifier. "Nice to know I'm moving up in the world."

"I'm just asking, 'Dro," I sighed tiredly. "Dude seems really distraught, and I know that'd be any one of us if we got separated from Mari. But I'll ask someone else if you're insulted or whatever."

"Nah, Reap. It's fine." Jandro pulled his hands out of the machine and quickly rubbed them in hand sanitizer. "I just wasn't sure if this was a friend's request or a president's order."

"A request," I answered. "I feel bad for the guy, that's all."

"Huh, you might have an empathetic bone in your body after all." Jandro rubbed his palms together. "Which one is he?"

"Bandaged head and eye." I pointed to the bed he was in. "Thanks, Jandro."

"Sure thing." My VP grabbed a pen and a notepad and headed toward the patient, whistling as he did so.

Meanwhile, I took over replacing the motor in the

air purifier. It was far less complicated than replacing the same part on a bike, and I was able to watch Jandro with the guy for my own curiosity.

Jandro sat on his bed like a friend would, the two of them too far away to hear, not that I would understand anyway. At one point, Jandro turned his head and looked back at me, his expression something between concerned and confused. He started writing on his notepad then, I assumed taking the man's information.

They spoke for about ten minutes before a medic came by to check the man's injuries. Jandro shook his hand gently before rising and returning back to me. He appeared even more confused than when he first looked at me.

"Well?" I asked.

Jandro shook his head and blew out a long breath. "Poor bastard's got noodle soup for brains. Must've been near too many explosions, on top of all the other shit cracking his egg. He wants us to find his wife and daughter, but can't remember their names."

"Fuck," I bit out. "Well, we can't help without knowing that. What's his name?"

"He doesn't know, but it gets even weirder." Jandro set the notepad down. "He's *pretty sure* his wife is a white lady originally from Texas, but as you heard," he jerked his head toward the guy, "homeboy doesn't speak a lick of English."

"So how could he be married to an American?" I rubbed my jaw.

"Exactly."

"Maybe she speaks Spanish?" I offered.

"Mm." Jandro made a skeptical noise. "I dunno, it seems like all kinds of things are jumbled in his head. When I asked him what was the last thing he remembered, he said his most vivid memory is his daughter being born. However, he's again *pretty sure* she's an adult now, so his sense of time is all fucked too."

"Damn." To my uneducated brain, it sounded a lot like dementia, which the man had to be too young for. He looked to be in his late forties, early fifties at the most. But then again, he seemed in better shape than the majority of those from that unit. "Poor guy went through the ringer."

"Yeah," Jandro agreed sadly. "Who knows if he'll be able to remember those details."

"Maybe as he recovers, he'll remember more. He's strong enough to sit up and talk, at least." I folded my arms, watching as a medic gave the man a dose of something and tucked him into bed. "Mari might know how to help him."

"I dunno, man," Jandro sighed. "He might even be above her pay grade. Like if he forgot all this stuff, maybe he forgot how to speak English too. Does that even happen with head injuries?"

"No idea, but I don't think any of what those guys are dealing with is normal."

"True. It sucks either way." Jandro leaned against the table next to me. "We don't even know if his family are prisoners, dead, or just figments of his imagination."

"If he can tell us more, we should find them," I said, determined.

"Huh, look at you." Jandro shot me a look of

surprise. "If Mari had said that three months ago, you'd chew her ass out for wanting to save everybody."

"Yeah, well," I shrugged. "I know what it's like having my family torn apart and not knowing if they're alive or dead. Nobody should go through that."

Jandro sniffed and pretended to wipe a tear. "My little Reaper's all grown up and matured."

"Shut up." I knocked my shoulder into his. "I gotta finish my rounds. You're welcome for the new motor in that thing, by the way."

"Aw, sweet!" Jandro rounded the table to look inside the air purifier. "And you're welcome for me being an interpreter, by the way."

"Yeah whatever, thanks man." I hesitated before grabbing my cart. "Would you be cool with checking in on him? See if he remembers any more?"

"You don't even need to ask," Jandro said while screwing the panels back on the machine. "I already told him I'd be by to chat again later."

"Thanks, 'Dro."

"Yeah, go on." He made a shooing motion at me. "Get back to grumbling and barking at people before they start thinking you're actually nice."

———

"SO WHAT DO you suppose we do with you?" My dad peered shrewdly at Captain Lance, the hostage that Blakeworth had refused to take back. That couldn't have been good news for him, to not be wanted by the territory you served and lived in.

We were in the main conference room at City Hall —a small, informal meeting with a few people present. Dad, Gunner, Mari, and I all sat on one side of the table, with Hades at my side. Lance and the soldiers who escorted him sat across from us, Lance's wrists still cuffed as he scowled at us.

He'd been given royal treatment for a prisoner, despite complaining constantly about his accommodations. Every other day, he seemed to come down with a migraine or an asthma attack, and the medics quickly figured out it was just an excuse to get out of his cell. They were laughably bad escape attempts and he was apprehended quickly every time.

Still, we asked Mari to be present at this meeting as a courtesy. We didn't know what the captain was capable of, and wanted to ensure we had a professional in the room if he tried anything crafty.

"You could let me go," Lance suggested, his tone bitter, like he already knew how we'd respond to that idea.

"Explain to me how that would be advantageous to either of us," my dad offered patiently, as if talking to a child. "You spied on us, attacked us, captured our citizens, and now your territory is disinterested in having you back. So where would you go?"

The captain shrugged, his cuffs clinking as his shoulders raised. "I'll find my own way, like everyone does."

"You're lying," Gunner cut in sharply. "You have some contingency plan you're not telling us. If you really had nowhere to go, you wouldn't be so eager to leave."

"You ambushed *us* and took my people captive too!" Lance shouted. "Four Corners isn't the peachy little village you pretend it is. You're just as bad as us, so why would I stay?"

"We don't kidnap women for forced marriages." I started counting off my fingers. "Using said kidnapped woman to blackmail another territory for labor and supplies, using our own citizens for slave labor while we get rich. Shall I go on?"

Lance scoffed and shifted in his seat. "Someone like you wouldn't understand."

"Someone like me?" I repeated. "What's that supposed to mean?"

He sneered at my patches, eyes tracing over the word PRESIDENT. "A filthy road pirate who doesn't know the first thing about building a prosperous city."

"I suggest you think very carefully about what you say next." My father folded his hands calmly on the table but I could feel his temper, so much like mine, simmering below the surface. "That's my son you're insulting."

The color drained from the captain's face as he realized his mistake. Generals were powerful and highly respected in his world, only a few steps down from the governor, who he seemed to regard like a king. He couldn't fathom General Bray in his pressed uniform, decorated with stripes and medals, ever existing in the same world as an outlaw biker, much less sharing blood with one.

Lance's eyes snapped back to me and for a moment, I thought he might actually apologize. His mouth opened but only a soft rasp came out. His cuffed hands flew up to his neck, eyes growing wider until they bulged.

On Gunner's other side, Mari leaned forward. "Is he choking?"

"Wait." Gunner placed a hand on her forearm. "He's doing his dumb faking shit again."

"No, I don't think so." Mari stood. "The blood vessels in his eyes are popping. He's not getting air."

She'd just started rounding the table, heading for the captain when I felt Hades' dark, oppressive presence weigh down on me like a boulder. The whole world seemed to darken and slow down when his voice came in the next moment.

Reap.

His life is yours to take.

Reap him now.

I didn't hesitate this time. I had learned my lesson before.

My hand swept over my gun, finding the grip with ease as I pulled it out of my holster. I already had a finger on the trigger when I extended my arm across the table, aiming the barrel at Lance's forehead.

I squeezed, firing off my shot before anyone could react.

Lance's head threw back from the force of the shot, his hands falling limply into his lap. He was dead instantly, but that didn't concern me. I was given an order and I carried it out.

What turned my stomach was my wife's horrified expression, her face speckled with the captain's blood.

TWENTY-ONE

MARIPOSA

It took a few seconds for me to catch up and figure out what had happened. In one moment, I was approaching a choking man to assist him. In the next, a gun had fired and there was a bloody hole in the man's forehead. His head had thrown back, dead, empty eyes staring up at me.

I looked across the table to see Reaper with his arm stretched out in front of him, weapon in hand and pointed at the now-dead Blakeworth captain.

Everyone seemed frozen for a long time, even Reaper was looking like he couldn't believe what just happened.

General Bray moved first, rising from his seat at the table. "Thank you, lieutenants. You are dismissed. We'll handle this from here."

The two soldiers who had escorted the captain turned and stiffly marched out of the room. Their faces didn't betray any shock or horror, so who knew what they were thinking.

As soon as the door closed after them, Reaper lowered the gun to the table, staring at it like it would bite him. "He told me to. I had to obey."

"Hades?" Gunner asked.

Reaper nodded, his expression numb.

"Then you didn't do anything wrong." Gunner reached over and grabbed his shoulder, giving it an assuring shake. "You had a reason. He must have been faking it and planned to do something nefarious with Mari."

"I know...I know." Reaper rubbed his forehead, the shock of the event seeming to quickly fade. "It just... feels like I murdered someone in cold blood."

Because you did, a small voice inside me whispered.

"Mari, honey." Finn's voice drew my petrified gaze away from the dark hole in the captain's forehead. "You've, um, got some blood on you. Do you want to wash up?"

"Okay," I answered flatly, turning like a robot toward the bathroom. "Yes, I will."

"Do you need help?" Gunner and Reaper both moved to get up from the table.

"No!" I raised my hands, moving faster toward the bathroom. "I'm fine. I just...need a minute."

Their stares weighed heavily on me as I closed the bathroom door behind me. The electricity in here was old, and the bulb flickered and hummed when I hit the light switch. The dim light struggling to stay on didn't help with the glimpses I caught of myself in the mirror, the dead man's blood speckling my face like morbid freckles. It didn't feel real, more like I was in an old horror movie as I struggled to keep the contents of my stomach in place.

I tried to breathe deeply and opened the faucet. The water trickled out pathetically slowly, and I was forced to look at myself again as I wetted a paper towel and wiped at my face.

"Why are you freaking out?" I murmured, watching my own blood-speckled lips move.

Hades ordered Reaper to kill. It was what they did together, and always for some justifiable reason. Captain Lance was our enemy. Maybe he was going to try something when I got close enough, and Hades gave Reaper the command to protect me.

I had seen men get shot. I saw them die mere feet in front of me. So why was I having this reaction?

My trust in Reaper was shaky at best, but had been slowly getting to a better place. Even when we were in a good place, I knew what he was capable of. I knew he wouldn't hesitate to kill someone if they threatened anyone he loved.

Was it the fact that it came without warning? That he was just sitting in a meeting in one moment, then a killer in the next?

Did I really believe Hades had ordered him to do it?

That question made me pause, my damp paper towel hovering next to my face. It was a cold, eerie realization that I wasn't sure if I could believe it. No matter how badly I wanted to, I knew Reaper was brash and impulsive.

And that side of him almost cost us our marriage.

Maybe it still would.

When I couldn't see any more blood on my face, I dropped the paper towel in the small trash can and washed my hands vigorously. I didn't want to go back out there, didn't want to face them and the dead man who had been alive mere moments ago.

But there was no other way out of this bathroom, so I opened the door reluctantly and stepped out. Gunner and Reaper immediately looked at me, while Finn zipped up a long bag on the floor.

A body bag.

Again, I'd seen them before. So I couldn't place why it was so jarring to watch as two soldiers lifted the bag at either end and carried it out of the room.

"Are you okay, sugar?" Reaper sounded apprehensive, like he was worried he upset me.

"I should go to the hospital," I said, bypassing his question. "Some blood might have gotten into my eyes or mouth and I should get tested just in case…"

"I can take you." Reaper started coming toward me and I found myself backing away before I realized it.

"No, thank you. I'll drive myself." I could barely bring myself to look at his face but from one darting glance, I saw the rejection and hurt he wore plainly.

"Mari, are you afraid of…" He let the question trail off as if he couldn't believe it, much less say it out loud. *Afraid of me hurting you?*

I wanted to shout *no* and wrap him in a hug. Reassure him that he did the right thing, and that I was glad he reacted so swiftly to protect me. But that small, nagging part of my heart that still couldn't trust him fully, kept me nailed to my spot.

"I'll see you guys at home," I murmured, heading stiffly for the conference room door.

———

IT WAS a fast blood draw at the hospital lab, but I wasn't ready to go home right away.

"We'll let you know by the end of the week, Mari," Jarrod, the lab tech, informed me as he carefully sealed and labeled my blood vials.

"Thanks." I pulled my sleeve down over the band-aid inside my elbow and stood from the chair. As I stepped out into the main corridor, I spotted a familiar, bearded man walking with a medic, his hand trailing gently along the wall for balance while the medic chatted away at him.

"Grudge!" I hurried toward him, relief and elation flooding my system at the sight of him up and about. It had been a few days since I had time to check on him "You're looking so much better."

"Mah!" His face lit up with a smile, the bruises and swelling mostly gone as he held an arm out to me.

I hugged around him carefully, taking note of the thick bandages still wrapped tightly around his torso. "You taking it easy, big guy?"

"Mm-hm." He looked to the medic, a woman named Becky, who elaborated.

"Always gotta get his exercise in." She rolled her eyes, but it was affectionate and playful. "He likes to walk fast to increase his lung capacity, but these ribs aren't gonna heal overnight, mister." She poked the dimple in his cheek and it was cute seeing the friendly banter between them. Despite the communication barrier, Grudge was just likable and always seemed to make friends easily.

"Mah?" Grudge looked back at me and pantomimed writing with his hand.

Becky reached into the pocket of her scrubs to hand him a notepad and pen, then smiled at me. "Seems he wants a private conversation with you. I'll be back in a few."

"Thanks, Beck. What can I do for you?" I stood back while Grudge turned to the wall to write his message.

S said you can tell if we're related from blood? he quickly scrawled out.

"Yes," I answered. "It's a simple test. We'd only need a little blood to find out. I just got mine taken." I pushed up my sleeve to show him the bandage on my elbow.

He nodded, stroked his beard for a moment as if pondering, then returned to writing.

T & D are my family. You & Demons are too. But I'd like to know if me & S share blood.

"Of course. We can do it now if you'd like. And I'll let Shadow know and test him too."

Grudge nodded but his mouth pressed into a frown. His hand hovered over the notepad, hesitating before he wrote his next message.

I don't like being injected with stuff. Or the opposite, w/e that's called.

"Okay. So no syringes." I nodded, trying to conceal my disgust. Not at him, but the people who gave him those phobias. Knowing what gave Shadow his fear of being cut with knives, I could only imagine what had been done to sweet Grudge.

"Do the medics give you IVs?" I asked him. "The needle in the back of your hand? It's attached to a long tube with a bag at the end."

He nodded and returned to writing. *Yes, that's not so bad. It's different…in my brain. But when the doc said I needed a shot, I couldn't do it.*

"I completely understand," I assured him, placing a hand on his arm. "We could do a blood draw with an IV needle and a long tube. Would that be okay?"

Will you do it?

"Yes, if you'd like me to."

"Mm-hm." He nodded eagerly before writing again. *Becky is nice but she's not you. You're my sister.* He underlined the final word with a firm stroke of the pen.

"Aww, Grudge!" I was grinning from ear-to-ear, the shock and numbness of what happened in the confer-ence room far away from my mind. "Don't tell the other two, but," I leaned closer to him and whispered, "you're my favorite Son of Odin."

He huffed and smirked, rolling his eyes slightly as if to say, *obviously.*

I laughed and took his elbow. "I'll walk you back to your room and we can do your blood draw there."

"Hm!" he agreed and followed my lead down the hallway.

———

REAPER WAS PUTTERING around the kitchen when I got home. Not drinking, but he seemed to be rearranging the contents of our cabinets—something to keep him busy until I got there, perhaps.

"Hey," he called softly, setting a series of whiskey tumblers down on the counter. "Did you find out anything?"

"I won't get results until the end of the week." I hung my jacket on the back of a dining chair, going around him as I went to the refrigerator.

"They can't do it any faster for you?" he pressed. "Since you're medical staff?"

"I'm sure it's the fastest Jarrod can do it," I answered. "He's by himself and backed up. Everyone else going in for tests is waiting weeks to get results back."

"Oh. Okay."

The silence was heavy between us. Me trying to ignore him, him trying to act like everything was normal. What was normal between us anymore?

It dawned on me right then how silent the whole house was, not just the lower floor. No one else was home, and I wondered if that was intentional.

"Can we talk about earlier today?" Reaper broached quietly.

Of course. The others had cleared the house so we could have *this* conversation.

"Sure," I answered dryly, my tone betraying just how much I *didn't* want to talk about this.

"You just seem shaken up by what happened."

Green eyes watched me warily. "I want to make sure you're alright."

"I'm…not." I swallowed heavily, trying to work out the knot that tightened my throat.

"Okay." I was staring at my own fingernails on the kitchen counter but could hear the heavy breath cycle through his chest. "Can you tell me why?"

"Because I never really enjoy being splattered in a patient's blood and brain matter while on my way to treat them."

I was being snippy, defensive, and we both knew it. Reaper drew in a sharp breath and I saw his hand close into a fist before flattening his palm again.

"I don't want to get into another fight with you," he said softly. "Hades gave me a command and I obeyed. Hesitation has only cost me in the past, so I chose to act swiftly this time. That's all it was. I'm sorry for upsetting you."

"You didn't *upset* me. I just…" I brought a hand to my forehead, my frustration mounting. At myself for purposely being difficult. At him for being the calm, reasonable one for once. Where was my impulsive, hot-headed Reaper? And why was I getting pissed that he seemed to be missing from this conversation?

"He hadn't even done anything." I felt like I was grabbing at straws, and maybe I was. Why did I even care? The captain had been the enemy. "You condemned him to death for doing nothing that justified it."

"That's not my decision to make, sugar," Reaper said. "The God of Death gave an order, and I'm the instrument." He straightened up. "Eduardo had also done nothing when I was ordered to kill him. My hesitance then put four people in danger, including the *governor*. I promised I would never make that mistake again." His face hardened with determination. "Especially not if you were the one at risk."

"Did you really do it to protect me?" I fired back, lifting my eyes to his. "Or did you just *love* the chance to shoot and kill someone without a second thought?"

Reaper reared back like I'd struck him, his brows knitting together and making his eyes narrow. "I've *never* enjoyed killing anyone," he snapped. "Not once in my life, even when they've deserved it. If that's who you think I am, you are badly mistaken."

"Am I?" I challenged. "You wouldn't have enjoyed killing Shadow if you had the chance?"

Reaper's eyes closed softly, his chin dipping down until he stared straight down at the ground.

"No," he finally answered, barely above a whisper. "Because I'd be murdering a brother and hurting the woman I love."

"Killing, not hurting," I corrected. "You might as well have killed me too."

"Yes, I know." He looked up to meet my gaze, eyes pained and mouth set in a hard line. "You're still angry at me for what I did. And I'm sorr—"

"I know you're sorry." I turned away from him, hand on my forehead to rub the ache that seemed to settle there permanently. Anger throbbed through me— at myself? Him? I didn't know anymore. I was being unfair to him, I knew that. But I got a twisted sense of satisfaction from lashing out at him like he'd done to me several times before. And I hated that I enjoyed cutting him down like that.

What's wrong with me? I'm no better than him.

"I thought we were getting to a better place," Reaper said quietly.

"And what place would that be?" God, why could I not *stop?*

He flinched at the question. "One where you can trust me again. Where we're happy and in love like we used to be." His fingers dragged across the counter. "I know I still have a long way to go before we reach that point."

It felt like I was kicking him while he was down, and he just kept silently taking my hits and asking for more. I hated that he was being so passive like this, but wasn't it also what I wanted? For him to stop being so bull-headed, to show more kindness, empathy and patience?

I fell in love with a hot-tempered, passionate man who took without asking. Was it possible for me to love him any other way?

"Are you so sure we'll get there again?" I whispered, focusing on a small crack in the tile. I'd fall apart if I kept looking him in the eye.

It took a long time for him to answer. "I'm willing to try, as long as you are."

Those words should have reassured me, satisfied me to some degree. But the knots in my stomach only increased as I walked off, leaving him alone in the kitchen.

TWENTY-TWO

JANDRO

I was usually a solid sleeper, so I couldn't place what woke me up in the middle of the night. Being in a different bed, maybe. Or maybe sleeping in a different part of the house just fucked with my senses.

My eyes adjusted to the darkness as I lay awake, the two figures in bed next to me becoming clearer. Shadow was reclined on his back, one massive arm wrapped around Mari, who was draped over his chest. The sheet had been pushed down to waist level, just covering her ass and his lower half. Unsurprising, since the big dude gave off heat like a furnace. Even so, he and Mari seemed content wrapped up in each other, their bodies rising and falling gently with steady breaths of sleep.

For a moment, I wished I had Shadow's artistic skills. The two of them made for a pretty sexy picture.

But more pressingly, I was wide awake at an ungodly hour and probably too hot. With the sheet kicked down around my legs and my throat dry as a bone, I might have to talk to the big dude about cracking a window.

Especially if I was going to be spending more nights in his room.

I swung my feet down to the floor and found my shorts, pulled them on, and felt my way blindly to the bedroom door. The kitchen light was on, an unwelcome surprise as I quickly shut the door behind me so it wouldn't flood the bedroom.

"Who fuckin' left the light on?" I grumbled, rubbing my eyes and squinting as I padded barefoot to the kitchen.

"I'll get it before I pass out," answered a gruff voice.

I blinked, surprised to see Reaper hunched over the counter on a barstool, a recently purchased bottle of whiskey now half-empty in front of him. Like me, he was shirtless and barefoot, only in a pair of sweatpants.

"The fuck are you doin' up?" I went through the cabinets in search of a glass, then filled it from the sink.

"What's it look like I'm doin'?"

I drained my water and refilled it. "Being a sorry sack of shit."

"Bingo." There was no humor in Reaper's voice as he lifted the whiskey and drank straight from the bottle.

With a sigh, I grabbed a stool and settled across from him. "Alright, so tell me why. Before you need a liver transplant."

Reaper shook his head and let out a rattling breath, which quickly turned into a cough. *And a lung transplant, Jesus,* I thought. *He needs to cool it with those cloves.*

"You heard about the thing that happened today?"

"You shooting the Blakeworth captain in the middle of a meeting? Yeah, I heard."

"Right." Reaper passed the bottle between his two hands on the counter. "Well, it shook Mari up. She got kind of…distant. I tried talking to her afterward and I think I just made things worse between us."

I grabbed the whiskey from him and took a quick swallow. It wasn't like he needed it anymore. "I thought you two were getting along. Working through reconciling."

"I thought so too, but…" With nothing to occupy his hands now, he flattened them on the countertop. "I always seem to fuck it up."

"What did you say?" My tone came out more accusing than I intended but at this point, Reaper had come to expect that from me.

"Nothing bad, I don't think. I was listening. I didn't raise my voice or lash out. I thought…I thought I did okay, but she just seemed to get angrier."

"Dude, it might not actually be your fault for once. She's stressed out. You're stressed out. We're all fighting for our lives here and none of us are in the best state of mind."

"She and Gunner got past it," he grunted out. "She's happy with literally everyone but me. And it's not about *me*, I know that. It's just…" He took a long pause, leaning back in his stool as he scrubbed his hands down his face. "I don't know if we can make it work, Jandro."

"Don't say that," I snapped. "Don't you dare give up on the best thing that's ever happened to you. To all of us!"

"I don't want to. But if she gives up on *me*, what else

can I do?" His hands flopped down by his sides. "I want her to be happy even if…even if it's without me."

"She'll be heartbroken without you, man. She needs you just as much as she needs any of us."

"Does she really?" he countered. "It seems like all I do is make her miserable. I'm a constant reminder of what I did to Shadow." His eyes looked off in the distance, focused on nothing. "I told Gunner this too. All I've ever done is hurt her."

"You really want to test that theory?" I leaned across the counter toward him. "You really think that if you're gone tomorrow, she'll be skipping along without a care that you're no longer here?"

He didn't answer. Of course he wouldn't.

"You *really* want to kill what's left, you go right ahead and do that." I pointed to the front door. "That'll be exactly what she needs, one of her husbands walking out on her in the middle of a war, during the most stressful, painful time of her life. 'Cause we all know how well that went last time."

"And I was the cause of that," he argued. "The blame for Shadow leaving lies solely on me."

"And now he's back, and you're atoning for it," I said. "Yeah, it sucks you're still being frozen out by her, I know. But she's your wife. You gave her your mother's ring."

"I know," Reaper sighed heavily. "I know."

"This whole war going on right now, on top of what happened between you two," I tapped my finger on the counter, "is probably the hardest thing that will ever test your relationship. Hopefully this is the last big war of our lifetimes. If you show her you're willing to stick through this, then you can start mending things properly. But if you bolt now? Dude." I shook my head at him, hoping I was conveying how serious this was. "There is *no* coming back for you."

"I want to stay, Jandro. There is no question in my mind about that. I'm just becoming less confident that it's what *she* wants. And I..." he groaned and rubbed his eyes. "I don't want to pressure her about us right now and add to her stress. I'm also scared to death of what her answer might be."

I leaned back and took a long swig of whiskey. "I know you never believe me when I tell you this, but *man* you're sensitive."

"Am not." He reached across the counter and swiped the bottle from me.

"You are. She's under a lot of pressure and you're taking what she says super personally. Don't." Reaper lifted the bottle to take a drink and I snatched it back from him. "Because Medic Mari is exhausted and over-worked just like all of us are. She's not at her best. You're not at your best." Reaper lunged across the counter and belly-flopped on the surface as I held the booze out of reach. "Are you even listening?"

"Yes," he grunted, settling back into his seat. "Basically the same shit Gunner told me—don't make any big life decisions right now."

"Exactly." I returned the bottle to the counter, placing it right in front of him while he eyed me warily. "You gotta hold on, man, for all of us. It's not just her that needs you."

"Yeah, yeah. Enough of your sweet-talkin'." Reaper upturned the bottle and took a long swallow. "I'm not going anywhere."

"Better not."

He nodded, nudging the whiskey back toward me. "I just wish I knew how much longer this is going to go on for."

"Don't we all." I wasn't much of a whiskey guy and was already feeling it, so I idly spun the bottle on the counter. "Want me to say anything to her?"

Reaper pondered it for a moment, rocking back on the rear legs of his stool. "Nah," he decided. "She knows what I want…and how I feel. I just need to be patient, consistent. Show her that I'll stick around during the hardest time of all our lives, like you said."

"Good man." I pointed to the bottle and decided to take one last swallow. "And that's the core of it, really. You're irritable, short-tempered, overbearing, and yeah, kind of a dick, but at the center of it all," I set the bottle down and spread my hands, "you're a good dude who loves his woman and just needs to get laid."

"Huh," Reaper scoffed, reaching for the bottle. "Rub it in, why don't you?"

"Nah, I'm good. That's on you to rub 'em out."

He shook his head, smiling ironically. "It's been months and honestly, I never even feel up to doing that." He paused before taking a sip. "It's just not the same."

"I hear you," I said sympathetically.

Reaper choked on his next swallow. "I sure as fuck hear *you.*"

"That's mostly Shadow's fault. He's addicted to pleasing her and she gets…enthusiastic."

Reaper laughed lightly before setting the bottle down, pushing it away with a touch of finality. "Thanks, Jandro."

"You feel better, buddy?" I got up to put my water glass in the sink, slapping his shoulder along the way.

"As better as I'm gonna feel," he sighed.

"Drink some water," I said, grabbing a clean glass and filling it up from the sink for him. "Or you'll feel like hell tomorrow."

"Thanks, Dad," he snorted.

I turned to hand him the water just in time to see Shadow's cracked bedroom door close with a soft click.

TWENTY-THREE

MARIPOSA

I parked my dirt bike in the small, roped-off clearing a few hundred feet from the field hospital. We created a makeshift parking lot further away from the main tent because the noise of vehicles upset the patients. I was checking on the overflow today, mainly Blakeworth citizens and a few from Tash's army. Maybe this lot would have some whose recovery was on par with Robert's, but I wasn't terribly optimistic.

The bulk of my workload had been at the main hospital in town, and this was actually my first time visiting the overflow hospital since we got all the patients and volunteers streamlined. My stomach flipped nervously as I headed for the large white tent. I knew Reaper had been assigned to volunteer here, though I didn't know what shifts he worked.

For being unable to sleep after hearing his conversation with Jandro last night, I was surprisingly alert. Maybe I was finally getting used to the sleep deprivation of the last several weeks. That, or it was my wounded husband's words running through my mind, leaving me unable to focus on anything else.

He's thought about leaving. That was the bell that rang endlessly in my head, no matter how much I recalled Jandro chastising Reaper, convincing him to stick around, especially with the war still going on.

But what if he doesn't actually want to stay?

The thought sent my stomach clenching as I approached the tent. Every beat of my heart was painful. I needed to talk to him, but it seemed like an insurmountable task after that last conversation we had.

I was a major bitch to him. It's no wonder he's thinking about taking off.

Reaper wasn't likely to approach me again, so it was on me to apologize and to have a constructive conversation without lashing out.

How the tables had turned.

I hurried into the tent and went straight for the medic station, a small area sectioned off from the rest of the patients. "Rhonda!" I couldn't help but beam at the head nurse, flipping through charts like she hadn't nearly lost her life in a battle a few days ago. "Good to see you."

"Gonna take more than a little ambush to get rid of me," she smirked back. "How you doin', honey?"

"Fine." I wasn't about to complain about being overworked and sleep-deprived. We all were.

She nodded, accepting that answer. "How are the patients faring at the main hospital?"

"Blakeworth citizens and our people are pulling through their injuries just fine. As for the John Does, recovery is still slow except for the one, Robert. He's remembering more every day. A third of them still haven't shown any signs of improvement."

Rhonda made a few notes as I spoke, nodding as she did so. "Pretty much the same story here. One is improving much faster than the rest, though he's still muddled on some details. He's only been speaking Spanish, so your hubby's been translating for him."

"Oh no," I snickered. "Do we have a second interpreter? You never know what Jandro's gonna make up."

Rhonda laughed. "He's actually been very helpful. No nonsense about chickens or anything X-rated."

"Well, that's good." My laughter died quickly as I thought of those who weren't so lucky to be speaking or moving. "Have you thought about what we should do for the ones who are still catatonic?"

"Only every single minute," Rhonda muttered. "Dr. Brooks and I need to discuss this at length and exhaust all options of treatment that we can."

"And if you run out of options?" I chewed my lip, remembering how Freyja told me she couldn't save them. If a goddess couldn't, then I didn't have much hope for modern medicine.

"Then we'll keep them as comfortable as possible," Rhonda said softly. "They are victims of this war just as much as anyone else."

"You're right about that," I said, setting down my backpack. "Alright, so what do you need from me, routine check-ups?"

"Yes, dear. The John Doe your husband's been interpreting for has had trauma to his eye, if you could take note of the swelling and any infection. John Doe number-6 needs his leg injury looked at."

Rhonda handed me a small stack of charts and I flipped through them quickly to become acquainted with each patient's needs. The moment I stepped out from behind the divider and looked out at the main patient area, my heart did that painful beating again.

Reaper was here.

He was standing at the foot of a patient's bed, talking and smiling like he was cracking jokes. I hadn't seen him smile like that in months, and that made the ache in my chest cut even deeper. He certainly hadn't smiled at *me* like that in a long time.

Reaper said something that made the patient laugh uproariously, clutching his stomach and causing other people to look his way. When Reaper grinned and leaned over the bed to fist-bump the man, his eyes caught mine and all his laughter died.

His eyes dropped just as quickly as they lifted, his lips forcing a smile out at the patient, but the bright glow was gone from his face.

I did that.

And I *hated* that I did that.

I looked down at the patient charts in my arms, trying to focus on the job I came to do, not on my husband across the room who felt hundreds of miles away. *Tonight*, I decided. *We'll talk tonight and figure this out.*

With that in mind, I set to checking on everyone that Rhonda had assigned to me. I caught glimpses of Freyja walking around as I worked, her tail in the air between the beds or jumping up on someone's bed for some healing and head scratches. She settled at the foot of the Spanish-speaking man's bed, where he and Jandro talked softly.

The man was at the end of my rotation, but his voice reached my ears several times while I tended to other patients. I couldn't catch everything he said, but there was something warm and comforting about how he spoke. The cadence and inflections of his words reminded me of my dad, which compounded the ache in my chest already put there by Reaper.

Jandro was speaking rapidly by the time I approached, his wild gesticulations making it clear that he was telling some dramatic story. His accent and tone were slightly different from the other man's and I found myself grinning as I walked up. It was so sexy when he spoke Spanish. I needed to remind him to speak it more at home.

"Mariposita!" Jandro returned my grin as I approached the bed from the other side.

"Guapito," I returned.

The patient, at first engrossed in Jandro's story, swiveled his head to look at me. He had gauze pressed to one eye and medical tape to hold it in place. Part of his head was shaved, revealing a long incision held together with surgical staples. But there was no mistaking him.

All of my patient files fell to the floor as our eyes met. My hands, my legs, and my mouth refused to work.

No, it couldn't be.

But it couldn't be anyone else. No wonder his voice had sounded so soothing to me from afar.

"Dad…" I managed to squeak out before my knees

buckled, hitting the edge of his mattress. I managed to grab the bedframe before collapsing completely to the floor. "Dad!" I cried louder, his face blurring from my tears. "Oh my god, Dad?"

He looked at Jandro and then back at me. *"Tu eres mi hija?"* he asked with a puzzled expression.

"Dad!" I grabbed his hand and he startled at the touch, pulling away like I was some stranger. "Dad, it's me, Mari! You…" I felt like I was crumbling. It was nothing like any other heartbreak I had experienced before. "…You don't recognize me?"

"Hold on, hold on." Jandro came around the bed to help me up, but I barely felt him past my father's confused expression cutting straight through me. "Mari, are you sure this is—"

"Yes, I know it is!" I cried. I knew this man's face almost as well as my own. We had the same nose. He had a scar on his chin from one of the first battles he got drafted for. I *knew* that mouth frowning at me, it looked exactly the same as when I'd get in trouble as a teenager. "Dad, come on. You know me."

He just kept staring at me with a confused expression while Jandro rubbed my arms. "It's okay, babe. We'll figure this thing out. We always do."

"Dad!" My husband's words were little more than background noise in my head. "Dad, you can speak English. Why are you only speaking Spanish?"

"We don't think he's remembered it yet," Jandro said into my ear. "He's remembering a few things since I started talking to him, but it's slow-going. Please don't take it personally, Mari—"

"Dad," I sobbed, shaking with the urgent need to hug this man, to hear him call me *mijita* again and tell me where he'd been all these years. "How can you not know who I am?"

"What's going on?" Reaper walked up to us, his brow pinched in concern.

I was making a scene in the middle of the hospital but couldn't hold back my relief, my grief, and my heart breaking, all rolled into one. My father was alive but was he, really? His chart had indicated he was one of Tash's army. I sank to the floor, sobbing as I stared at the man in his bed while Jandro held and rocked me.

"Found homeboy's daughter," Jandro muttered dryly, wrapping around me tighter as if he could protect me from this pain in my body that swallowed me whole.

"What, *Mari?*" Reaper gasped, looking between me and the patient. "*She's* his, his…"

"He doesn't recognize her," Jandro elaborated. "At least, not yet."

"Oh fuck, sugar." Reaper covered his mouth, like he was holding back a sob himself. "Fuck, my love. I'm so sorry."

My dad was looking at all three of us now, the confusion deepening in his face. He spoke rapidly in a soft voice, mostly under his breath, and the sound only made me want to cry harder. That was my father's voice, and the fact that he didn't know who I was made it feel like knives in my ears.

"He's…very apologetic." Jandro interpreted awkwardly. "It's not that he doesn't believe you. He knows he has a daughter and a wife, he just can't recall their names or faces."

I swallowed hard, taking a deep breath as I locked my gaze onto the man in the bed.

"Your name is Javier Luis de los Angeles. Your birthday is February twenty-seventh. You were born in Guadalajara, Mexico and moved to Texas when you were fifteen," I said. "You married Emma Wilder on September sixth, and had me, your daughter, Mariposa Wilder, on March twenty-first." The important details of his life came rushing out of me in a single breath, but his eye shifted to Jandro as I spoke.

My husband repeated everything I said, but neither of our accounts brought a spark of recognition to the man's face.

"Lo siento, lo siento mucho." He muttered the apology with a sad shake of his head.

I didn't know it was possible to crumble anymore, but it was only Jandro holding me up as I collapsed into tears.

"We should get her home," Jandro said softly.

"I can take her," Reaper offered. "I rode the fat boy today."

They talked for a little bit longer but it was just noise to me. At some point, someone pulled me to my feet and gently dragged me away.

TWENTY-FOUR

MARIPOSA

I was barely aware of the ride home. Reaper kept one hand over both of my palms resting on his stomach the whole way. Whether that was to comfort me or make sure I didn't fall off the bike, I wasn't sure.

His hand stayed connected to mine when we arrived and headed inside. I followed his lead numbly, not resisting nor hurrying. Reaper directed me to the couch and sat me down without a word, then headed down the hallway. I heard some distant noise as he did something but none of it was registering in my mind. All I could think about was my own father's clear lack of recognition when he saw me.

Never for a moment did I consider this as a possibility. Not from the man who taught me how to drive, how to be a hard worker, and how to appreciate tequila. Him, me and my mom—our little family was everything. It was all we had as the Collapse approached, and what kept us going afterward. Finding out he got drafted for the border wars, and faced prison time or death if he refused, was the first big heartbreak of my life.

What Reaper did to Shadow, and Shadow's leaving, was the second. And this…this was the third and the worst one of all.

"Sugar." Reaper's hands enveloped mine again as he kneeled in front of me. "I'm running a bath for you. Come and get in."

I was grateful that he didn't ask, and just told me. I didn't want to be making any decisions right now. If he had asked me, I would have just said that I wanted my dad back.

Reaper gently pulled me up from the couch and led me down the hallway to my favorite bathroom in the house. This one didn't have a shower, only a luxurious standing tub that I once loved soaking in. I couldn't bring myself to love anything right now. Not even my small collection of soap bars and scented oils that Reaper was thoughtful enough to place on the tub's edge for me.

"I'll be in the kitchen if you need anything," he said stiffly before turning to leave.

"Wait." The word choked out of me, my throat raw as my hand reached out to grab his wrist.

He turned back to face me, eyes concerned and a little curious. His throat bobbed with a heavy swallow.

"Is…is anyone else home?"

Reaper shook his head. "Gunner and Shadow are in a meeting with my dad. Jandro's trying to finish up his work at the hospital so he can come home early. But that still might be a while."

I hugged my arms around myself, standing awkwardly next to the tub. "I don't want to be alone right now. I'll just think about him too much and—"

"Then I'll stay with you." Reaper turned his back to me in an offer of privacy. "Get in whenever you're ready."

I took my clothes off slowly, feeling an odd mixture of gratitude and slight that Reaper chose to not see me naked. He was my husband—we'd spent countless hours naked together. Rationally I knew he was being respectful, considerate of the distance between us in recent weeks. But a smaller part of me felt rejected that he didn't want to see me.

Reaper turned slowly after I sank into the water. A thin layer of bubbles floated on the surface, covering me from the shoulders down. Still, he kept his eyes on my face.

"I'll be right back," he said, heading for the door. "Just going to grab a few things."

"Okay." I leaned my head against the edge of the tub, sinking a bit lower.

He returned mere moments later with his arms full of three bottles—one water, one whiskey, and one tequila. "Wasn't sure what you're in the mood for," he said, carefully sitting on the floor next to the tub. "So I brought the unholy trinity."

"Isn't there a song about this?" I mumbled, watching him set the bottles next to him.

"Not quite. You're thinking of One Bourbon, One Scotch, One Beer."

"Oh, right." A dry snicker escaped. "I'll just have

water." As tempting as it was to drink myself into oblivion, I'd have many more long shifts ahead of me. Possibly in that same tent with my father who didn't recognize me.

By the time Reaper handed me the water, I was already crying again. At least it was quieter this time. I took sips of water between soft, hiccuping sobs while Reaper pulled from the whiskey bottle.

"He'll remember you, sugar." Reaper scooted closer to the tub, leaning his shoulder against the outer edge. "You're not easy to forget."

"You don't know that," I whispered, staring at my knees poking through the bubbles on the water's surface. "He hasn't had an MRI yet. We don't know how extensive the damage to his mind is."

"He's improved by miles since last week. And anyway, you're his daughter, his only child. There's no way his memory of you is completely gone."

"I know you're trying to make me feel better but please don't." My gaze shifted toward him, drifting over his forearm resting along the edge of the tub. "I know more about this than you do. And it...it doesn't look good. I'd rather face reality than have false hope."

"Okay. You're right." He shifted away, his arm dropping next to him as he took another swig from the bottle. "I'm sorry, sug—Mari."

We sat in silence for a few minutes, only taking small sips of our drinks.

"I heard you last night," I said, clutching the water bottle between my hands. "When you were talking to Jandro."

Reaper barely moved. Only his chin tipped up slightly in surprise. "What did you hear?"

"Everything."

I didn't know what made me bring it up. I wasn't anxious or sad about what I overheard like I'd been earlier that day. I felt numb, just a body sitting in a bathtub and trying to stay alive by drinking water. Maybe it felt less risky to bring it up when I already wasn't feeling anything.

Reaper let out a long breath but the silence stretched on.

"I was a total bitch to you the last time we talked," I began.

"No, you weren't—"

"I'm sorry for shutting you out while you've been trying to make things work. I didn't mean to make you feel like you'd be better off leaving." At least I could recognize and say that, even while feeling like an empty shell in the moment.

"You didn't make me feel that way," Reaper said. "How you feel, everything you said to me that day, is completely justified."

More silence passed between us, and a sliver of feeling cracked through my numb shell—the need for answers. An intense desire to know *why*.

"So why did you want to leave?" I hugged my knees, not looking at him as I whispered out the question.

"Because I've been a bad husband to you. Even before exiling Shadow."

That drew my gaze up. His brow was pinched with pain, with regret. "What?"

"Even in the very beginning, I mistreated you." Reaper gripped the edge of the tub, as if stopping himself from reaching out to touch me. "I did and said things that hurt you. I let others hurt you, like with Heather at Fight Night."

"Reaper." I leaned toward him unconsciously, my shoulder brushing against his fingers curled over the lip of the tub. "That was so long ago. We barely knew each other."

"But it wasn't the only thing." He inhaled sharply, fingers gripping tighter. "There's something else you don't know. Something I was going to take to my grave, but you deserve complete honesty."

"What?" My voice was small, my chest felt like it was collapsing around my heart. My biggest fear came to the forefront of my mind—another woman. That he'd been with someone else while I was gone, or when I wasn't speaking to him.

"I...*did* try to kill Shadow." Reaper said each word slowly. "I would have, if Hades hadn't stopped me."

The silence between us now was oppressive, creating a distance that stretched wide, like two canyons on opposite ends of a valley. I waited for the response in my body, the irreparable heartbreak. The final twist of a knife that this news was supposed to bring. But it never came. I only felt more of the same, a constant numbness tinged with a painful ache.

My eyes lifted to Reaper's, filled with fear and regret. He was desperate for me to say something, but would never ask me to. Like me, he was probably expecting this to be the end of everything between us.

"On some level, I think I already knew that." The realization came to me slowly, clarity emerging from the sharpness of many painful weeks.

"H-how?" Reaper blinked in surprise. "Did Hades tell you?"

"No. I just know you." My arms wrapped tighter around my knees. "You don't take half-measures. Exile wouldn't have been your first choice."

His head hung low. "You're right," he sighed out quietly. "And it wasn't."

"I've felt so angry and hurt for so long, I just…" A heavy sigh rushed out as I brought my hands to my forehead. "I'm tired of feeling this way. I'm tired of wondering whether forgiving you is the right choice or…" The sentence died on my lips before I could finish speaking it. I still couldn't bring myself to consider the alternative.

"I've asked you for forgiveness too many times already. Now after what I did to Shadow, to you…" Reaper shook his head—a slow, pained, back and forth movement. "It's too much to ask. I love you more than anything in the world, but all I do is hurt you."

I remained still in the water, soaking up everything he said while fighting the urge to reach for him. To reassure him and tell him no, none of that was true. I fell in love with him the fastest, the hardest. But he wasn't saying it in hopes of falling into my arms again. He was just being honest. And there was truth in what he was saying.

"Do you want to leave?" I asked quietly.

"I want you to be happy and to never feel a betrayal like what I did again."

"That wasn't my question."

Reaper sighed and rubbed at his face. "No, I don't want to leave."

"What *do* you want?"

"What I want doesn't matter," he said gruffly. "My selfish wants shouldn't factor into any decisions you make."

"Tell me, please."

He sighed again, tilting his gaze up toward the ceiling. "I want to see you smile at me again. I want to hear you tell me you love me. I want to wrap you up in bed at night and make you feel safe. I want to feel trusted and needed by you again." The back of his head touched the wall as he spoke, his gaze somewhere far away as his throat worked in a hard swallow. "And I know I have no right to ask for any of that. I'm not entitled to anything from you."

"You're still my husband." The declaration seemed to come out of nowhere, like a final thread I was desperately trying to hold on to.

"And you have three other very capable ones who treat you as you deserve."

"This isn't about you versus them," I argued. "This is about you and me."

"Then I leave the decision up to you." His gaze finally turned to me, a resigned calmness in his green eyes, like he already accepted his fate. "Keep me as a husband or not. Choose what'll make you happy and forget everything else." He pushed himself up to standing, looking down at me in the tub with such longing, it made my chest ache.

At least I could feel again.

"Take all the time you need to decide." Reaper picked up his liquor bottles and started for the door. "Whether that's tonight or when the war's over, I'll accept your decision either way, Mari."

"Reaper, wait." He was almost out of the room when I stood up, water sloshing onto the bathroom floor. He glanced back, then faced forward again when he realized I was standing and naked. That made me hurt even more. Every day, every moment of missing him and longing for him seemed to culminate in this moment and it felt like I was shattering again.

My dad. My fallen medics. Him. This whole fucking war. I was breaking apart at the seams and all I wanted was for my husband to make it stop hurting.

"Why won't you look at me?" I cried out at Reaper's back. "I'm your wife! I'm *yours!* Why…"

He was across the room in a flash, rough hands pulling me into his chest. I was dripping wet but he didn't seem to care, holding the back of my head so my face was against his shoulder so I could scream and sob. I gripped his cut to pull him closer, inhaling the whiskey and cloves with every rattled breath through my chest like I was an addict. My legs threatened to give out from underneath me but he held me up, like an oak tree rooted firmly in the onslaught of a storm.

He's shaped by storms, I realized. The losses Reaper had endured gave him armor that sometimes hurt those at his sides. He was strong, there were no doubts about that. But only now was he seeing that armor did more harm than good. He didn't need armor to be strong. He just had to be brave enough to lower those defenses.

And now, he had been. There was no ego, no pride left in him. He'd been more honest with me here next to this bathtub than probably any other moment in our relationship. I wanted more of that. I wanted my Reaper who was strong enough to be raw and vulnerable with me.

His hand continued running up and down my back as my sobs quieted. His other palm on the back of my head was a comforting weight, holding me to his shoulder.

"You'll be alright, sugar," he whispered gently. "I know it doesn't feel like it now, but you will be."

Not without you.

The thought made me clutch him harder, like he would be ripped away from me at any moment. He held me tighter in response, the hand on my back pressing me into his chest while staying a respectful distance above my ass.

I didn't want him respectfully distant. I wanted his claim on my body, consuming and without apology.

"Reaper…" I whispered his name along his neck before bringing my lips to his skin there. My tongue flicked against his pulse, the thrumming doubling in speed. His skin was so warm and mildly salty.

Reaper let out a surprised hiss, jerking in my arms at the contact. The swelling in his pants was immediate, an insistent need pressing against my lower stomach.

"Mari…sugar, are you *sure?*" His voice was a husky

rasp, just further proof that he truly hadn't been with anyone but me. My husband's desire was only for me.

"No, I'm not sure of anything," I admitted, watching his skin prickle in reaction to the breath from my mouth. "Except that you're here and I want you. I've missed y—"

He moved away from me only enough to bring his mouth down on mine. The two of us groaned into the kiss, like a couple of addicts hitting a fresh high. And that was exactly what it felt like. Sparks shot through my brain and every nerve ending in my body. I never wanted to come down from this, never *not* feel the rough scraping of his stubble, the demanding presses of his tongue, his wild and passionate way of loving me.

Reaper's hand finally slid down the curve of my back to squeeze my ass, my bare skin still wet from my bath and burning hot, first from the water, and then from him. Our kiss broke for a dizzying, gasping breath and a cocky smirk filled my vision, a glimpse of the Reaper I first met and fell in love with.

"Do you want to step out?" he asked in a husky whisper, gliding a rough palm over my waist and hip. "Or I could come in."

"Out." It was the only coherent word I could say at the moment.

Reaper moved back, holding my hands for support as I stepped over the tub ledge. "Want to towel off?" He turned to grab a bath towel from the rack on the wall but I was faster, grabbing his cut and pulling him back until my mouth was locked on to his again.

He let out a moan that was more of a growl and

lowered his arms, palming my ass with both hands and lifting up until my legs wrapped around his waist. In a few steps, he walked us to the vanity, perched me on the edge of the counter, and rolled his jean-clad erection against my spread open center.

"Sorry for getting you all wet," I blurted out the apology as he bent to kiss my neck, running that sinful mouth to my shoulder, where he nipped me.

"Shouldn't *I* be the one apologizing for that?" His grin was wicked, eyes dilated and hungry as his hands ran up the front of my body. He touched and looked at me like it was our first time again, like I was something precious he wanted to both treasure and defile.

"Stop," I groaned with a playful smack to his shoulder, but I regretted that word in the next moment. He kissed me again, deep and dizzying as a hand ventured leisurely down my belly.

"Stop?" Reaper teased the word against my lips as his fingertips found my clit, running over it with the lightest possible contact.

"No," I begged, holding him in place with my legs around his hips and an arm around his shoulders. "Don't stop."

"Hm, I could've sworn you told me to stop." His hand moved away and I whimpered in protest. He touched the edge of the tattoo on my hip and leaned down to inspect it more closely, fingers tracing the vines and lengths of the petals. "Is this his gift to you?" Reaper's tone was lighter, curious. "Shadow's?"

"Yes," I answered, watching his reaction carefully.

"It's well done. 'Course that goes without saying." His gaze lifted to mine. "Do you like it?"

"I love it," I breathed. "For me and him, it's perfect."

"I have to agree." Reaper smiled, his forehead nudging mine. "I'm glad that you have him. That we all have him."

"Me too."

Reaper brushed the back of his palm against my cheek. "He loves you."

"He does," I said. "And I love him."

For a moment Reaper looked like he was going to say something else, but opted to kiss me instead. The coolness from our brief conversation gave way, our passion reigniting like gasoline on a fire. His kiss started off gently but soon became a deep, demanding tongue-fucking. I felt fingers brush my clit again and whined into the kiss.

"Don't stop," I pleaded, nearly teetering off the edge of the vanity with how hard I bucked toward his hand. "Please don't stop."

Reaper pressed down on the bundle of nerves, his thumb circling it as his fingers stroked through my folds. "It feels so good to hear you beg for me," he rasped. "Fuck, I've missed you."

"I've missed you so—ohh!"

Two fingers filled me, spreading wide to caress my walls while his thumb kept the steady, circular motion right above. My head tipped back as I gave in to the sensations of him, so familiar, like I was coming home and yet so new that it gave me such a rush. With his hands busy, he placed more of those kisses on the column of my throat. Some were so soft, they felt like whispers. Others were rough and biting. Exactly like the man who gave them—so full of love but with hard, jagged edges.

I wanted so badly to touch him, to take him out of his wet clothes and feel his bare skin on mine. But my hands braced behind me on the counter, my only support under him conquering and devouring me. The steady driving of his fingers through me sent my pleasure soaring, and it wouldn't be long until my strength gave out.

"Reaper," I whimpered, head tossing as my control began to unravel. My hips and his hand crashed against each other, meeting in the middle with loud smacks of flesh. Anyone listening at the door could have mistaken it for sex.

"Mari," he rumbled, lips skimming mine. "I don't have it in me to deny you. I want you coming for me every time you choose me." He smothered my moan with another bruising kiss, fucking me harder with his hand. "And if I please you every day until I die, it still won't make up for how I hurt you."

I shattered around him then, clutching around his fingers with a release that sent my cries echoing off the bathroom tiles. He kept driving into me, prolonging my pleasure while murmuring praises in my ear about how good and sexy I was. My body sucked around his fingers when he finally removed them, both of us panting.

Reaper kissed me again with more gentleness than before, but I still had to break away to breathe. My pulse raced and I felt exhausted, but my mind felt much clearer than before. And to my shock, the most persistent feeling was a wave of intense remorse.

Reaper straightened up, that cocky smirk returning as he unsnapped the button on his jeans. The motion sent a jolt through me, but not of pleasure. My body was still feeling the effects of physical pleasure from moments ago, but right then my brain was screaming, *I don't want this. I'm not ready.*

"I don't expect to last very long." Reaper yanked his zipper down, oblivious to my internal conflict. "But I have also been dying to taste you again."

"Wait." I held a hand up when he reached for me.

He froze, brow pinching in confusion. Or maybe it was concern. "Something wrong, sugar?"

"I don't…I…" My throat tightened and I was hit with the overwhelming urge to cry again. Like I hadn't been doing enough of that lately. "I'm sorry, but…I think this was too soon."

Reaper backed away and refastened his pants immediately. He grabbed a towel and quickly returned to wrap it around me, rubbing my arms through the fabric for a moment before yanking his hands away like he shouldn't have been touching me.

"Thank you," I said, holding the towel securely over me. "I'm sorry, I'm just—"

"Don't apologize. You have nothing to be sorry for." He seemed unsure of what to do with his hands, either rubbing his jaw or crossing them over his chest. That worried, pinched expression never left his face. "Did I hurt you?"

"No." I shook my head and tried to smile at him, but it faltered and he only looked even guiltier. "No, I think I just had a moment of clarity and…physically, I'm just not ready to jump all the way back in yet."

"Of course. Yeah, of course. I understand." Now *he* tried to smile, but it looked equally as strained as my attempt. He stood several feet away from me now, the space between us feeling as wide as a canyon again.

"I'm gonna lie down, I think." I slid down from the vanity, holding the towel to my chest while the throb of my orgasm still pulsed softly throughout my body.

"Okay. Let me know if you need anything." Reaper then turned and left like he couldn't get away fast enough.

TWENTY-FIVE

MARIPOSA

"I'm sure this comes as no surprise." General Bray held a folded letter above his head, barely able to contain his grin. "Blakeworth has *graciously* sent us a formal surrender and offering of peace."

The conference room erupted in a mixture of cheers and raucous laughter. Soldiers hugged each other, made obscene gestures, and shouted various forms of, *Suck our dicks, Blakeworth! Bend over and take it up the ass!*

"How kind and diplomatic," Gunner mused to my right. "Right after we handed their asses to them." His feet were propped up in the chair on the other side of him. The whole feel of the room was relaxed, if even happy after hearing this news.

"You'll love this part." Finn opened the letter and scanned for a certain section to read. "We hope you will join us in leaving behind the pains of the past and move forward in a mutually beneficial relationship."

Gunner made a farting noise with his mouth that

stretched on for several seconds, until I slapped his arm. "Okay, really though," he laughed. "What happens now?"

"Their infrastructure is crippled, so their economy will be limping along for several years." Finn leaned back and put his feet up in an empty chair as well. "We can offer them aid, with strict terms. Remember, it's their working class that will suffer the most. The elite families have probably all fled to greener pastures."

"Also no surprise," I muttered.

The general nodded. "How are the hospitals doing, Mari?"

"Okay." I forced a tense smile. I hadn't felt great since yesterday with my dad and Reaper, but I shoved it all down to get an early start before attending this meeting. The patients needed me. "We're good on supplies at the moment. All current patients are stable. The volunteers have been a tremendous help. The only thing is, both hospitals are full and we are still understaffed." I clasped my hands on the table. "If we have another big battle, it could overload our capacity. Our resources are going to be spread extremely thin."

"I'm glad you brought that up," Finn said, his mouth tensing. "Because there is still New Ireland to deal with."

"Have you tried communicating with them?" Gunner rolled his chair closer to me, grabbing one of my hands.

Finn shook his head and lowered his voice. "After what we've seen with Andrea and the soldiers from there, sending a messenger is not something I'm willing to risk. I never thought I'd be saying this but…I don't think we're dealing with a *person*."

Gunner and I nodded in agreement.

"For now, we have to stay vigilant," the general said. "We'll plan an attack for when the hospital has more space, so we don't overload our medical staff."

"Truthfully, sir," I squeezed Gunner's hand, "that could be weeks from now."

"Yeah, what if they ambush us again?" Gunner leaned forward in his seat, placing his chin on my shoulder.

"That's where staying vigilant comes in," Finn answered. "Samson has the Jerriton army posted around the perimeter of Four Corners. They've been briefed on what to look for. Nothing will get past them, no matter which direction it comes from. We won't be surprised again. But for us?" He smiled a little more easily. "I feel like we could use a bit of a break from fighting, don't you?"

Gunner cleared his throat. "Respectfully sir, I feel like waiting too long gives them too much time to prepare."

"I see where you're coming from son, but you heard your wife. Medical staff are already carrying a huge burden. Our soldiers are exhausted. We won't be the superior army if we keep going until we're dead."

Gunner leaned back, conceding to the general's point. "You're absolutely right, sir."

"Don't get me wrong, we will push back if we see Tash's army approaching," Finn added. "We just shouldn't get too far ahead of ourselves."

Gunner nodded his agreement, letting the conversation die as the general stood to talk to a small group of soldiers across the room. With the two of us now alone at one end of the long table, I reached for his hand to clasp it in mine again.

"I know how you feel." My other hand ran through his golden strands as I leaned in, talking low to keep our conversation private. "It feels like we're stopping right when we've gotten good momentum, but Finn is right."

"Yeah, I know he is." Gunner tugged me closer until I slid out of my chair and into his lap. He hugged around me from behind, resting his chin on my shoulder again. "We can only ride high on adrenaline and morale for so long. It's good to take a small break." He squeezed around my waist and planted a kiss on my neck. "We should ride out to the hot spring and camp for a few days."

I turned to look at him. "'We' being who, exactly?"

"All of us," he answered quickly, a grin pulling at his lips. "It can be like a honeymoon for you and your four husbands."

His grin was infectious as I played with his hair some more. "As nice as that sounds, I can't get away from the hospital for that long."

"One day, then. Just an overnight trip." Gunner pushed my hair aside, dragging more kisses along the back of my neck. "Think about it," he whispered, his breath sending shivers along my skin. "Sleeping under a sky full of stars. The hot water relaxing all your aches and pains away."

"*All* of them, huh?" I snorted.

"Whatever the spring misses, your devoted husbands will take care of." He dug his thumbs into my upper back right then, circling them into the knots of muscle that had settled there for weeks. "We'll attend to your every need, baby girl. We can even be like real cavemen and hunt food for you."

I laughed at that, leaning into his hands working their magic on my back. "You make a tempting offer, captain."

"Then accept it." I felt his smile on my skin before he kissed behind my ear.

I squirmed in his lap, unable to keep my own grin away. He was turning on the charm and it was fun seeing this side of him again. A full day away from everything, just me and my men, with no responsibilities, sounded like utter bliss.

"I'm not sure if I can get away from work, even for a day." I twirled a lock of his hair around my index finger. "But I'll try," I added when he pouted and turned on the puppy dog eyes.

"Even an afternoon would be enough," Gunner said. "I just want some time to spend with my favorite people and no one else."

Horus, who had been perched on the back of Gunner's chair, now leaned down with a chirp to nip at his hair.

"Yeah, that includes you too, you little shit." Gunner reached up and let the falcon walk onto his hand, then brought him down to perch over my lap.

I tensed at the sight of Horus' talons so close to my

leg, but the bird seemed to take care and be gentle, releasing Gunner's wrist to walk toward my knees. "We'd never exclude you, Horus," I said, using the back of my hand to lightly stroke his chest feathers.

"You critters are my favorite people too." Gunner returned to hugging around my waist, dropping a kiss on my shoulder. "At least until we have kids."

"Is that so?" I leaned back to kiss his cheek.

"It's one of the things I'm looking forward to most, after all this is over." Gunner placed a soft kiss on my nose. "I want to be a better father than my dad ever was."

"You will be," I assured him, touching the stubble on his cheek. "I already have zero doubts about that."

He inhaled sharply, like me saying that caught him off-guard, and I wondered if anyone had told him that before. Then he smiled, the motion slow and unbelievably sweet like melted honey. "Thank you, baby girl."

"I love you, Gun."

Horus flapped his wings and fluttered onto the table as I shifted in Gunner's lap, turning to face him.

"I love you, Mari." He whispered it reverently, forehead on mine and holding me like I would slip out of his arms at any moment. "And thank you for trusting me with your heart again."

"Thank you for owning up about being a dick," I chuckled, darting my tongue out to the tip of his nose.

"It won't happen again." He remained serious even after I tried to crack a joke. "Who you love and who you keep—those are *your* decisions to make. We had no right to force an outcome you didn't want." He swallowed. "We had no right to treat a brother like that."

"Thank you for acknowledging your part in it," I said. "With you, I'm ready to move past this. Shadow is too."

Gunner gave me a long look. "And with Reaper?"

My heart immediately picked up a thunderous rhythm, beating against my sternum like a fist. I was taken back to yesterday, talking to Reaper while sitting in the bath, and then what we did afterward.

I could still taste the roughness of his kiss, the grip of his hands on me, and how expertly he played my body. And I remembered how quickly he stopped, his guilt-ridden face after he saw I was no longer enjoying myself.

Why did I suddenly not want to keep going? I could only determine that, physically, I still didn't trust him completely. Even if I was mentally and emotionally ready to have him as my husband again, my body, even after yearning for weeks, had rejected him.

Damn that post-orgasm clarity.

The hurt on Reaper's face had been crushing. He probably took the rejection personally, he always did. If I peeked into his bedroom, I'd probably see a packed duffle bag ready to go—just waiting for me to say the words.

But I couldn't be certain. I hadn't seen or spoken to him since he walked out of the bathroom. If I had a chance, I'd tell him I wanted him to stay. I wanted him as my partner and my lover, just that my body-brain connection was being weird about sex. I wanted to get back to trusting him fully again, with his help.

"I guess that's a 'no'," Gunner mused softly after I hadn't said anything for a while. "Or at least a 'not yet'."

I let out a long sigh, resting my forehead on his. "I want to, but it's not as simple with him."

"I know." Gunner leaned back, looking at me with a loving smile. "That's part of why I want all of us to get away. So we don't have to think about," he waved his arms around, "all this. We can just focus on us."

"You're right. And it's a good idea."

"'Course it is." He smirked. "All my ideas are great."

I snorted and began sliding off of his lap to stand, but got hit with a sudden sense of vertigo and found myself crumbling to the floor.

"Mari! Are you—agh, fuck!"

Gunner must have felt the same pain that I was feeling right then, like a sledgehammer pounding at my skull.

Something was trying to get inside my head.

"No, no!" I clutched my head, all sense of direction gone, but I must have been rolling around on the floor.

Whatever barriers I had against the previous attempt to fracture my mind were failing. I could *feel* them buckling under the weight of the mental attack. Fear struck me, thinking of my dad and all the mindless, controlled soldiers walking to their death under General Tash. *This* was how they were broken and kept to heel like dogs.

Who or whatever General Tash was, it would not stop. It hurt so fucking bad that I saw in a single clear moment that I had vomited on the floor. My hands were covered in blood, probably from grabbing at my ears.

And then whatever was attacking me broke through.

The pain stopped and I heard a clear, otherworldly voice in my head, dripping with smugness.

Aha, there you are. Bring me the underworld, the sky, and the thread that ties them together.

TWENTY-SIX

MARIPOSA

I rolled, pushing shakily to my knees. Remnants of pain still throbbed in my head, but overall I felt okay.

Someone clutched my arm—Gunner. Blood trailed down the sides of his neck and darkened the ends of his hair. He was sweating and breathing hard—I imagined I was doing the same.

"You okay?" he asked in a pained rasp.

I nodded. "Did you hear that?" We said it at the same time.

"Yeah." Gunner's hands floated over my face, my neck, and shoulders, as if checking to make sure I really was okay. "What does it mean?"

"Hey, you two."

I looked up to see General Bray and a group of soldiers forming a circle around us, their faces drawn tight with concern. "What was that?" My father-in-law knelt at my side, staring at my bleeding ear.

"It…happened again," Gunner said with a tight breath. "The pain in our heads, the—"

"I thought you were certain it *wasn't* going to happen again," Finn clipped out. "You said you were protected."

"I thought we were, but—"

"Get them to the hospital," the general cut him off curtly. "Tell Dr. Brooks it's an emergency. They're encountering the same symptoms as the Tash soldiers."

"Right away, General," a lieutenant responded.

"Finn, wait." I climbed shakily to my feet, reaching for my father-in-law's arm to steady myself. He allowed me to lean on him but looked as though he'd rather throw me in a prison cell than let me touch him. "We need to find the others—Shadow, Reaper, and Jandro. The last time this happened, we were all affected."

"I know." Finn's gaze was hard, his mouth a thin line. This wasn't my warm, kind father-in-law at the moment. He was one-hundred-percent general. "I'm afraid we'll have to hold you at the hospital until we get to the bottom of this. If the others are affected, we'll hold them too, when they come to see you."

"Hold us?" Gunner repeated, his gaze narrowing. "You mean, against our will?"

The general turned stiffly to him. "We talked about this. We agreed that if you were to display these symptoms again, you had likely been compromised by the enemy." His gaze softened just a fraction. "I'm sorry, to both of you. But we still don't know what we're dealing with, and I need to keep the territory safe."

"Wait, wait!" I slapped away the hands of the soldier who tried to take my elbow.

"Ma'am, please don't resist." The soldier's throat worked in a swallow. "I don't want to force you, but I must follow the general's orders."

"Don't touch her!" Gunner hissed. Then to Finn, "Sir, I understand what we said. We'll cooperate, but you need to understand something."

"I'm sorry, but I don't know if it's my son-in-law talking to me right now, or…something else." Finn gave a defeated wave of his hand toward the exit. "Take them."

More hands grabbed my arms on either side and forcibly started moving me in that direction. I pulled my arms away and kicked out my feet, but it was no use.

"Mari, Mari, it's okay." Gunner was trying to be calm, but I heard the undercurrent of panic in his voice. "Don't fight them, we're still on the same side. Once we see the other guys, we'll figure something out."

With a huff, I stopped trying to get away, but still turned my head to yell back at the general.

"Something's going to happen!" I hollered over my shoulder. "They're coming! They want something and you need to be ready."

After that, I allowed the soldiers to escort me without issue. We walked down the long corridor without a word, boots scuffling over the carpeted floor. We were almost at the exit, two soldiers holding the doors open up ahead, when a sudden screech sent us all ducking.

A light breeze on my back was the only indicator of Horus' flight. He made no sound as he sailed through the corridor and out the open doors, the two soldiers darting out of the falcon's way.

They took Gunner and I to one of the army's SUVs, which we got into willingly. We huddled together in the backseat on the way to the hospital, trying to be strong for each other while I knew that voice still haunted us both.

———

"IT'S GOT to be something to do with Hades and Horus, right?" Reaper ran his thumb over his lip, pondering the message that had rattled through our heads. "What else would be the underworld and the sky but those two?"

He, Jandro, and Shadow had been notified of what happened to us, and immediately rode over to the hospital, where they were greeted by more soldiers. All five of us had been escorted and crammed into an exam room at the hospital. The door wasn't especially secure like a holding cell, but all of those rooms were taken by the worst-off of Tash's soldiers—the ones still screaming and bleeding from the ears. Finn's soldiers stuck us in here and were standing guard on the other side of the door.

None of us had resisted. They were just doing as they were ordered, and Finn believed this to be the best course of action. But if we needed to get out, I was confident my four men could break their way through.

"But what's the thread that ties them together?" Jandro sat on the exam table, legs swinging back and forth like a child. "Fuck, I hate riddles."

"Remember when we were looking up the gods in books?" Shadow said to Reaper. "Back in Sheol."

"Yeah, and?"

"The underworld and the sky are like two ends of a spectrum. The darkness and mystery of death on one end, light and higher knowledge at the other." Shadow held his hands out in front of him, roughly two feet apart. "What's in the middle?"

"I dunno, dude. That's what we're trying to figure out."

Shadow's hands fell to his thighs as he shot Reaper a disappointed look. "Life, Reaper. Humanity. Not dead, and not in a higher state of consciousness. Where we are *right now.*" The room fell silent as Shadow looked around for someone else to chime in. "The underworld is below us, metaphorically speaking. The sky is above us."

"I get it, man. But I'm still not sure what—"

"Freyja," I broke in, the understanding clicking into place like a puzzle piece. "Humanity. Life and love in all of its forms. This is Freyja's domain. She's the link between the underworld and the sky."

"Yes," Shadow beamed as he nodded at me. "Our companion gods form a trinity, of sorts."

"Okay, so this thing," Jandro pointed at his temple, "wants *our* gods? Why?"

"Because they're protecting us," Gunner piped up. "They're naturally opposing forces, right? Chaos versus life, death, higher learning—we have the natural order of things. Chaos wants to disrupt that. Our gods are what's standing in the way of chaos taking over."

A brief silence filled the room before Jandro slapped

Gunner on the back with a loud *whack* on his cut. "Look at you, smart guy. Way to break it down for us."

"So, what? We have to round them up and protect them?" Reaper rubbed the back of his neck. "Hades is back at the house. We've seen some coyotes around, so I told him to guard the chickens."

"Aw thanks, dude." Jandro nodded at him.

"Freyja is usually wandering the hospital," I said. "But I don't know if she's here or at the field hospital."

"Horus took off," Gunner frowned. "I can look through him and see where he is, but getting him to land might be another matter."

"Once we do round them up, what do we do with them?" I asked.

"City Hall has a basement," Reaper answered, the first words he said directly to me since yesterday. "It's heavily reinforced like a bomb shelter, in case of attacks on the city."

"What about our babysitters?" Jandro jerked his head toward the doors. "Do we just tell them we forgot to feed our animals?"

"We're gonna have to force our way through them, unfortunately." Gunner rubbed his jaw. "Three of us should take them on, one of us should guard Mari."

"I can handle myself," I huffed.

"Lover, they're armed and we're not," Shadow said gently. "We'll have to subdue them and take away their weapons. Those of us who take them on need to overpower them quickly."

"You three take 'em, then," Jandro said. "You're the strongest fighters. I'll cover Mari."

"I dunno about this, guys." I chewed my lip, tapping my foot on the ground to release some nerves. "I'm gonna have to run up and down the halls to look for Freyja. If they call for backup, we could get boxed in."

"Once we get our guards out of the way, we'll have guns," Reaper pointed out. "Nobody wants to hurt our own allies, but I feel like this is a risk we have to take." He pinned me with a hard stare. "We *need* to protect those gods. The survival of Four Corners needs them. Shit, the whole fucking world might need them."

Trust him or don't trust him?

The question echoed in my mind, and not for the first time. Only this time, I did feel a clear, single answer. My heart, mind, and body were all in agreement for the first time in months.

Trust him.

"Okay," I said with a deep breath. "You're right. You're—"

A crackling sound from the ceiling drew everyone's attention upward. The hospital's PA system was so old and fickle, no one used it. It was easier to use radios to call each other across the building, but someone was in the control room and attempting to broadcast a message to the entire hospital.

"Attention, I need…I need every available military and medical staff in the secure holding area." The broadcaster was panting, groaning slightly like they were in pain. "John Does number eighteen through twenty-four have fucking lost it."

The use of language would have been funny if the

situation didn't sound so dire. All five of us stood frozen as we listened.

"The patients have become violent toward staff without warning. Sedatives are no longer effective. Medical staff have sustained injuries trying to subdue them, and I fear some are dead. They…ah, oh fuck… patients are trying to break out of holding cells and we need help!"

"Shit." My hand flew to my mouth and I moved instinctively toward the door, only to be stopped by Reaper with a light touch on my wrist.

"Mari, who are the John Does number eighteen through twenty-four?"

"Seventeen through twenty are the mostly unresponsive ones," I answered. "With the ear-bleeding and screaming symptoms. The rest are the catatonic ones. Freyja said she couldn't do anything for them."

"So they're still being controlled. Fuck." Reaper turned to the door, a hand on his jaw.

"They must have heard the same call that we did," Shadow said. "A broadcast to every mind this Chaos thing has access to, maybe."

"Why would it tell us too?" Gunner's brows pinched. "It doesn't make any sense."

"The very definition of chaos is not making sense," I said dryly. "Are we going to help or what?"

The doors and walls were thick, but we could hear some commotion out in the hallways. Medics and soldiers must have been racing to assist, shouting as their footsteps pounded just outside of our door.

"Stand back." Shadow's light touch drew me and

Reaper away from the door. My biggest husband raised a booted foot and crashed it against the door's locking mechanism. It opened easily. Shadow's kick looked effortless, like he was passing a soccer ball.

"Fuckin' show-off," Jandro chuckled, but patted Shadow's back as he slid off the exam table. "Did our babysitters take off?"

"Looks like it." Shadow stuck his head out to look both directions down the hallway. "It's pretty empty. They must have all responded to the call."

"You guys check and see if they need more help," I slid out from behind Shadow and started down one length of hallway. "I'm gonna find my cat."

"I'll go with you." Jandro followed after me.

"Meet back here," Reaper called after us. "We grab Hades from home, and take them to City Hall together."

"Okay!" I turned a corner, Jandro right at my side as I headed for one of the hospital wings that Freyja liked to hang out in. "Freyja? Freyja!"

"If you haven't tried seeing through her, now would be a good time," Jandro suggested.

"Tried it, doesn't work," I said, breaking into a jog. "But yes, that would be useful right about now."

"Freyja!" Jandro's voice echoed through the halls. "I'll feed you Foghorn if you come out!"

We ran up and down the halls, peeked into rooms, and even checked closets and supply cabinets. It felt kind of ridiculous, looking for a cat like it was the most important thing in the world. But damn it, it kind of *was* the most important thing in the world. And I hated the thought that kept popping up in the back of my mind—that she was trying not to be found.

"Let's head downstairs," I said to Jandro after nearly ten minutes of fruitless searching. "Maybe she's in the lobby."

We headed for the stairs, in too much of a hurry for the elevator. On the wall next to the staircase, a long bay of windows stretched from the ground floor to the top floor of the building. It caught my attention as we headed that way, because the landscape outside looked strangely dark, despite the sunny day.

"Oh…fuck." I stopped in my tracks the moment I realized what the blackness was, making Jandro crash into me from behind. He gripped my shoulders, sucking in a sharp breath once he saw what I did.

"Holy…fuck, that's not possible," he breathed. "How…"

"I don't know." I tried to swallow, my throat dry, like sandpaper. "We have to find Freyja."

"Yeah."

But neither of us could tear our eyes from the massive swarm of black-clad soldiers marching on Four Corners.

TWENTY-SEVEN

SHADOW

"Where the fuck even are the holding cells?" Reaper's head swiveled around, looking for a sign as we took off down the opposite hallway as Mari and Jandro.

"Probably that way." I nodded toward an unmarked door, the small window in it only showing a narrow stairwell going up. "They'll be isolated from the other patients."

"How would you know that?" Gunner asked me.

I shrugged before trying the doorknob. It was only a standard deadbolt, so I stepped back and kicked it in. "It was where they kept me before transferring me to the mainline at the prison."

"Alright, thanks, Donkey Legs." Reaper clapped me on the shoulder once. "Let's move."

I led the way up the stairwell, with Reaper after me and then Gunner in the rear—quite the shift from our usual formation.

"This is what I get for skipping fucking leg day,"

Gunner groaned, despite keeping a good pace behind Reaper.

"Told you," I muttered.

"Yeah I know, dude. Put me on your workout plan once all this shit is over."

The holding cells must have been on the very top floor of the hospital, because the stairs just kept going up and up.

"You sure this is the right way?" Reaper was starting to pant behind me. "I think this is an emergency stairwell."

"I wasn't sure, it was just a hunch," I said. "We can —whoa, Freyja!" I stopped right before the next landing, where the black cat waited patiently for us. "Mari's looking for you," I said, lowering to a crouch. "Tash, chaos, whatever it is, is coming for you and the other gods."

I'm afraid you're incorrect. The goddess' voice was soothing through my head, unlike the feeling of jagged knives through my brain matter like the other voice. *It isn't coming for us, but for you.*

"Me?"

All of you, collectively. The ones we've touched.

"Us?" Reaper nudged his way forward to stand next to me. "What does it want with us?"

The five of you are our ties to humanity. To cut us off from you is to weaken our connection to humankind as a whole. We exist without our animal vessels, but we cannot bond with other humans as we have with you.

"They mean to kill us?" Gunner came up on my other side.

Yes, if they cannot turn you into instruments of chaos first.

"Fuck, we have to get Mari and Jandro." I started backing up to head down the stairs the way we came.

"Uh, guys?" Gunner was pale, staring out the small, square window next to the landing. "You might wanna see this."

Reaper went next to him and I walked up the steps to see over their heads. "Holy…fuck."

The landscape just beyond the territory border was black as far as the eye could see. Thousands upon thousands of Tash's soldiers were marching on us, packed so tightly together that they looked like a single entity, and they *still* swarmed the landscape. The army looked like a slow-moving ink spill creeping closer to the city.

I moved in closer behind the other two, and looked to the south. The army spread that way too, as far as I could see. Looking the other direction told the same story.

"This window faces west," I noted. "New Ireland is east of us."

Reaper and Gunner turned around slowly, their faces stunned and harrowed. The previous attacks from Tash were a drop in the bucket compared to what was coming right now. Within an hour, they'd be tearing through Jerriton's perimeter like paper. Once they made it through, they'd sweep through Four Corners just as quickly.

We never stood a fucking chance.

"We have to get Mari and Jandro, and get the fuck out of this territory," Reaper said. "All of Four Corners is about to get slaughtered because they're looking for us."

"Reap, no," Gunner argued. "I get leading them away, but the five of us can't take on *that*." He pointed out the window. "And how would we even get out? You heard Shadow, they somehow made it *west* of us. We're fucking surrounded."

"I dunno." Reaper's jaw ticked, arms swinging stiffly at his sides like he wanted to punch something. "Fuck, I don't know what to fucking do!"

"Let's find Mari and Jandro," I said. "They might have already seen that," I nodded toward the window, "and started moving faster to get the animals."

"What about the medics and soldiers here?" Reaper wondered.

"I hate to leave them, but there should be enough of them to manage without us."

"Shit, I just thought of something." Gunner paled again. "Last time they marched on us, they burned down the field hospital. I'll bet you Mari and Jandro are heading that way to evacuate people."

"Fuck, I bet you're right. Mari's dad's in there," Reaper muttered before leaping down the stairs, taking three at a time.

I followed in the rear this time, glancing over my shoulder for a moment to see that Freyja was gone. I didn't know if she teleported or had uncanny speed, but doors and physical barriers didn't seem to slow down our god companions.

Please, please tell them what you told us, I thought—or prayed, I suppose. *Let them know and keep them safe.*

"They better not have touched our fucking bikes," Gunner announced as we made our way down.

Once we reached the first floor, we ran through an empty lobby to the parking lot outside. Jandro's bike was missing, leaving only mine and Reaper's.

"Get on," Reaper said to Gunner without hesitation as he turned on his steed, the machine rumbling to life. "Just hold on to me, don't make it weird."

My bike sounded like it was roaring out a battle cry. I backed it out of the space and turned toward the road, accelerating hard once it was clear. Traffic and signs went ignored as I weaved through the roads toward the field hospital. I only watched for pedestrians, but everyone within a mile heard us coming and no one dared to get in our way.

The field hospital was on the outer edge of town, close to the border. I kept hoping, praying that they weren't already being attacked. General Bray should have caught sight of the threat by now. He had no idea yet what they were really after, but hopefully his army would buy us some time.

I saw the top of the white hospital tent from the road and pushed my bike harder, knowing Reaper and Gunner weren't far behind. Everyone in town still acted normally, from what I could see speeding by. No one was running in a panic, there weren't any soldiers trying to evacuate large groups of people. A sick sense of dread turned my stomach and I could only grip the handlebars harder.

Something terrible is going to happen. Either thousands of people are going to die, or we are.

I crested a small hill and saw the field hospital straight ahead. What I saw beyond it nearly had me slamming on my brakes.

Blackness covered the landscape like a shadow. Seeing it closer now, without a window in front of me, was a completely different experience. I thought it looked bad enough from up there, but down here it felt utterly bleak and hopeless.

Rather than braking, I accelerated harder, pushing my bike to its limit. My teeth ground in my jaw as the wind whipped past me, eyes focused on that white tent where my wife was likely helping others before herself.

I spent the first twenty-odd years of my life in bleak darkness and hopelessness. I would not meet my end that way, or let it take my family from me.

I came to a hard stop in front of the field hospital in a cloud of dust and smoke. The smell of burned rubber followed me as I tore through the tent door, finding chaos within.

Medics were running around in a mad rush, packing up supplies in a hurry. As I suspected, many of them were moving patients as well. That was slow-going, considering many were still badly injured.

"Mari!" I barked at the rushing medical staff. "Is Mariposa here?"

"She's getting patients evacuated," someone said, pointing to the main hospital floor.

I started moving that way, brushing past people as I searched the sea of faces for hers. *There!* I didn't have the luxury of feeling relieved when I spotted her holding the arm of a man to help him out of bed.

"Mari!"

Her head snapped up at the sound of my voice. "Shadow, they're coming! Can you carry him?"

"We have to leave," I told her in response. "They're not coming for the gods, but for us."

"Us?" Her brows knitted together in confusion.

"You and your men, the ones the gods have touched. Freyja told us," I said in a rush of breath. "Where's Jandro?"

"He's driving one of the vans to get patients out." All the while, she continued helping the patient to his feet, bringing his arm around her shoulder while she held around his waist. "Shadow, we can't just leave these people here."

"Here, let me." I crouched low and wrapped my arms around the man's leg, lifting up when he was adequately slung over my shoulder. "I'm sorry if this hurts, I don't know where your injuries are."

Mari and I turned back toward the exit while the man muttered quietly in Spanish, seemingly confused, but at least he wasn't one of the violent ones.

Shit, the violent ones.

My heart nearly stopped before I turned to my wife. "Mari, how many of the catatonic patients were here?"

"I thought there were four but none of them—" She was jerked away from me in the blink of an eye. An expressionless man pulled her into his chest, covered her mouth with one hand, and wrapped the other around her throat.

"MARI!"

I set the patient on my shoulder down as gently as I

could, but it wasted precious seconds as Mari's attacker started dragging her away, completely unaffected by her kicking and squirming.

He was fucking fast, even with her resistance. In seconds, he was nearly at the other end of the tent when I ran toward him, leaping off of abandoned beds and shoving wheeled carts out of my way. Others were trying to stop me, I could see them in my peripheral vision. Empty shells of people with no expression on their faces, eyes blank and hollow as they moved to cut me off from either side.

Our guns had been confiscated by General Bray's soldiers the moment we showed up to the main hospital. Thankfully, they hadn't known about my hidden knives.

I grabbed the handles hidden at my lower back, waiting for the perfect moment to send them out to my left and right. My eyes stayed on Mari when I threw them, but I never missed. My knives hit true to their targets.

Even with knives in their torsos, the controlled soldiers never stopped.

"What?" I breathed the word as I dared to look, sliding my gaze away from Mari for a fraction of a second before returning it to her.

She was getting red in the face, like she was struggling to breathe, the patient dragging her away with impossible speed. I was fast on my feet, but it felt like I couldn't catch up. And the other two bleeding from their knife wounds were creeping up faster on me.

And where the fuck were Reaper and Gunner?

With the next bed in front of me, I picked it up by

the metal frame and tossed it to the side, hoping to slow down one of the fuckers coming at me. I grabbed a cart and tossed it toward the other one, then kept running. Even slowing down that tiny amount put more distance between Mari and me.

Fuck, I would've killed for a gun right then. I didn't trust myself enough to throw a knife from this distance. A stab wound wouldn't kill her, but with a gun I could be far more accurate.

Mari's attacker hit the far wall of the tent, and there he stopped. My heart leaped and I pumped my arms and legs harder to reach my woman. The man holding her seemed to be messing with one of the support poles holding up the tent's frame. He released Mari's mouth to tamper with it, but kept the other arm tightly wrapped around her neck. Mari was either trying to scream or take a breath, her hands digging and clawing at his arm.

I reached them just as the tent started to fall.

He had ducked under the canvas siding, Mari's feet scrambling and kicking as he dragged her along. The entire tent groaned as its support system began to collapse. I had a knife ready, slicing through the canvas like butter to make my way through. I had covered enough ground to reach them, and didn't hesitate.

The knife left my hand, sailing forward until it found its mark in the back of the man's neck, cutting cleanly through his spinal cord.

His feet kept moving for another few steps but his arm had gone limp, releasing Mari to collapse in a heap on the ground before he dropped dead soon after.

"Mari!" I hit the dirt next to her as she coughed and wheezed for air, quickly scooping an arm under her legs and wrapping the other around her back. "I got you," I grunted out as I rose to my feet and headed back toward the collapsed tent.

"Stop," she coughed out weakly as I made my way around the fallen structure. "We have to get the rest of them."

"I'm sorry, love. We can't help everyone, especially when we're the targets." My head whipped around in search of Reaper, Jandro, anyone. *What the fuck? They were right behind me!*

"Shadow, watch out!"

I looked just in time to see the two that I stabbed, now moving slower and uncoordinated from blood loss, stumble out of the hole I ripped in the canvas. One dragged a lame ankle behind him, but they were both still hell-bent on catching up to us.

"Fuck. Can you run?" I asked Mari.

"I think so."

I placed her feet gingerly on the ground, keeping hold of her hand. "Let's go."

We bolted together, me keeping a slow enough pace for her to stay at my side. I didn't know where to go, except away from them. With my free hand, I reached into my cut for another knife, pulling it out just as the fourth and final zombified patient stepped out from behind a van.

I pulled my arm back to throw my knife, stopping abruptly when I saw the gun in his hands.

"Get behind me!" I skidded to a stop and shoved Mari behind my back.

"The other ones are still coming!" she cried, clutching the back of my cut.

I didn't dare take my eyes off the one in front of me, who raised his gun slowly. "Throw the knife away."

The way he said it was eerily calm, almost like he was bored. He wasn't dead but there was no *life*, no adrenaline running through him. I gripped harder on the knife handle, and hated knowing that I couldn't throw it right into his chest. I didn't know how fast or accurate he was with a gun. I was Mari's only shield and couldn't take that risk.

He cocked the weapon and walked closer. "Throw it away."

"Okay…okay."

I widened my hands and tossed the knife into a bush without looking. I had more, of course, but couldn't reach for them without him seeing.

"The Sha wants you alive to begin with," he remarked, lowering the gun barrel. A small relief. "But the Sha does not mind if you are brought in pieces." He pointed at my legs and a single shot rang out.

I braced myself for the impact. Pain was not an issue but it would disable me, especially if I bled a lot. But the tearing of my flesh, the odd sensation of a foreign object cutting through muscle and tissue never came.

Instead, the man fell to his knees, teetering there for a moment before collapsing forward as dead weight. A tell-tale hole was perfectly centered in the back of his head. I looked up to see Gunner roughly fifty yards in the distance, waving a rifle over his head in victory.

"Jesus, fuck…" Mari and I ran toward him instantly. She released my hand to leap on to him in a hug. "Where the fuck did you guys go?"

"Made a pit stop at the armory for some essentials." Gunner held Mari with one arm as he tossed a rifle to me. "Still think I'm losing my touch?" he asked with a grin.

"I'll never talk shit about you and your guns again," I said, quickly checking and loading my weapon. Jandro and Reaper were a few yards back at their bikes, arming themselves to the teeth. Two rifles crossed each of their backs, sat at their hip holsters, and each man even had one strapped to the front of their bodies amidst all the ammo in their tactical vests and slung over their shoulders. Reaper even had the automatic rifle mounted to his handlebars that he used in the first battle against Tash.

"Do we have a plan?" I asked, making my way over to get myself strapped.

"Shoot as many of them as you fucking can. Don't get captured." Reaper inserted and locked a long magazine into the assault rifle. "That's the plan."

"Everyone seems to be evacuated," Jandro remarked, noting the now misshapen tent a few yards away.

"My dad! Did he get out?" Mari squeezed in between me and Jandro and started loading a rifle.

"I got him on a truck and handed him to a medic," Jandro assured her.

"The army is mobilizing to help, but…" Gunner came up on my other side with an apprehensive shrug. "I think we're front line, guys."

"And *we're* the ones they want?" Mari blinked. "How did that happen?"

"Let's start to fan out and move backward toward the city as we start to engage them." Reaper's eyes were on the horizon, watching the enemy get closer. "Hopefully we'll make a dent, but the five of us can't take them in an open field for long. We'll need cover, so hopefully dad's troops move their asses."

"Even if they do." Gunner shook his head with a worried frown. "There's enough of them to turn the landscape *black*. I can't even estimate numbers, but they've gotta be in the hundreds of thousands. We've *never* gone up against anything like this."

"The only other option is to not fight as we go down," Reaper shot back. "Which would you rather do?"

"The one about to shoot us said we were wanted alive," I said. "So it's not a death sentence right away."

"If we get taken by them, it might as well be," Gunner said. "We'll be like *them*. Fucking zombies."

"Guys! They're really close now." Mari had followed Reaper's gaze and I looked the same direction.

Fuck, they were no longer marching but running. I could make out facial features and hair colors from this distance.

"Fan out and move back when I say," Reaper ordered. "Mari, stay between Gunner and Shadow."

We spread out, still close enough to cover each other.

To keep higher ground, we all stood on top of abandoned vehicles or equipment left behind by the medics. Only Reaper was closer to the ground, and the center of our firing line.

There was no preamble, no motivating speech, or quick moments of affection with our woman. We had no time. Reaper confirmed with each of us that we were ready before he roared out, "FIRE!"

I focused on my targets, popping off clean, fast shots to the sound of bullets spraying from Reaper's automatic rifle. I could tell that Mari and Jandro were aiming for the upper bodies, while Gunner and I picked people off with head shots.

It seemed efficient for the first few minutes. Reaper mowed down the front line, giving obstacles for the people behind to step over, and the rest of us shot those moving in. But there were so many. We were only dealing with the ones right in front of us, and not the ones to the sides that crept closer into my vision.

They were still running, coming closer on three sides with no regard for fear, pain, or their fallen comrades they were literally trampling over.

"Move back!" Reaper ordered. "Back toward the city!"

I jumped down from the van I was standing on and looked for Mari, who was slower to climb down.

"Come on!" I grabbed her hand when she hit the ground and started running, with Jandro right alongside us. Only Reaper stayed put, swinging his handlebars around to spray bullets at our enemies in a wide arc.

"Reaper, come on!" Mari yelled at him.

He started easing the bike backward, still shooting, but he'd have to turn his back to catch up with us, and I was not about to let my president take that risk.

I stopped running but shoved Mari forward. "Go, I'll catch up."

"What are you doing?" she demanded, spinning and returning to my side.

"I'm gonna cover him so he can move back. Now go!"

"What about you?"

"I'll be fine. Run to Jandro and Gunner now!" I shoved her again, more forcefully. "Do not follow me." I ran back toward Reaper without another word, pulling my second rifle from my back holster as I did so.

He was swinging the machine gun more wildly, face set in a hard grimace as he sprayed back and forth in an effort to keep the enemies from getting too close. An endeavor he was quickly losing. They were close enough to shoot with handguns now, a swarm of blackness threatening to swallow us up.

"Go, I'll cover you." I came up beside him and started shooting, swinging my rifles in the opposite direction as him to cover more ground.

"You can't hold 'em off," he argued before his shots abruptly stopped, a soft *click-click-click* following in their wake.

"Just get cover and reload!" I moved in front of him, squeezing my triggers as fast as my guns could allow, which was much slower than his.

Reaper finally turned the bike around and drove toward the city. I followed after him, running backward as I fired shot after shot at blank-faced, black-clad soldiers. I was shooting men who were, in all likelihood, completely innocent. None of them deserved to be shot so callously. It wasn't their fault their bodies were being controlled by something else.

What did that one soldier call it? The Sha?

I couldn't afford to think, only act as they came closer. As I swung my rifle barrels, I almost snagged some of their uniforms. They were close enough to reach out and grab me, and some of them did. I started throwing my elbows out, trying all I could to create some distance so I could keep shooting, but there was just so fucking many.

I didn't look back. I'd be done for if I did, so I kept moving my feet back while facing forward. If they surrounded me and the others were getting away, good. I had to believe Mari and her other men got into the city and had adequate cover.

I thought I could hear someone shouting my name, but it was impossible to tell over the hundreds of footsteps all encircling me. Hands were grabbing at me, pulling my weapons and ammo away. Arms pulled at my shoulders, my biceps, weighing me down. Kicks hit me in the knees and shins, and I felt my strength faltering. I gathered up what I could with a loud bellow of effort and threw some of the Tash soldiers into the crush of people closing in on me.

But it was all for nothing.

An arm wrapped around the front of my throat, cutting off my air. My vision went to black dots as I planted my feet wide apart, refusing to fall. I'd be dead on my feet before they took me down. I'd protect my wife, my family, until there was nothing left. I'd be emptier than all of them before I stopped.

An odd sensation on my neck had me spinning, reaching to land punches on the soldiers behind me. It felt like the prick of a needle, like when Mari drew blood from me. I continued to struggle until my arms felt impossibly heavy, like boulders at my sides.

And then my legs stopped working, refusing to hold me up any longer. My eyes weren't even closed when all I saw was blackness.

TWENTY-EIGHT

MARIPOSA

"SHADOW!" Someone's arm was around my stomach, pulling me back as I fought with all my strength to reach my husband. "Let me go, he needs help!" Tash's soldiers were swarming Shadow by the dozens—climbing and grappling as they tried to bring him down. Nothing they were doing was lethal, but there were *so* many. He was stronger and taller than all of them, but he couldn't overpower their sheer numbers.

"Shadow!" I screamed again, then drove an elbow back into whoever was holding me.

It was Gunner, who immediately pinned my forearm behind my back. "I'm sorry, baby girl. I'm so sorry."

"Why aren't you shooting?" I bellowed at Reaper. "Do fucking something!"

"I could hit him by accident," Reaper shouted back, his face pained and scowling. "We gotta keep moving into the city, get some cover!"

"FUCK YOU!" I screamed with all my might. "We are *not* leaving him!"

"Mari, there is nothing we can do right now." Reaper looked over at me and nodded at Gunner. "Don't let her go. Move further in and I'll cover your back."

Only Jandro was still shooting, but to no avail. As much as I hated to admit it, Reaper was right. Aiming at the mob that descended on Shadow ran the risk of hurting him, or worse, killing him.

"We'll get him back," Gunner whispered as he started to drag my limp, exhausted body away from the scene I couldn't tear my eyes from. "Maybe not right now, but we will. I promise you."

"Shadow…" His name became a weak sob, tearing from my throat. I couldn't see him through the crush of bodies piling on anymore. I hated that we were leaving him—us, his family. Even if it was a death sentence for us.

"Fuck, they're in the city limits now!" Gunner turned me around to face him, taking my face gingerly in his hands. "Baby girl, I need you to drive for me. Can you do that?"

"…Drive?" I only realized then we were standing next to a pickup truck. The engine was running but no one was inside.

"Mari, I really, really need you to focus right now." Gunner tapped his fingertips lightly on my cheeks, just enough to bring my attention back to him. "Drive to the City Hall building. We're gonna hide out in the base-ment there and figure out what to do next. Okay?"

"…Okay."

"Good girl. Drive fast." He smacked a quick kiss on my forehead, drew a new gun from one of his holsters, then hopped in the truck bed. Jandro followed him, his face a hard mask. He couldn't afford to feel anything about losing Shadow right now and neither could I.

Tash's soldiers had gotten one of their targets. Now they needed two more.

I got into the driver's seat, not bothering with the seatbelt as I hit the gas hard. As the truck jerked forward and I was forced to pay attention to the road, the scene in front of me was the complete opposite of the calmness from earlier.

People were panicking. Screaming and running in the streets. In the distance, I saw several dark smoke plumes from fires near the eastern border. Jerriton's army must have tried to stop them. It was a war zone right here in the city. We'd been trying to avoid this outcome, to keep the carnage as far away from the civilians as possible.

Now it was coming for us, and we had no option but to lead it straight into the heart of the city.

My gaze flicked to my guys in the rearview mirror every other second. Jandro and Gunner were shooting to cover Reaper, who followed behind us on his bike and turned to shoot behind him at every opportunity.

City Hall. City Hall. Make it to City Hall. That's all you have to do right now. I whispered it to myself as I white-knuckled the steering wheel through town. If my mind drifted anywhere else, I might not be able to get us there.

A hard thump on my door made me startle. Then there was another on the passenger side door, and more alongside the truck. I realized with horror that Tash's soldier's were throwing themselves at the vehicle.

"Keep going!" Jandro yelled at me from the back. "Don't slow down!"

I pressed down harder on the gas pedal, my hands already aching around the steering wheel in my fight for control of the truck. Another quick glance in the mirror showed me Reaper driving over the bodies that threw themselves in front of his motorcycle. They came up on all sides and tried to grab him, or the bike. Some of them held on and dragged behind him as he drove.

Fuck…Would we even make it to the building?

It was less than a mile away now, and most people seemed to be off the streets. I thought I caught sight of the Four Corners army shooting, but I was going too fast to see.

So close. So fucking close…

I couldn't tear my eyes from Reaper now. They must have figured out he was the most vulnerable and continued to pile on him. He was getting smaller in my mirror as more of them jumped, grabbed, and tried to drag him off the bike. One of them caught hold of his handlebars right in front, and he fired some rapid shots of the machine gun at point-blank range into the man's stomach.

We're here! We made it!

City Hall came into view, along with a long line of Four Corners soldiers and Jeeps right out from.

"Get out of the way!" I yelled, slamming on the

horn as I made a beeline for the sidewalk right in front of the buildings.

Soldiers quickly dodged the truck and reassembled after I was past their line, forming a barrier between us and the mindless black swarm.

But Reaper was still out on the street.

I hopped out of the cab and climbed into the truck bed, where Gunner handed me another rifle. I took it and started shooting alongside my men, alongside the soldiers now raining fire down on the enemy, the mindless pawns of someone or some*thing* powerful enough to control thousands of minds from a distance.

We avoided shooting directly at Reaper, but I aimed as close as I dared. Jandro, Gunner, and I focused on the ones grabbing for his bike from the sides, while the army fired at the mass at large. But I couldn't ignore the heartbreaking reality that they were all centering on one target—my husband.

Reaper was fighting to shoot and keep control of the bike, which wobbled dangerously every time someone tried to grab it. When someone jumped on the seat behind him, my heart stopped.

"REAPER!" My voice was already weak from screaming for Shadow, so it didn't carry over the commotion and gunfire.

The Tash soldier wrapped an arm around Reaper's throat, taking my husband by surprise. Before Reaper could break out of the hold, the attacker stabbed him with something in the neck. The continuing struggle sent them both careening off the bike.

"NO! Reaper, no!"

I didn't realize I had jumped down from the truck bed and was running straight for him until I was being pulled back. Arms wrapped around my stomach and pinned my arms down as I lost sight of *another* husband in a pile of bodies.

My kicking and screaming was to no avail. I screamed at the sky, at Hades and Horus for not protecting my two men. I screamed at the pain splitting through my body from the knowledge that two of my husbands had just been taken from me. My voice stopped working and I still screamed. Everyone's ears had to be ringing from all the gunfire, so it wasn't like they could hear me anyway.

The binds holding me eventually loosened and I broke free at the first opportunity, picking up the first gun I saw and quickly wiping my eyes clear. Holding the rifle against my body, I spun around in confusion.

"Where…what…?"

They were all gone. Tash's soldiers had vanished like smoke, leaving only their dead behind. I turned back toward the building to see Jandro and Gunner approaching me slowly, their faces just as shocked and pained as mine must have been.

"Where'd they go?" I asked, my voice little more than a raspy whisper.

"They left," Jandro said numbly. "They took him and just fucking *left*."

"How…why?" I looked at Gunner. "Why didn't they come for us three?"

"I dunno." Gunner stared at Reaper's motorcycle

lying on its side. "I don't fucking know." Anger bled into his voice as his lower lip trembled.

The gun, now a useless, dead weight in my hands, clattered to the ground as I turned in a slow circle. None of it made sense. The more I looked at the scene all around me—bodies, guns, blood, and bullet casings—the less sense it made.

"What's going to happen to them?" The mere thought of that question made me want to scream and cry again.

Neither Jandro nor Gunner answered. They stepped in closer to me, shielding my view from our surroundings. Jandro brought my head into his chest, settling my ear over his racing heartbeat. He stroked the back of my neck with trembling fingers as Gunner came up behind me. Gunner let out a rattling sigh as he lowered his forehead to the back of my head, his shaking hands resting on my waist.

Together we could only stand, supporting and being supported by each other. None of us needed to speak to know that without each other, we wouldn't just lose.

We would crumble.

Epilogue

"Ah, fuck!" The pain in my shoulder woke me up. It throbbed with a sharpness that felt like I was getting stabbed repeatedly. I deduced pretty quickly that the thing was dislocated, probably from falling off my bike.

"Okay, get this thing back into place, then figure out where the fuck I am." I was mainly talking to myself to make sure I was still alive, in case my shoulder wasn't a clear enough sign.

I was sitting on a concrete floor and figured out there was a brick wall behind me. When I tried to stretch my legs out, I realized that the shackles around my ankles, connected by a chain bolted to the floor, prevented me from extending my legs fully. As I became more aware of my body position, I realized my other arm was pretty sore too.

Both arms were shackled above my head. "Ugh, no wonder this fuckin' hurts."

I shimmied and scooted as much as my thrashed

body would allow to press my back against the wall. Like a toddler learning to walk, I pressed slowly up to standing until my arms were in a more natural position. It hurt like a motherfucker, but I hissed and ground my teeth, pressing that shoulder into the wall until it popped back into place. The stabbing pain faded right away, lowering to a dull throb that I just knew would continue to haunt me as long as I was in here.

With that taken care of, I started looking around the room. The large, looming figure on the adjacent wall caught my eye first.

"Hey," Shadow greeted unceremoniously.

He remained sitting on the floor, heavy chains wrapped around his ankles and wrists. I wondered if the shackles didn't fit him, they were already pretty tight on me.

"Hey," I returned. "Got any idea where we are?"

"New Ireland, I assume," he mused. "Tash's compound."

The rest of the room wasn't much to look at. A concrete floor, four brick walls, a tiny square window too high up to reach, and an iron-barred door, like a jail cell.

"How long you think it's been?"

"I dunno, maybe a day?" Shadow's chains clinked as he shifted his position. "I woke up not long before you."

"Fuck." I tipped my head back until it touched the wall behind me. "We're fucked, aren't we?"

"Probably."

"You sound awfully calm about it."

Shadow shrugged, the motion moving some of his hair to reveal that a chain was also wrapped around his neck. "I'm used to dungeons, I guess. How did you get caught?"

I recounted everything that happened after he went to cover me, from the moment the others got in the truck, to getting jumped on my bike and passing out.

"Do you think the others got away?" Shadow's brows furrowed and I knew we were thinking about the same person.

"They should have, they were behind the army lines." I cleared my throat and looked around, feeling thirsty as a motherfucker but of course, there was no water in this shithole. "The inner chamber of that building is like a fortress, and they have basic necessities for a couple of weeks. They'll survive, figure something out."

"Mari will want to come after us," Shadow said.

"She better not," I barked. "She's the missing piece —the thread that ties the underworld and the sky together. If they get all three of us, I bet we're more than fucked. At least right now, we might still have a chance." I blew out a long sigh, wondering how much longer we'd be kept without water.

Hahahahaha...

Shadow and I jerked away from our walls at the same moment, staring wide-eyed at each other. Yeah, we definitely both heard that.

An odd swishing sound pulled our gazes toward the door just in time to see a forked tail dragging along the ground on the other side.

TO BE CONTINUED IN MERCILESS - BOOK 9 AND THE FINAL BOOK OF THE STEEL DEMONS MC SERIES!

PRE-ORDER MERCILESS:

http://books2read.com/SDMC9

Acknowledgments

Don't hate me yet, we've still got one more book! Thank you once again for reading this far into the series. It's been such a journey and we are *so* close to the end. I promise these characters will get the ending they deserve.

For regular updates, exclusive teasers, and excerpts, join my reader group, Crystal's Coven. We're a friendly bunch, and I'm always posting in the Coven first before anywhere else online.

A special thank you to my pack--Kathryn, Aleera, and Lana for listening to my whining and keeping me accountable. I love you babes.

Telisha, Janet, and Izzy, thank you for being such amazing cheerleaders, friends, and confidants throughout the evolution of this series. You all help me write the best books I possibly can!

Thank you Mr. Ash, my quietest yet biggest supporter. I'll never not be embarrassed when you tell coworkers what I do, but thank you for being proud of me. I love you!

See you all in the next book!

-Crystal

Also by Crystal Ash

For a complete list of books by Crystal Ash, visit her Amazon page.

About the Author

Crystal Ash is a USA Today Bestselling Author from California. From an early age, she's been obsessed with magic, heart-wrenching love stories, strange animals, and the people who turn into them.

When she's not writing, she's probably in her garden of crazy-looking plants or drinking craft beer with her husband and cat.

She loves interacting with her readers so don't hesitate to reach out!

authorcrystalash@gmail.com
CrystalAshBooks.com

facebook.com/Crystal.Ash.Romance
amazon.com/author/crystalash
bookbub.com/profile/crystal-ash
instagram.com/crystalashbooks

Made in United States
Orlando, FL
08 November 2024

53597423R00214